CHANGE

A sudden chill ran through Theresa's body.

'Now hold on Paul, let's get one thing straight here . . . you don't think for a single minute . . . you don't, do you . . . you couldn't . . .'

She rounded on him in a fury.

'You *couldn't* . . .'

He shifted. 'I don't know what to think,' he said.

But that wasn't what she wanted to hear.

She leapt to her feet.

'You do . . . you do! Paul, for God's sake! You know I wouldn't do anything like that. Why on earth . . . what do you think . . . oh, sod the lot of you!' she said suddenly and turned and started walking away towards the silver sea.

Also by Christine Purkis in Red Fox

The Shuttered Room

Sea
CHANGE

CHRISTINE PURKIS

RED FOX

A Red Fox Book

Published by Random House Children's Books
20 Vauxhall Bridge Road, London SW1V 2SA

A division of Random House UK Ltd
London Melbourne Sydney Auckland
Johannesburg and agencies throughout the world

1 3 5 7 9 10 8 6 4 2

First published in Great Britain by
The Bodley Head Children's Books 1996

Red Fox edition 1997

Printed and bound in Great Britain by
Cox & Wyman Ltd, Reading, Berkshire

RANDOM HOUSE UK Limited Reg. No. 954009

Papers used by Random House UK Limited
are natural, recyclable products made from wood grown in
sustainable forests. The manufacturing processes conform to
the environmental regulations of the country of origin.

ISBN 0 09 963401 5

For Mopsa, Mum, Dad and Pentire

With special thanks to
E. E. Morton Nance

BRISTOL

1

It was a temptation, an irresistible temptation, to a girl who didn't see the point in denying herself whatever she wanted.

Every time Theresa walked through the open-plan lounge to the kitchen, there was no way to avoid seeing the cocktail cabinet, fixed at eye level on the wall above the dining room table. Her mother kept all the glasses on the top shelf and the smaller shelves down the right hand side. But on the left were the bottles: the vodka, the gin, the Campari, the whisky and the rum.

Of course there were usually lagers and beers in the fridge, Sam, Theresa's stepfather, being more of a beer-drinker; and there were always assorted wines laid on their sides in the rack next to the sideboard, quite accessible, but less attractive, to Theresa anyway.

She was getting ready to go out. Her mother had warned her. Sam's boss and his wife were coming for supper. Debs had said she could sleep over at her place. No plans had been made except the Arcade. They'd just hang out. See what came up.

Theresa felt good, excited as she pulled her black bomber jacket over her grey lycra top and black leggings. She stooped to tie the laces on her black trainers. Ready for anything. Nearly.

In the hallway, she hesitated. Her mother was clattering pans in the kitchen and Theresa stuck her head round the door. Sam was chopping yellow peppers over the sink. Rosie, neat in matching cotton shorts and T-shirt, was sitting at the kitchen table, inspecting her felt tips, putting them in some kind of order – all the blues together, and all the greens, and all the reds, chattering to herself as she did so. She didn't see her elder sister sneaking up behind her. As Theresa pinched Rosie on the left cheek, making her turn her head, she took a handful of pens with her right.

Falling for that one made Rosie madder than anything else in the world.

'Mummy!' she screamed as Theresa threw the pens back along the table like nine-pins, scattering the orderly designs.

'Bye. I'm off. See y'all!'

Her mother turned round quickly, wiping her hands on her tracksuit bottoms.

'Oh – have you got everything?'

'Like what?'

'Toothbrush?'

Theresa flipped open her jacket. The head of her red toothbrush protruded from her inside pocket.

'Have fun!' Theresa called over her shoulder as she left through the door to the lounge.

At the door to the cabinet, she paused, sucked in her lower lip, and, without making a sound, levered open the cupboard door and took out the gin bottle.

Quickly, she unscrewed the top, put the bottle to her lips and tipped back her head.

She hadn't intended to take more than a sip.

'Damn it,' she thought, holding the bottle up to the light. Looking quickly round, she saw a vase of fresh sweet peas on the table. She lifted them out and poured some of the water into the bottle before returning it to the back of the cupboard, moving the vodka and the whisky bottles firmly forward.

Quickened by the bitter gin which rushed through her body like electricity, she threw her bag on the floor behind the table, and deliberately crashed the vase over on the table top.

'Whoops!' she cried loudly, scooping up the straggle of sweet peas, and sticking them back in the righted vase.

'What's going on?' her mother appeared instantly.

'Sorry – knocked the flowers over ... trying to get my bag ... got it now ... might need a bit more water ... got to dash!'

'What about my table top!' she heard her mother saying as she slammed the front door behind her.

They met outside the Amusement Arcade as arranged. Theresa was late but Debbie was used to that.

'Let's go. What are we waiting for?' Theresa greeted her cheerfully.

It was cool and magical inside – the low ceiling and the flickering lights giving the impression of perpetual night and perpetual promise. Debbie went straight to The Terminator, Theresa to The Demon Driver.

By seven-thirty, money was spent, pockets empty, and the effects of the gin had left Theresa feeling dissatisfied and ill-tempered.

'What are we going to do now?' Debbie asked. Theresa was standing holding an inactive lever of a fruit machine, concentrating on the symbols: two lemons and a cherry.

'Damn it!' She slapped the sides of the machine so hard the lights flickered and the palms of her hands tingled.

'Heh! Don't take it out on my machines! OK?' It was Stefan the manager, a charmer with all the girls, but mean as mean could be and had never been known to lend out so much as one measly token.

Theresa felt an iron weight round her neck, pulling her backwards, off balance.

'Heh!' she half laughed, dodging out of his armlock. 'Get lost, Stefan.'

He smiled at her and put a long cigarette between his lips, lighting it with a heavy gold lighter.

'Wassermatter huh?' He leant easily against the glass back of the machine. He always wore a leather jacket and a neat red turtle neck, summer and winter.

'Oh, nothing.'

'You lose?'

'Yeh – but that's not it.'

'What then?'

'It's all so *boring*!' Theresa suddenly felt like crying as she voiced the words.

'Boring! Wassermatter with all you kids, eh?' he

asked Debbie. 'It's all I hear: boring, boring, boring! When I was your age . . .'

'Yea, yea, yea. Save it for your grandchildren, Stefan.'

'Oi you, cheeky!'

At that moment, their attention was diverted by a commotion on the pavement outside. Blinking into the light, they saw a lanky boy in cut-offs and a vest appear in the doorway.

'Heh, Stefan! Seen Vince?'

Stefan shook his head.

The boy whistled through his teeth in annoyance.

'Pete?' Theresa thought she recognised the silhouette.

'Heh! Trees-r-green! Debs! How y'a doin?'

Debbie nudged Theresa. They exchanged an excited glance.

'Thank you, God,' whispered Theresa to the ceiling.

It was the same Pete Sweet who had occupied much of her head and her heart for the last thirteen months, five days – ever since she had first bumped into him at a school detention, she a troublesome third year and he an uncontrollable fifth former. Although she'd contrived to meet him many times since, he'd never taken much notice of her, but his name had been written over and over, next to or entwined with her own in her exercise books. And although maybe he hardly knew her, she knew him intimately. After all, he had shared her fantasies every night as she dropped off to sleep, not to mention her waking hours. And now, suddenly, here he was.

Theresa's face had broken into a wide smile as she moved towards him, Debbie following a little more reluctantly, and then they saw the buggy, up on the pavement and attracting disapproving looks from pedestrians.

'That yours?' she asked, trying to sound casual.

'In a way . . . temporarily . . .' he bragged. 'Wanna ride?'

Caution went to the wind. Stefan was left shaking his head but Theresa was up there in the back seat, squashed between two boys she'd never seen before.

'Come on,' she called to Debbie who was still standing on the pavement, undecided. 'Give us your hand. Budge up,' she told the boys and Debbie squeezed herself in next to Theresa. Pete was in the driver's seat and roaring off up the street, bouncing off the pavement and screeching his tyres as he swung the buggy round in an illegal U-turn.

The boy in the passenger seat had a pack of Budweisers at his feet and, unbidden, tossed four into the back. The quadraphonic speakers pounded out Ice-T so loudly that people they passed froze to the spot like rabbits in headlights.

Up the streets they sped, through a just-amber light, swerving round an old man on a zebra cross-ing, taking a roundabout on two wheels before racing off round the Downs at faster and faster speeds.

Theresa's hair pulled back from her face, forcing her chin up. She was laughing like a child. Tears were running down her cheeks. The wind was battering her eyeballs; it was hard to keep them open but she liked the feeling. She couldn't say anything. If she opened her mouth, the wind pushed against her teeth and made her think of the windscreen of her mother's car years ago after the long ride up from Cornwall, thick with the bodies of insects – yellow and white slimy smudges and smears of blood.

Debbie's hand was clutching Theresa's knee, fingers digging in painfully.

They stopped once for a reshuffle. The boy in the front, called Jerry, took the wheel. One of the boys in the back swung forwards, and Pete got in next to Theresa. She could feel his thigh against her own and then, on a particularly tight corner, he threw his arm round her shoulders and pressed his body against hers. It was she who dug her fingers into Debbie's leg at that point and the two exchanged a look of brilliant excitement.

There was another issue of Budweisers. The boy on their left took their empty tins and started shying them at targets they hurtled past: the notice-board outside the Catholic Church, 'Bull's-eye!': an old Airedale dog carrying a shopping basket, which he dropped immediately with a yelp as his rear-quarters seemed to catch up with his front legs.

All the boys laughed, including Pete, and Theresa tried to, though she felt awful. Turning round, she caught the owner's eye staring in a fury at the racing buggy. She felt her insides cringe as Debbie's fingers dug even more painfully into her knee.

9

'Ow!' Theresa protested. 'Give over, will you!'

But Debbie knew by the look on her face that Theresa didn't like it any more than she did.

At that moment and with one empty can still to be disposed of, they raced past a stationary police car.

'Oh no.' Theresa closed her eyes.

Debbie gulped.

'Swing by one more time!' yelled the boy with the can.

Luckily there was no policeman in sight, and the boy with the can pitched a perfect lob.

'L of Lice!' he crowed as they speed away, jeering and whooping. Miraculously, there was no sudden wailing of sirens, no blue flashing light, no chase, and the buggy came to a sudden halt outside the Tapas Bar. Theresa and Debbie almost fell out onto the pavement.

The buggy sped away with an awesome squeal of tyres. Theresa saw Pete adjusting his sunglasses and sinking back in the seat, his arm stretched along where she had been sitting. He didn't turn back.

They stood for a moment, propping each other up on legs which felt weak and rubbery. Theresa's hair was one huge tangle, standing out from her head like a bush. Debbie's short bob, in contrast, had been flattened by the speed and clung to her skull like a bathing cap.

Still numb, the girls stumbled off down the road, swigging the last warm mouthfuls of lager, laughing as they went, as much from relief as anything.

2

Debbie and her mum lived in the High Street above the Bank, in two rooms, 'camping' they called it, while Debbie's dad served his time for having been caught with his hand in the firm's till. A tiny galley kitchen led off the main room, but there was standing room only there. They ate at the one table in the next room, which doubled as Debbie's work place and her mother's sewing space.

'Hungry?' Debbie asked Theresa.

'Famished.'

'Spag. OK?'

Debbie opened the jar of sauce and put the Easy-cook spaghetti into boiling water on the stove while Theresa wandered into the lounge and picked up the TV Guide.

'There's a film on at nine – "woman, forties, with husband a victim to multiple sclerosis, has 16-year-old daughter up on manslaughter charge ... a powerful and moving account of one woman's bravery in a fight to save her family and her own sanity. Made for TV. One Star." Sounds good.'

'What's on now?'

'Just rubbish! Shall I nip out and get some cider,' Theresa suggested, 'before the film?'

Debbie hesitated. 'Got any cash?'

Theresa shook her head. 'Sorry – I'm wiped! I'm sure and certain Stefan fixes those machines.'

'Expect he does. Hang about.'

She didn't like doing it, but Debbie knew her mother always had loose change in her coat pockets.

'£1.55 – here's another twenty – and a ten – that's enough.'

It was Norfolk Classic she bought, being 30p cheaper than the other brands. As she stood at the till, Theresa picked up some cheese and onion crisps from the box on the counter.

She hadn't meant to, but she actually finished the last one as she climbed the stairs to the flat. She screwed the packet up and stuffed it in her pocket but forgot the crumbs on her coat.

'You greedy pig!' Debbie cried.

'Cheese and onion. You don't like them.'

'Well, why didn't you get salt and vinegar then?'

Theresa made a gesture as if to say 'Obvious!' and Debbie swiped at her with the tea towel.

'Come on. Ready. Help me serve out.'

They were sitting on the settee, their empty bowls stacked in front of them on the floor, deeply engrossed in the film, when Debbie's mum arrived home just after ten, and the phone began to ring as her key was in the lock.

It was only necessary to hear the one side of the conversation.

'Hello – yes – oh – yes, she's here . . . told me you knew . . . oh I see . . . she what? . . . oh dear – empty? . . . water! How embarrassing! . . . yes . . .

no, thank God . . . well, she wouldn't dare . . . had my fill of those kind of problems, thank you very much . . . don't have any alcohol in the house . . . well, it's not right is it . . . what do you want me to do? . . . I'll send her packing if you like . . . no I suppose not . . . see what you mean . . . she can stay put if that's what you want . . . you say . . . all right then . . . I'll tell her.'

There was a click as the receiver was replaced and then a pause, just long enough for Debbie and Theresa to exchange anxious looks.

As the door opened, both girls were concentrating fixedly on the screen.

Deb's mum sniffed loudly.

'Hello! I'm back!' she said.

'Hello, Mum,' said Debbie dutifully.

Tomkin, the cat, jumped down from his cushion and wound through her legs. As she stopped to stroke him, she noticed the bottle lying on its side on the floor.

'What's this? Cider! This your doing, Deb?'

She flushed.

'I brought it round,' Theresa rescued her friend.

Deb's mum gave her a long hard look.

'I would have thought you'd had enough for one evening . . . that was your mum on the phone, nice evening she had entertaining your dad's boss!'

'He's not my dad . . .'

'Whatever. Well, Debs should have told you what I think about alcohol in the house . . . at your age . . . it's wrong, that's what it is . . . I mean, you, Debs,

13

of all people, you should know that . . . look what it did for your father.'

'Give over, Mum,' Debs said quietly.

'Oh.' Her mother turned to Theresa. 'Can't say diddly squat about her precious father, can I?'

'Leave off, Mum.'

'Sor–ry!'

'We're watching this film . . . can't concentrate when you're talking.'

'Oh hark at her . . . too late to be staying up on a school day anyway.'

'It's only another few minutes,' Theresa said quickly. 'It's really good. Come and watch it,' she suggested, sketching the plot outline briefly and enticingly.

'Is he a goodie or a baddie?' Deb's mum asked doubtfully, perching herself on the arm of the settee as the accused girl's social worker took the witness stand.

'Good question,' Theresa muttered.

As the credits rolled, Debbie's mum was sitting eyes closed, slumped over Tomkin who was fast asleep on her lap.

'Come on – better let the old duck sleep!' Debbie whispered.

'What happened?' she said, snapping awake.

'Innocent,' Theresa told her, standing up and stretching.

It was dark when Theresa first rose to the surface of consciousness, pitch dark. Assuming it to be the middle of the night, she closed her eyes and let herself sink, which she was just doing when she felt a sharp kick in her back.

'Wake up!' It was Debbie. 'Alarm's gone.'

Theresa's head was right under Debbie's bed, among old pairs of shoes and empty suitcases waiting to be taken away again.

'Whatsertime?' she moaned.

'Seven-thirty.' Debbie swung her legs over Theresa, just managing to find a piece of floor space and wandered off to the bathroom.

Theresa tried to shut her eyes again but her heart was thumping and the sinking feeling was in her stomach not her head.

'Oh no,' she groaned. 'Can't face it.'

Debbie gave her a friendly kick as she came back into the room.

'Get up! Mum'll have a fit! Don't risk it,' she warned. Theresa sat up suddenly like a jack-in-the-box.

'OK. OK.'

As she leapt up, her sleeping bag fell in coils round her feet. Stepping out she pulled on yesterday's clothes, turning her knickers inside out.

'You can borrow some of mine,' Debbie offered.

'Don't bother.'

In the tiny bathroom she sloshed cold water onto her face, rubbed toothpaste round her teeth with her finger, her toothbrush still in her jacket in the bedroom, and tried to pull her fingers through her hair. She picked up Debbie's towel and she rubbed her head and neck vigorously, before letting the towel drop. Instead of falling, however, it hung heavily from her wrist, caught on the silver catch of her identity bracelet: 'Theresa Bird: March 25th 1980'. The engraved words were looped and delicate. A christening present from her grandmother, it had lain in its blue velvet box until her arms had grown to teenage thickness. Now, it was just part of her.

'Must get that mended,' she thought as she unhooked the snagged towel and pinched the sharp ends of the clasp together.

There was a pot of tea, three mugs, a cornflake packet, three bowls and a milk bottle on the table. Debbie's mum was just selecting three spoons from the drawer when the doorbell rang.

'Who the hell's that?' she asked as she rushed to answer it.

It was Sam.

Theresa recognised his voice and swung round, eyes blazing.

'What are *you* doing here?'

Sam, embarrassed, turned his eyes towards Debbie's mum for help. His smile was apologetic.

'Your mum's idea, Theresa. She thought it would be best to sort all this out . . . she'll run you in to school later on . . . best to face the music.'

'Well, I'm not coming. Not with you.'

The muscles in Sam's face started to tighten.

'Come on Theresa – I've got the car – let's just get it over and done with.'

Deliberately, she turned her head away and stared at the picture of white racing horses, nostrils flared, galloping through the spray on a deserted beach.

He had two choices – drag her away by force – or leave her.

'Have it your own way then,' he said lightly. 'Forgot the handcuffs!' he explained to Debbie's mum, who put her hand on his arm as they exchanged a look.

The air was full of awkwardness after he left. Debbie's mum was obviously angry; Debbie, hating scenes, embarrassed; and Theresa felt even more twisted up inside.

It was a silent trio which walked out of the flat and down the stairs, to emerge by the bank. Debbie caught the bus one side of the street, her mother the other, and Theresa started to walk.

3

Theresa never had the slightest intention of going straight home.

'Let them stew!' she thought, hating the bitter taste in her own mouth.

It was automatic as she passed the off-licence at the end of the road, even though it was only just nine o'clock and Mr Patel was still unlocking the metal grills on the window. She walked in. He hurried in behind her and stood anxiously at the counter observing her every move. She knew he was looking at her, knew also that her pockets were empty, knew that she had no intention of actually taking anything, although she would dearly have loved to tuck a bottle of Smirnov under her jacket or to fill her pockets with cans of Red Stripe.

It was enjoyable though, just removing a bottle from the shelves; turning it round lovingly in her hands; studying the label; turning her back deliberately so that Mr Patel's agitation filled the shop before replacing it carefully on the shelf.

The jangling bell alerted Mr Patel to the arrival of a couple of customers, two middle-aged women. One engaged Mr Patel in a loud conversation about the relative merits of a Portuguese and Spanish wine. It would have been easy to slip something under her shirt at that moment; she liked knowing that she could have done so, and then resisting the temptation and walking decisively out of the shop.

When she reached the lakeside, she slumped down onto the bench, stuck her legs out in front of her, hunched her shoulders and stuck her hands into the side pockets of her jacket.

A few mallards and pochards were conducting their morning ablutions on the edge of the water. Seeing her, a small flotilla of assorted ducks, including her favourites, the dumpy tufted ducks with their yellow eyes and unkempt heads, swam towards her.

'Dumpy divers! Dumpy divers!' she used to shout when she came here with her parents as a little girl. It had been a favourite spot, she with her bag of crusts, left over from her toast or her sandwiches.

Didn't like the swans though – never had – silent and deadly – with wings strong enough to break a man's arm according to her father. Hateful the way they chased away the ducks just by fixing them with a dark eye and stretching out their long necks – and then they'd get the bread she had specifically thrown for the ducks.

And then there was that time a squirrel had jumped out of the rubbish bin when her father had bowled the crunched-up paper bag into it, cricket style. What a shock! But worse for the poor squirrel, as her father had pointed out. There was the same bin now, updated and upgraded in a natural wood surround. In late summer it had always buzzed with wasps. How she had hated putting her ice lolly stick into it.

'You do it, Dad!'

'No, you do it!'

'Mum?'

She'd usually do it – save the fuss.

Sometimes they'd bring a picnic, sandwiches and apples and fizzy drinks and sit on the car rug under the willow tree, but then Mum had gone off the idea after the episode with the ants' nest.

Although it was a bright June morning, there was a cool wind which was ruffling the surface of the pond and bouncing the willow branches up and down. It made Theresa restless and unable to draw attention away from a gnawing in her stomach. If only she'd had the cornflakes, at least, instead of feeding off her righteous fury at Sam.

'I just can't sort this out,' she explained out loud to the ducks. One was standing on splayed orange feet quite close to her, wiping his beak to and fro under the feathers of his wing as though sharpening it.

For a moment, she wished she had seized the opportunity and helped herself in the shop. But she'd been that way before, got found out, and it had taken her down a path she vowed she would never go down again . . . police, social workers and all that hurt and pain from her mother. She shuddered.

A few little sparrows were still finding microscopic crumbs, overlooked by the larger birds.

'See – even you have got more in your stomachs

than me,' Theresa spoke to a brazen sparrow who had hopped right up to her shoe.

Jumping suddenly to her feet, she sent the last birds scooting across the path.

'See you, birdies!' she called out.

There was no place else to go. At least the fridge would be full and if she was crafty she could get to the drinks cabinet.

'*Not* the gin', she reminded herself.

She wondered as she turned into her road, just for a fleeting moment, if she should play it differently. Could she? Just say 'Sorry Mum' like she used to – 'mea culpa' – one of Grandma's favourite phrases, and bury her head on her mother's shoulder and allow herself to be reunited, pardoned, hugged as they both wanted.

The moment was fleeting.

No key. She went round the back. There was no one in the kitchen so, in passing, she opened the fridge and took out a piece of quiche. She was caught mid-bite.

'What the hell do you think you are doing?' Her mother's voice was ice though her eyes were puffed from crying.

'Eating a piece of pie – whoops, sorry, *quiche*!'

'And just where do you think you've been?'

'I *know*, I've been by the lake . . .'

'The lake!'

'Where we *used* to go, remember?'

'Oh, don't start.'

'I didn't start it.'

Her mother bit her lip. 'Why didn't you come with Sam?'

'You should have worked that one out.' She swigged back milk from the bottle.

To Theresa's dismay, her mother sank heavily into a chair. There was a catch in her voice. 'He's tried so hard.'

'Oh no,' Theresa thought. 'Not this one.'

'I know,' she said.

'Why, why, why are you being so poisonous, Theresa?'

'That's just what I am – poison!'

'That's not true.'

'You said it.'

'What's happened, Theresa?'

She shrugged.

'What are we going to do?'

She shrugged again.

'I'm at my wit's end . . . I feel such a failure . . . what have I done? . . . if only I knew . . . and I've got all these people on my back . . . the school, the social worker, and now this . . . I just can't defend you any more . . . there's nothing more I can say.'

'I don't want you to.'

'Well, what are you going to do? Aren't you even going to talk about it? Ruined the dinner party, by the way. They said nothing at all of course . . . too polite . . . if Sam hadn't decided to break with tradition and have a gin . . . it was pure water.'

Theresa couldn't stop a grin from spreading over her face.

'Not that pure – sweet pea water!'

22

'It's not funny, Theresa.'

'It *is*, Mum.'

'What's wrong with you, Theresa? I mean this is becoming a serious problem. Have I now got an alcoholic as well as a shop-lifter for a daughter? You tell me!'

'That's not fair. That was just once a long time ago and you know it!' Theresa flushed angrily.

'Well, where do we go from here?' her mother asked wearily, dabbing at her nose with a tissue.

There was no need to reply, however, because at that moment the doorbell rang. Even before her mother opened the door, Theresa could see the distorted shape of the policeman's uniform through the bubble glass. Having nothing to fear, she stood in the kitchen doorway, more curious than nervous.

'Morning Mrs Cussons – is Theresa at home by any chance? Can I have a word?'

Mrs Cussons motioned the policeman into the hall. Theresa saw her close her eyes as though she were about to faint as she closed the door behind him.

'Ah, Theresa.'

She had had dealings with Sergeant Miller before.

'I haven't done anything,' she said quickly.

'No, no,' he said implying the opposite. 'Shall we ...' he inclined his head towards the dining room.

'Oh yes, by all means.' Theresa's mum recovered her composure enough to lead him into the room. There were no traces left of the previous evening. The sweet peas were in their vase in the centre of the table and the air smelt of Fresh-air spray. Sergeant Miller sat himself down at the head of the table and Theresa perched at one side, staring absently at the cocktail cabinet on the wall opposite her. Her mother hovered behind her.

'Can I get you coffee?' she offered.

'No, no thanks. Now Theresa . . . not at school . . .' he observed.

'Ah, that's my fault,' her mother intervened with a false laugh. 'I told her to come home so we could . . . have a chat about a few things . . . I said I'd run her in to school before break . . .' She was picking at her finger nails. 'I know I shouldn't . . . but, you know . . . exams are over . . . and it's so difficult to find time to talk to one's children nowadays . . . I was entertaining last night, and Theresa stayed with a friend . . .' she trailed off lamely.

'No, no, none of my business, Mrs Cussons . . .' His words *always* implied the opposite, Theresa thought. 'No, I've just had a phone call from a Mr Patel at the off-licence, Theresa . . .' he glanced up at her sharply.

In spite of herself, Theresa felt a prickly blush flood her neck and cheeks.

'Have you been in there this morning?'

'Yes, I have actually . . . but I didn't buy anything.'

Her mother bit her lips.

'No, I don't think he mentioned the word "buy". "Taking" was what he was complaining about, Theresa.'

She shook her head furiously. 'No way. No . . . never!'

'Said you were behaving suspiciously, taking bottles off the shelves, turning your back on him so he couldn't see, and then while he was engaged by a customer, you slipped out . . . and that's when he realised a couple of bottles of his best malt had gone from a display case . . .'

'No way . . . I don't even like whisky much, do I Mum?'

'No, that's certainly true, Mr Miller. I have never known Theresa to choose whisky.'

'Perhaps you can tell me, Theresa, where you went after you left the shop?'

'Look, I went to the lake, didn't I . . . witnesses: lots of birds . . . and no I was not swigging malt whisky, you can check the bins can't you . . . anyway, I'd be staggering by now and you can tell I'm not . . . I'll walk a straight line if you want!' she said, jumping up. 'Or you can smell my breath . . .' She leaned over Sergeant Miller and huffed a huge breath into his face.

He grimaced and waved the air away with his gloved hand.

'I'll take a breathalyser if you want . . . you can search me,' she said, opening her jacket.

'That won't be necessary, Theresa . . . we're old acquaintances,' he said in a more friendly manner. 'You've always been truthful with me . . . in the end . . . I think I know when you're having me on. I'll believe you this time . . . can you shed any light on this, then?' he asked as he got to his feet.

'There were a couple of women in the shop when I left . . . one was talking to Mr Patel . . . I expect the other was pinching the whisky at the same time.'

He smiled. 'You could be right. But a suggestion . . . keep out of Mr Patel's shop for a bit eh, Theresa . . . he's not forgotten yet . . .'

At the door, he stopped on the front steps, turned and said quietly to Theresa's mother, 'Keep an eye on her, Mrs Cussons . . . we're not quite out of the woods yet . . . needs to be kept on her toes.'

'Yes . . . thank you, Sergeant . . . I'm doing my best!' she said.

Theresa's mum turned round slowly, breathing deeply, trying to calm her racing heart. She walked towards the dining room but at the doorway stopped, gripping hold of the door jamb, catching her breath in disbelief.

'STOP THAT!' she screamed.

Theresa, down on her hands and knees behind the dining room table, had just removed the top from the Campari bottle. She managed to steal a hasty mouthful before wiping the top slowly on her sleeve and returning it.

Her mother burst into tears.

'That is *it*! That is *it*! I'm not having any more . . . what's the matter with you?'

Theresa shrugged her shoulders and gave her mother a look.

'And don't look at me like that! I thought we'd got this all sorted last time . . . God knows I've tried to be liberal . . . I've no objection to alcohol as such . . . show by example . . . an occasional drink, a celebration or something . . . when I think of the times I stood up to your father . . . introduce them when they're young, that's what I always said . . . moderate social drinking . . . take the glamour out of it . . . kill the mystique . . . seems like I was wrong and he was right all the time then . . . is that what you're trying to demonstrate . . . I just don't know what else to do!'

'Oh, don't fuss!'

'You see!' her mother screeched. 'Fuss! Fuss! When I catch my sixteen-year-old daughter, an alcoholic, stealing from her own mother, and without a shred of remorse I might add, not to mention ruining an important dinner party.'

'There was plenty of other things besides the gin!'

'That's not the point!' snapped her mother.

'And I'm no more of an alcoholic than you are, Mother!'

'Don't be ridiculous, I'm three times your age for goodness' sake . . .'

She jumped up decisively raking her hand through her hair. 'This is getting nowhere . . .'

'You said it!'

'I wash my hands of you . . . I've done everything I know how . . . you're going to your father's . . . at least his is a dry house . . . see how you like that for a change . . . I've talked to him on the phone, I've warned him and it's all arranged – you are going – *now* . . . as soon as possible . . . sooner . . . you have *no choice* this time, Theresa . . . *no choice!*' She underlined the words in the air. Her voice was high-pitched and hysterical.

Theresa turned towards her slowly.

'That's great.'

'Not so great, young lady. Naomi, may I remind you is in her seventh month of pregnancy and your precious grandmother is ... well, never mind ... there'll be plenty to keep you occupied. And your father is well aware of just how *odious* you have been. I didn't spare him this time – or you –' she added '– or me!'

And with that she sobbed loudly once, put her hand to her mouth, turned and ran out of the room.

'I'm changing my shoes and we are going *straight* away to the station!' she yelled after her.

CORNWALL

4

Until the train pulled slowly over the Tamar bridge, Theresa had sat curled up tightly in her seat, eyes screwed shut, brain numb, not looking, not feeling, not thinking, as unaware as it was possible to be.

She uncurled, opened her eyes, and sat forward, however, as the train pulled slowly over the bridge, and peered through the metal cross-hatching into the water far below.

Once over the divide and into the promised land, she began to feel that old thrill of excitement. Kernow! Cornwall! Still here, still the same after all this time. Everything would be all right now, with the sea and the sand and the rocks and the gulls. And Grandma.

Grandma would always have been there when Theresa was a child and they'd travelled down for holidays, waiting at the station with the ancient Rover parked in the yellow-striped 'buses only' spot. She herself would have been on the platform of course, dressed in something weird and wonderful, waving a parasol madly or a huge golfing umbrella, or even once an enormous fan of peacock feathers.

Today, there was no Grandma, but even so Theresa stepped much more lightly from the train feeling skippy, almost free. Her father was standing behind the safety of his newspaper, in the lee of the tiny red brick buffet. She could tell from his face and the way he folded the paper that he was unsure what note to strike.

Seizing the initiative, she bounded up to him, threw her arms round his neck and kissed him rather fiercely on the cheek.

He was startled, she could tell, because he winced and pulled back and she instantly let go. He tried to pat her on the shoulder but her hands were already back in her pockets.

'This it?' He indicated her rucksack.

She nodded.

'Right.' He picked it up and led the way through the gates to the car park, protected on the side by deep rhododendron bushes.

'Good journey?'

They swung out under the railway bridge and onto the main road. He adjusted his mirror.

'Mum OK?'

'Not really.' Well, one of them had to broach it.

'No – I s'pose not. A pity. All of this,' he said vaguely.

'Yep.' She could only agree.

There was a pause.

'Mint? You'll find some humbugs in the glove compartment. Unwrap one for me, will you?'

Popping it into his mouth, feeling his lips on her hand, like a horse nibbling on a sugar lump, sent a shiver up her spine.

'We must have a talk sometime, you and I . . .'

'Yep.'

'But not tonight,' he added hastily. 'Might take the boat out or go for a walk or something.'

'OK.'

'Got the gear?'

'Nope.'

'Oh, not to worry – you can borrow Naomi's – she's not needing it at the moment,' he laughed.

'How is she?' Theresa asked politely.

'Pretty good I'd say – tired, you know – big as a bus,' he laughed again, 'complains of this and that – but she's fine really.'

'And Grandma?'

'Ahh.'

She looked at him quickly.

'What?'

'No – she's fine – you know her, out every day, come wind come weather, pottering about the garden and so on.'

'Well, shoot then,' Theresa persisted.

'Bees in the old bonnet . . . you may not even notice anything. I'll be interested to know. Gets very tired. Still,' he reached across and patted her knee, 'she's getting on. Aren't we all?'

There was something dark in what he said, more so in the spaces between the words, that chilled Theresa and set her heart fluttering.

The familiar landmarks passed like a film set: the deserted showground, the clock mender's pink cottage, the humpback bridge where she always left her stomach behind, the climb up the narrow lane flanked by stone walls and dark laurel trees, and, finally, the descent down to the village, a left turn beyond the gates to Chilcott House, and there they were crunching over the gravel forecourt.

Her father cut the car engine, secured the handbrake and they sat in silence for a moment. No one opened the old front door, set back under its stone porch.

He patted her knee again. 'Good to see you Trees – pity about the circumstances.'

'Cuthbert!'

The first, the *only* member of the welcome party appeared round the side of the house. He walked stiffly as though his legs were in splints. His back was as broad as a tree trunk.

Theresa threw herself down to his level and flung her arms round his neck. 'I forgot all about you. How could I have done that?'

From the broad doggy grin on his face she knew that forgiveness was instant. He licked her face and his entire back-quarters wagged from side to side.

'He remembers you,' her father said admiringly.

'I should hope so. Pooh! His breath stinks.'

'Yes – altogether a bit unsavoury aren't you, old chap. What are we saying, eh?' He fondled the old grizzled head but the dog's smile was unaffected.

'Well – come on in. Make yourself at home – you know the ropes. I'll put the kettle on. Mary's done us some scones. We can take them in the garden, I think,' he said, looking up at the cloudy sky.

Theresa had always occupied the same room at the top of the staircase, a lovely sunny room which looked out over the lawn, over the fields, to the sea itself. She threw open the door to find it transformed – white and apple green paintwork, a new carpet and in the corner a whicker cot still wrapped in polythene.

'Ah – sorry,' her father appeared behind her, 'forgot to say. You're in the spare room – next to Grandma. This . . . well, you can see whose room this is.'

Theresa tried not to feel anything as she sat down on the bed in the spare room which was too soft and had that hateful maroon eiderdown covering it. Nothing matched in this room: some old oak veneer wardrobe, a dark chest of drawers out of a junk shop, a dark patterned carpet, blue flowery sheets, yellow and brown patterned wallpaper, pink chintzy curtains. The little hand basin in the corner was pale blue, and surrounded by tiles with ugly blue fishing boats on every fifth one. The ceiling bulged and sagged and there was a dark stain over near the window. Pulling back the curtains, she looked out over the gravel drive to the yew trees in the lane – north facing – no sun.

'How can I make myself at home in the *spare* room!' she said angrily, throwing her clothes over the coverlet, putting her toothbrush in the glass above the basin.

'Tea's up!' she heard her father calling.

It was better, slung in her favourite deck chair, its faded canvas seat fraying ominously across the wooden crossbar under her knees. There was the same old brown teapot under its stained knitted tea cosy too, and the same assortment of bone china cups, most with cracks and the handles stuck back clumsily with brown glue.

'Naomi's due back any minute – don't quite know where Grandma is . . . Scone?'

'Who's Mary?' Theresa helped herself to a large floury scone and buttered it thickly with the funny little squat-bladed butter knife.

'Ah, Mary's our life-support system. Comes to help with Grandma really, but knocks up a batch of scones now and again, peels the potatoes, does the floor, that kind of thing. Have some jam – goose-berry I think,' he said, squinting at it and holding it up to the light. 'Naomi's good at jam – good at most things in that line actually. Well – most things, as you'll find out.'

Theresa ate without replying. She'd met Naomi of course, even before the wedding the previous spring. She was OK. Didn't like being called step-mother, though, which she'd made quite clear through the champagne flow of the wedding.

'Ah – this is the life, eh?' Andrew sat back in his chair and shut his eyes.

Theresa had forgotten the way he was always pretending to sleep, or hide anyway, behind news-papers and books, his VCR if not his eyelids.

'Garden's looking good.'

The roses were in abundant bloom, the flower beds of lavatera, sweet pea, hollyhocks and tall blue delphiniums had neatly trimmed edges, and the dark soil was free of weeds.

He opened one eye. 'Isn't it – can't take any credit, Naomi's doing.'

'Doesn't Grandma still do her roses?'

'Likes to think she does. More of hindrance, so Naomi says ... dead-heading the new buds and so on.'

Theresa tried hard to reject this idea. It was too precious an image of her grandmother, straw hat on her head, trug over her arm, wielding her secateurs, her brown arms scratched with rose thorns.

'Smell that ... that is *heaven*! ... see that ... that is *perfection*!' she would say: and her savage attacks on black spot and spider mites had been safety in Theresa's young world.

Cuthbert lifted his head from his paws. He was lying under Theresa's chair. He had heard something, no doubt, but Theresa was surprised by Naomi's sudden appearance round the side of the house.

'Hello there! You've arrived safely. Had tea I see.'

She wore a white smock over pastel cotton trousers. Her feet were slightly splayed and her walk reminded Theresa of the ducks that morning. That morning! It seemed light-years ago.

Her father sprang up.

'Ah – you're back.' He kissed her on the cheek. 'I'll freshen up the pot.'

'No, no – I'll do it. I'm not *ill* you know,' she added, winking at Theresa.

When she returned, her father sprang up. 'Here, wouldn't you be more comfy here?'

'No, no – a good firm back is what a lady in my condition needs.'

She turned to Theresa.

'Things not too smooth at the moment I gather . . .' She made a wry face. 'Never mind – it'll pass. Things always do.'

Theresa bit her tongue.

'No Grandma, I see.'

'No.' Andrew tapped his teeth with his index finger somewhat anxiously. 'Haven't seen hide nor hair since lunch.'

'Well, thank heaven for small mercies,' laughed Naomi.

Theresa pulled herself up.

'Think I'll go for a walk. Might meet her.'

Naomi and Andrew exchanged glances.

'I'll come with you,' offered Andrew.

'No need.'

'Well – if you're *sure* . . .'

'Coming Cuth?' She slapped her thigh with her hand and the old labrador lifted his head in disbelief.

'Not too keen on walks nowadays, are you, old boy – just pootles around the garden. Occasionally we can persuade him to accompany us to the letter box.'

'OK, then.' She swung her bomber jacket over her shoulder. 'I'll just go down to the sea.'

'You remember the geography don't you, Trees? Nothing changes much down here. Turn right at the gate and follow your nose,' her father reminded her.

5

It was all familiar – as she remembered it, except for the scale of things and the odd detail. It had been five years since she'd visited, come to think of it. Five years – apart from the wedding, which didn't really count. The rickety gate at the top of the lane was new, a raw wood stile; the ruined barn in the field was more collapsed and more covered in ivy; the fields never used to be full of black polythene rolls, but straw bales, dense building blocks which you could stand on and jump off.

At the end of the field, she broke into a run. Faster and faster she went down the narrow footpath until suddenly there it was – the whole huge expanse of blue ocean stretching out for ever until it met the blue rim of the sky. Breathless with exertion and excitement, Theresa stood on the edge of the cliff. It was all even more sparkling and brilliant than was possible, the waves breaking over the grey rocks beneath her feet in an astonishing white spume.

She walked along the cliff edge over the spongy green grass, beside the herringbone flint walls which marked the fields from the path and which were covered still in the drying tufts of pink sea thrift and glossy green sea-spinach; then she turned into the estuary. The tide was out, exposing a broad stretch of sand, and the water lapping at its edges looked deceptively calm and inviting.

'Never go in above the ankle bone in the estuary!' her grandma had warned her darkly when she was young. 'Looks are deceptive.' And then she would illustrate the point by telling of the lives of young children lost who thought they knew better than their grandmothers.

This was the estuary she had sailed round with her father and mother, just once in the dinghy. But the blue skies had suddenly darkened and the blue water had turned from friendly to menacing as the wind and the turning tide whipped the waves into confusion. And the sails had flapped like giant wings above her head and the flying boom had nearly knocked her father out of the boat and he had yelled at her mother and her mother had yelled back. When they did finally reach dry land her mother had refused to help pull the boat up onto the trailer, an unforgivable sin, and she had shouted 'Never again!' and disappeared up the hill.

'Too right!' her father had called after her retreating form.

There were a few picture-book clouds, very white and bouncy, racing across the sky, and a fresh salty breeze, the kind which made Theresa's cheeks sting. She watched the seagulls soaring and chasing and squabbling, and a cormorant flying like a black dart low over the water.

Estuary Cove was a good beach for shells and stranded sea-creatures, crabs marooned on their backs and long dead, an occasional jelly fish, drying and globular in the sun.

Down at the water's edge, a couple of black-backed gulls were fishing something invisible to her from the water and on the low rocks below the old coastguard cottages, oystercatchers were piping.

She stood for a moment quite still and closed her eyes. Immediately her ears filled with the sounds of the mewling gulls, the roar of the sea; her nose with the salty, clean freshness of the sea air. A sea breeze seemed to be battering against her eardrums, the same noise the wind made in the sail on her father's boat.

She filled her lungs until they seemed to be bursting, so her body was gorged with the same goodness that surrounded her. Had she not anchored her toes deeply in the sand under her feet she felt she might take off and float away with the birds on the invisible thermals which contoured the air round the cliffs.

Theresa kicked off her shoes and walked barefoot, enjoying the textures of the sand under her feet – fine and warm near the sand dunes, gritty and coarser in the centre of the beach, soggy and cold nearer the water's edge. She never really liked the cold on her feet, though, Grandma; she was always trying to entice Theresa up onto the warmer sand. She even used to pull that spade along in the sand behind her, cutting a trail for Theresa to follow.

Had she not known that her Theresa was arriving? Had she been told not to greet her? Had she been informed of her disgrace? Theresa dismissed this idea as she wiped the sand off her feet with her hand, pinching it out from between her toes. Grandma was always the one she could run to when she knew she was being insufferable as a child – she'd give her a little job, a bowl to lick, a button tin to tidy, a skein of wool to hold. She'd play cards with her when her parents were reading, tell stories on demand, morning, noon and night without flagging. It wasn't that she didn't know that Theresa could be a little beast, a little madam, that she could lie and cheat and steal, but it didn't seem to matter to her like it did to her parents; it was just a small episode in a larger story.

The front door was open when she returned and there stood Grandma, a long ochre-coloured coat revealing just a suspicion of scarlet stocking above her stout ankle boots. Round her shoulders she had thrown a shawl patterned with brilliant greens and blues, like a rain forest. On her head she wore her old familiar navy straw hat. She was standing with her back to Theresa.

'Grandma!'

It took her a moment. She turned round, looking as though she'd been slapped in the face.

'Lord love us!'

Theresa threw her arms round her neck and the old lady hugged her so tightly Theresa could feel her bones.

'What a wonderful surprise! Come in! Come in! Let me look at you. My, my – how you've grown. What's this horrible black stuff!' She picked at her coat. 'Somebody died?' And she threw back her head and laughed. 'Andrew! Andrew! Look who's arrived!'

From out of the kitchen her father appeared.

'I know, Mother! I *told* you Theresa was coming.'

'You did no such thing! Not today anyway! He's always telling me he's told me something and he never has,' she complained to Theresa. 'Where are your things, my pet?'

'They're upstairs, Mother.' Andrew's tone was weary. 'She arrived just after lunch . . . on the train.'

'On the train! All the way? How long does it take now?'

'Just a couple of hours, Grandma.'

'A couple of hours!' That look of being slapped again. 'From London!'

'No!' Theresa laughed. 'From Bristol!'

'From Bristol – of course!' She laughed with her. 'How stupid of me! I do forget, don't I, Andrew?'

'Yes, Mother. You do.'

'He can't believe, for instance, that I simply don't remember where I've been this very afternoon . . . just been for a wander, I told him, just me and my old thoughts . . .'

'Mrs Carter found you half a mile away, stumbling along the grass verge of the main road,' Andrew said severely.

'Pah!' She waved her gloves at him dismissively. 'I certainly was not stumbling . . . I was on my way to the bus stop. And why not, pray, I wasn't doing any harm to anyone. It's a free country, isn't it?' She winked at Theresa.

'But I just don't understand what you were doing

there, Mother. I mean, if you want to go anywhere, I'd be more than happy to take you, you only have to say.'

Her tone softened. 'Dear boy!' She touched his arm gently as she walked past him. 'Must get out of this coat before I expire! Put the kettle on, there's a dear.'

'Can I leave this to you, Trees?' he asked her. 'Better go and see that Naomi's OK.'

By the time the old lady returned, Theresa had managed to locate a couple of scones in a tin and fill the tea pot. Her grandma's dress was strangely plain and unadorned, but round her waist she had a girdle of vibrant twisted silks tied in a loose knot.

'I remember that belt, Grandma,' Theresa said. 'I used to play with the end. Remember?'

'Probably why it's so frayed! Old and frayed – like me.' She sat down smiling, stroking the back of her hand with the tasselled end. 'Now – tell me – what have you been up to, dear Theresa . . . but spare me the boring parts . . . no school . . . have you been having fun? That's what I want to know.'

'Not really,' Theresa admitted, although it was the first time she had realised it herself. 'The walk on the beach just now was the best fun I've had really since . . . for ages.' She sighed, stirring two spoonfuls of sugar into her tea. 'I went for a drive in a buggy yesterday . . . and we went really fast . . . and I liked that bit . . . I seem to like doing things I shouldn't . . . but then things always seem to go wrong whatever I do . . . so what's the point?'

'I used to like going fast too, zipping across the

water with the wind filling the sails and blowing so loud you couldn't hear anything else. My clothes got drenched and I never even noticed. And my mother used to get so upset and I could never understand why.' The old lady's eyes had misted over. She seemed to have gone away from her.

Theresa wanted her back with her.

'I went down to Estuary Cove, Grandma, remember?'

She touched her hand which was on the table. It brought her grandma's attention back to the hand, to the touch, to Theresa, to the moment.

Curling her fingers round Theresa's own, she shook her hand and laughed.

'Of course! "Never above the ankle bone." Not so good for the paddling, dangerous for hot toddlers, terrible currents, and bad for grandmothers who had to explain the power of the sea to their wilful grandchildren, if I remember correctly.'

Theresa laughed. 'Good for crabs, though. Remember, I stuffed my pockets with them when you said I couldn't bring them home.'

'I will never forget.'

'But *I* forgot all about them,' Theresa continued.

'I believe it was our Cuthbert who found them.' The old lady looked over to the Aga where Cuthbert was lying. Hearing his name, he lifted his head and stared lovingly at his mistress.

'Yes, we're talking about you, Cuth . . . are your ears burning?'

Suddenly she leant forward, a look of intensity on her face. 'It's not easy being young, Theresa,' she said. 'And it's not easy growing up either; but one finds a way through somehow. And then you look back and realise that it was *all* pretty good fun. And you've got to have those tricky bits, something to pick your way through. You'd be a dull enough person otherwise.'

The change that came over her grandma's face was sudden, as though all the energy had suddenly flowed out, down through her body and into the earth beneath her feet. Her cheeks changed to grey, but it wasn't just the colour, the light faded in her eyes and everything about her sagged.

'You OK, Grandma?'

She managed to pat Theresa's hand, but vaguely and, though her lips parted, she didn't say a word.

'Ah here they are gossiping like magpies!' Naomi breezed into the kitchen on a wave of talc and body spray. 'Time for me to get the supper now ... and you know what I'm like about my kitchen, no one is allowed near me as I work,' she explained to Theresa. 'Now Mother.' She talked too loudly as though she were talking to someone stupid. 'Shall I turn on the tele for you? Or perhaps Theresa will take you.'

'She doesn't seem too well,' Theresa said.

'Oh, she often goes like this, don't worry. She's just tired, aren't you, Mother?' She raised her voice again. 'Just tired, aren't you?'

Theresa took her grandmother's arm and led her into the lounge. 'Do you want the News, Grandma? It's nearly six. Where do you want to sit – Grandpa's chair?'

Her grandmother turned, not understanding.

Theresa felt awkward. 'You know – this one!' She pointed to the big wing chair by the fireplace. 'We always called it Grandpa's chair.'

'We did, we did. Grandpa's chair!'

She sat down fingering the old leather arms tenderly. 'Grandpa's chair.'

6

Gradually, during the period of inactivity in front
of the television, and after the meal which Naomi
cooked for her, Grandma seemed to recover her
energy. Her face became flushed with colour and
the light came back in her eyes. When she appeared
in the kitchen where Theresa and her father were
stacking the dishwasher, dressed in her hat and coat,
it was hard to believe this was the same person
whom Theresa had lead into the lounge, shaking
and pale, just an hour and a half previously.

'Where are you off to, Mother?' Andrew asked
suspiciously.

'Nowhere in particular,' she replied. 'He'd keep
me on a lead if he could,' she confided to Theresa.
'There's a perfectly good one hanging up behind
the back door,' she told her son who attacked the
pot he was cleaning with fresh vigour. 'Cuthbert
doesn't need it these days.'

'I only asked because you have your hat on,
Mother,' he said calmly.

Her hand went up to her head quickly and after
a moment's hesitation she said to Theresa:

'Yes, my dear. I was going to suggest a stroll in
the garden. Inspect my rose trees. And there's quite

a wind today you know.' This last remark she threw towards Andrew.

'That's a good idea. I can finish off here. Naomi's got a NCT class at eight and I think I'll go along to support, just for half an hour or so, if you two can manage.'

'Of course we can, can't we, my lamb?' She linked her arm through Theresa's and together they strolled across the lawn in the evening sun.

'Adore this time of the year . . . so light . . . and just look at my roses . . . aren't they a joy?'

'Perfection!' Theresa replied.

The old lady smiled and squeezed her arm tightly.

'See those Princess Elizabeths . . . and my little Ophelia! I don't think I've *ever* seen the Bewitched looking more bewitching! My Indian Song's not doing quite so well . . . don't think it likes the soil . . . or the wind or something . . . or the company it keeps . . . well, beggars can't be choosers, we all know that in life. But let's see my Baby Darling, eh?'

The pergola, separating the roses from the vegetable garden beyond, was smothered in blush-pink blossoms.

'Andrew planted that when you were born, you know.' She squeezed Theresa's arm.

'I know.' She'd heard it all a million times. She knew just what her grandma was going to say next; but it was wonderful when she did.

' "Double blooms borne with great freedom", that's what the catalogue said.'

Theresa smiled and sighed deeply.

Her grandma turned towards her immediately. 'Now what was that for?'

'What?'

'That enormous sigh from the bottom of your boots.'

'I didn't even realise . . . it was a happy sigh, I think,' she said wondering. 'Happy to be here, with you.'

They both squeezed together.

It was when she relaxed her grip that Theresa noticed the way the arm hooked through her own became suddenly heavy. She seemed to stumble though the grass beneath their feet was as smooth as a snooker table. Her face was once more washed with that ashen quality and a fragility which scared Theresa.

'Grandma . . . Grandma . . . you OK?'

'Yes . . . yes . . . Just tired . . .' She tried to smile. 'Time for bed, I think.'

The clock in the hall struck eight sharp strokes. Theresa stood, hand on the newel post, wondering what she should do. Cuthbert came and stood beside her for a moment before sinking down on the rug and falling promptly asleep.

'I like your approach, Cuth,' she said to him gently.

She hadn't thought of it, it hadn't entered her head until this minute, but right now she would have murdered for a drink.

'Bet Naomi won't have it in the house,' she thought, standing in the centre of the lounge and looking about her for likely hiding spots. She pulled open a few cupboards. Surely, an odd bottle of sherry at least. She tried to remember. Had her father not taken a sherry on Sunday mornings after church, the odd whisky of an evening? Perhaps, in his study . . .

She was actually crossing the hall when the front door opened and Andrew came in. She stopped guiltily.

'Hi Dad! Did it go OK?' She could scarcely remember what at that second.

'Fine. What about you?' he asked anxiously.

'OK, she was fine. Then she sort of collapsed on me all of a sudden, said she was just tired. She's gone to bed.'

'Best place for her,' said Andrew decisively. 'I'm thirsty, how about you?'

'Yea!'

'Come on . . . I'll put the kettle on.'

'The kettle . . .' she repeated, trying to keep the inflection out of her voice.

'I'll have a coffee myself. How about you? There are plenty of teas . . . herbal, all that stuff, Naomi . . .' he explained. 'Difficult, old people you know . . . need more patience than I possess some-times, I'm sure you remember,' he laughed, pouring the milk into his coffee.

She *did* remember: those boiling rages, sudden, vehement, a tongue protruding from the side of the mouth, that hard jaw, those iron fingers and sometimes the flat of a hand, broad and hard as a paddle across the back of her legs.

'Naomi's wonderful I must say . . . can't imagine how it's going to be with the baby.'

Theresa shifted in her chair and stirred her coffee loudly, though she didn't take sugar, only in tea.

'She's taken to wandering off you see. I'm just worried about her, that she might set off somewhere and then not have the energy to get back, or forget where she is or something. Hence all the digs about the lead and so on . . . she just doesn't seem to realise she's a worry to me.'

He paused for a moment, a half smile fading from his face. Theresa noticed there were lines of fatigue round his eyes that she did not like to see, and there were grey streaks in the hair by his temples. She jumped up impulsively and put her arm round his shoulders. She'd have jumped into his lap if she'd not been too big.

At that very minute she heard Naomi's key turning in the front door.

'Hello there! I'm back.'

Theresa took her arm away immediately and went over to where Cuthbert was lying and, stooping down to his level, rubbed his tummy affectionately with her hand. He opened his eyes and groaned in an expression of ecstasy.

Naomi came into the kitchen, her face flushed with exercise. She sank into a chair and sat like Humpty-Dumpty, hands in the arch of her back, a gesture Theresa remembered from when her mother was expecting Rosie.

'Exhausted?' asked Andrew tenderly. 'Let me make you a tea.'

'Lime blossom please, it's the yellow box. Very relaxing,' she told Theresa. 'Try some.'

She shook her head. 'I've just had a coffee.'

Naomi wrinkled her nose. 'Terrible stuff . . . I've gone right off coffee, can't risk it. Not even real, can I, Andrew. That and alcohol. Strange, but I can't even bear to think of it.'

'Nor can I!' thought Theresa.

'It must be Nature's way of making sure he's getting just what he needs, eh Junior?' she said to her stomach. Why did all pregnant women seem to regress to the mental age of a six-year-old? Theresa wondered. Maybe it was all part of the necessary preparation. It would be impossible to deal with all those bottoms and nappies and squirming pink bodies if you had your wits about you.

She got up and yawned. 'Well, I think I'll go to bed. Long day. Got anything to read, Dad?' she asked, half hoping he might send her to browse along the book-shelves in his office.

'I've got just the ticket,' Naomi offered immediately. 'Just finished reading it . . . Mary Wesley . . . do you like her?'

Theresa had never heard of her.

'Is it suitable?' Andrew inquired mildly.

'Oh, all that sex and stuff. Don't be so stuffy, Andrew. There's nothing sixteen-year-olds don't know about nowadays, is there?' she said, winking at Theresa, who felt herself flushing with annoyance.

'Let me get it for you,' Naomi offered, half pulling herself up.

'I'll get it, if you tell me where it is, I'm going up anyway.'

'OK. It's right by the bed ... on the table ... wardrobe side ... Andrew insists on the window,' she said, toeing him under the table.

'Hang on a sec,' Andrew told her. 'Just take your grandmother up her tray for the night. Save me a trip.'

Quickly he assembled her night supports: a jug of water, a glass, two water biscuits on a plate, a thermos which he filled with hot water from the kettle; a little cup and saucer, white china with a pattern of purple violets.

For an instant Theresa hesitated, wondering whether or not she should kiss her father goodnight, but he handed the tray to her in such a way as to preempt her gesture.

'Well, goodnight then,' she called.

'Goodnight,' they answered in unison. 'Sleep well.'

She knocked quietly at first, and then louder on her grandmother's door and hearing no answer, tried the handle. It was unlocked. Her father's remarks had made her think it would be locked. Immediately she opened the door her grandmother's voice called out, 'Who's there?'

'Theresa. I've brought your tray.'

She was in bed, but the room was in darkness. Theresa could just make out the white handkerchief and the dark shape under the bedclothes, and then, as her eyes became more accustomed to the dark, the empty table by her bed.

'I'll put it here then. Anything more you want?'

'No . . . no thank you. Everything's as it should be . . .'

'I'll say night-night then.' She stooped over to kiss her grandmother's brow. It felt fragile as a rose petal, but smooth and fragranced.

'Goodnight, my darling!' Suddenly, surprisingly, she felt her grandmother pull her down with strong arms and kiss her rather passionately. 'My darling! My darling!' she said.

7

A beach; yellow sand. Blue sea with white bubbling waves chasing up the beach. Standing knee-deep in it – small hands in large ones – Dad to the right – Mum to the left. A wave, a heave of darker water, shapes itself and moves forward. Glee! Excitement! Sudden fear – it's too big – it will swamp them all! Then, with a one-to-three whee, up she goes, up and over, and the broken water runs harmlessly on to where Grandma stands with a towel slung round her shoulders, to just tickle her toes. Then, cold as a fish, blue as the water, teeth chattering, she is racing with the waves and now, folded in a huge, salt-stiff towel, Grandma's arms are pressing her to her stomach, a great wall of Grandma, wider than the sea, taller than the sky, safer than night.

It took Theresa some time to remember where she was when she surfaced from her dreams the next morning. There were no familiar sounds: just a seagull drumming on the slate roof over her head and cawing loudly; the wind in the yew trees; the sound of a vacuum cleaner the other side of her wall. There was a strange pinkish light in the room, and a peculiar smell too of mothballs and damp and lack of use.

The spare room! Those disgusting pink floral curtains, the maroon quilt which she'd rolled up and thrown into the bottom of the cupboard, and a musty smell of drains which seemed to be coming from a damp patch under the sink. She'd tell her dad about it.

What was Grandma doing, she wondered as she spat toothpaste into the blue basin, vacuuming her room at nine-thirty in the morning? She pulled on a pair of black cotton shorts and a grey T-shirt. Throwing cold water on her face, she remembered she hadn't got a towel. No sweat, she thought rubbing her face on yesterday's T-shirt, sniffing and grinning at her own joke.

She tiptoed along the corridor. Grandma's door was open. She poked her head round.

Someone was standing with her back to the door winding the electric cord round the vacuum cleaner which was now upright.

'Hello!'

The woman sprang forward as though she'd been shot.

'Sorry.' Theresa was embarrassed until the woman broke into a gale of laughter.

'My goodness, you gave me a shock . . . sent my old heart all of a patter . . . You must be Theresa . . . spitting image of your grandma! I'm Mary. She's told me all about you.'

'Oh dear,' said Theresa, secretly pleased.

'No, you've got a fan there, my 'andsome, won't hear a word against her Theresa.'

'Where is she?' Theresa asked.

'Having her breakfast in the kitchen, I hope,' she added crossing her fingers. She was plump, Mary, and wheezed as she worked, but nevertheless she never stopped swooping down to shake rugs, rearrange her grandmother's slippers, pull up the bedclothes.

Grandma was sitting at the kitchen table wrapped in a black silk kimono, orange dragons breathing red and yellow flames across her back, biting into a slice of buttered toast.

'Morning,' Theresa called cheerily.

'Morning, Pat! Sleep well?' her grandmother enquired without turning round.

'It's me, Grandma.'

The old lady swung round bodily and faced her with a look of complete astonishment on her face. 'Theresa, my darling . . . I forgot . . . but a wonderful surprise all over again.'

'I dreamt about you . . . on the beach . . . with Mum and Dad.'

'How lovely . . . what fun we had, didn't we? Remember all those sandcastles and mermaids we used to build in the sand? You were very fussy you know . . . difficult to please.'

'Was I?'

Theresa helped herself to a plate full of Cornflakes.

'The seaweed for her hair had to be just right . . . you didn't like the green . . . it had to be bladderwrack . . . and long strands, too . . . "Mermaids have long hair," you told me.'

'I thought you told me that.'

With some puffing and panting, Mary came into the kitchen carrying the Hoover.

'Now, I don't want to rush you or nothing, Mrs Bird, but chiropodist's coming at ten-thirty . . . your room's all ready . . . Now you just run along and get your stockings off and whatever you have to do . . . and I'll follow along direct . . . just got to do a pan of spuds for Mrs Bird. Naomi, I mean . . .'

The old lady sighed and clasped her gown at her throat. 'You see what it's like for me, Theresa . . . boss, boss, boss . . .'

With both her grandma and Mary gone, it was just Theresa and Cuthbert left in the kitchen and the silent old clock, whose hands moved visibly every second.

'I'll go down to the harbour, that's what I'll do,' Theresa said jumping up. 'Down to the quay and the sea and the boats. It's all just there waiting for me!' she told Cuthbert excitedly. 'Through the door and I'm in it. Magic! Coming?'

Cuthbert's ears flattened and conveyed the clear message that he had absolutely no intention of taking one step off his property.

It occurred to Theresa quite suddenly and with some annoyance that she had no money. It was her mother's last act of power and vengefulness, in her opinion, to buy her rail ticket on Access and then send her off without the price of a cup of tea. Trust her father not to think of anything so real. She'd have asked Naomi had she been around, or Grandma. She'd just have to go for a walk, do something and last out till lunchtime when she'd just ask

Andrew straight what the arrangements were going to be.

In spite of the virtually cloudless sky and a bright hot sun, Theresa swung her arms into her jacket and, leaving the house by the back door, which seemed permanently open, she crossed the gravel forecourt and set off down Mariner Street.

Up on the high pavements, at least half a metre above the road, Theresa could peer into the front rooms of the houses as she passed: a cat was sunning itself on the window ledge in one; a collection of china ornaments was displayed in another; spiders' webs and dead flies lay behind yellowed lace curtains in a third.

The fish shop was now a High Class green-grocer's; then there was the old butcher's, the saw-dust floor now replaced with lino tiles, she noticed; but the brick post office was still the brick post office, and the bank on the corner looked as incongruous as it always had. It pained her to have to walk past the fudge shop in the narrow street which led to the harbour.

It was the same as ever. Visitors, conspicuous in their shorts and holiday gear, eating ice-creams, strolled slowly around, pushing pushchairs, dragging unwilling toddlers who wanted to go at a different pace, spend longer gazing at the herring gulls which in turn were gazing at the toddlers' dripping cornets. The seats on the bandstand were already full: men reading newspapers, women, gazing up at the sun, with shopping bags at their feet, and, as always, whole families eating fish and chips out of greasy paper. At the side of the bandstand where an old slipway led down into the water, children with lines and hooks were fishing for crabs, as Theresa herself had done years before, putting her victims into a red bucket and then throwing them back into the water at the end of her fishing session, with a feeling of enormous good will.

On she walked, through the car park, past the stall which was selling raffle tickets in support of the Lifeboat; past where her father used to moor his dinghy before he got bigger ideas and a bigger boat, needing a change of mooring; past the Harbour Master's prefabricated office; and along the quayside to the fish tanks. You could always do this for free, go and watch the lobsters, armoured sea-monsters, brilliant blue in colour, their powerful claws humiliatingly secured with tape. It had been so thrilling, plucking up courage to touch the end of a feelers protruding from the water in that tank in spite of the notices telling her of the dangers.

Inside, the floor was wet and the air as cool and fishy as she remembered it. But to her astonishment and anger, the way to the tanks was barred by a notice demanding 50p entrance.

'What's going on?' she demanded out loud.

A visitor, a man in coloured Bermuda shorts and a Fat Willy's Surfing Shack T-shirt, was peeling off some notes from a considerable wad in his wallet; he answered her cheerfully.

'Don't get nothing for nothing these days.'

'Ain't that the truth,' Theresa muttered to herself in her mock American accent as she turned and walked out into the light again. Someone had put a notice up on a chain hanging across the quayside to her right.

DO NOT WALK THIS WAY – UNPROTECTED QUAYSIDE.

She'd always walked this way. Who did they think they were?

'Or who do they think we are, come to that,' she thought as she walked out onto the forbidden quay.

Mostly, it was deserted, being the working part of the town, where the rusted fishing boats moored and the boxes of fish and lobster were unloaded and put onto waiting trucks. But though the tide was coming in, there were no boats unloading at this time. Near the end of the quay, in a boat which was smaller than the rest, an old man was sorting out his nylon net.

'In the old days, I suppose he'd have been sitting there with his wooden needle, mending the holes,' she thought. At least now all he had to do was pull out the tangles and arrange it in some kind of pile. She stood on the quay watching him. He wore thigh-length boots and an old oiled sweater with holes in the elbows. He had a cap on his head, but his face was as wrinkled as a map, brown and creased by years of salt and sun. He had a grizzled white beard too – a real-life, grubby, rough Captain Birdseye.

The old man stopped his work and looked back at her. She felt suddenly awkward, staring at him as though he were an exhibit, and she was about to move away when he spoke.

'How do.'

She didn't know whether to reply OK, or to treat it as a hello. Instead she just smiled.

'On holiday are you?'

'Sort of.'

'Brought the fine weather.'

She nodded.

There was a pause when he lifted his cap and scratched his hair. 'Remember me?'

She shook her head.

'Well, I remember you. I'd know you anyways . . . Tilda May's granddaughter, aren't you . . .?'

Theresa nodded again.

'Spitting image you are. I knew her when she was your age . . . chums you might say . . . before she went her way and I went mine.'

Spitting Image, that was the second time she'd been told that.

'How's she doing?'

'She's OK.' It was easier to leave it at that.

'Don't see her these days.'

'She doesn't get out much.'

'No, no. That's what I heard. What's your name now . . . I clean forgot it, though I saw you once when you were a little scrap of a thing.'

'Theresa,' she told him.

'Ah! That's it. Not a Cornish name . . . that was your mother I expect. Theresa,' he repeated, trying out the sound, committing it to his memory. 'And I'm Joseph – not a Cornish name either, you're thinking, but the name don't tell you about the everything. Joe they call me. Tell your grandma: Joe sends his regards.'

'I will,' Theresa promised.

'Now, I got things to do and I expect you have too, better things than talking to an old salt!' he laughed.

'No,' said Theresa truthfully, but he wasn't going to believe her.

'I'll talk to you again Theresa Bird, if you want to.'

'Yes. All right.'

'And mind how you go,' he called after her.

She walked back past the notice prohibiting her entrance, but she didn't think he meant that.

Back round the harbour she retraced her steps. It was busier now, fuller, and there was quite a queue outside the Chippy. The smell was delicious and had Theresa had any money at all, she'd have felt tempted by the chips at least. However, she hunched her shoulders and moved on round the front, past the twee pink coffee shop, past the shop which sold the coloured sticks of rock she used to hanker after as a sweet-toothed child, to the shelter.

Inside, deep in the shade, stood and sat a group of young people of her own age. Their tatty jeans and jackets indicated resident status, not visitor. One boy was standing smoking and drinking from a can of Blackthorn. Theresa saw it all and noted it, but she hurried past, head down, knowing that they had seen her.

Instead of going on round the far side of the harbour as she had intended, she turned abruptly left round the side of the conical shelter, back past the fudge shop to the Bank and on up Mariner Street.

Naomi was already home by the time she re-entered the kitchen. She was showing Andrew an assortment of little Baby-gro's, sleep suits and cardigans she'd just bought.

'Dad,' she cut in ignoring the display. 'I forgot to say. Mum said can you give me some money. She was right out of change. I haven't got a bean.'

'Ah.'

Naomi continued to turn the tiny clothes over in her hands, folding and refolding them.

'Is there anything in particular . . .?' he inquired, putting his hand in his pocket.

'No . . . just don't like to have nothing at all . . .'

She saw him hesitate and look towards Naomi as though for guidance.

'I don't want much,' Theresa said, an edge creeping into her voice.

'Of course she must have something,' Naomi rose to her defence.'

'I don't need your say so,' Theresa wanted to say. She was beginning to feel stifled too.

'Look, I've only got a few coins at the moment. Here's two, three pounds. I've got to go to the Bank this afternoon. We'll get something more organised together this evening, OK?'

'Thanks . . .' a bunch . . . Theresa thought, pocketing the small pile of change.

'Aren't you hot in that old jacket?' Naomi asked. 'If you'd like something more suitable, I've got a whole wardrobe full of clothes that I can't wear at the moment. You're more than welcome.'

Andrew smiled at her generosity.

'It's OK, thanks,' Theresa declined.

Mary stuck her head round the kitchen door from the hall.

'I'm off now, one and all. She's on her way down. See you tomorrow.'

'Oh, Mary,' Naomi shouted after her, 'could you get me a few things from the shops on the way up tomorrow?'

Mary stepped into the kitchen. 'Why surely.'

'Just a couple of loaves . . . a wholemeal and a white sliced for Mother, and maybe a pie or something for lunch. What do you think, Andrew?'

'Sounds good to me.'

'Can you give Mary some money?'

'Ah yes of course . . . here.' And taking a bill-fold out of his back pocket, he peeled a five pound note off and passed it to her.

He didn't avoid Theresa's even gaze.

She swept out of the kitchen intending to go to her room, but met her grandmother coming down the stairs.

'Theresa, my lamb, tell me all . . . what's been happening to you while I've been having my feet de-bunioned?'

Theresa helped her down the last two steps.

'Nothing much . . . went for a walk . . . oh yes, met an old friend of yours . . . asked to be remembered . . .'

Her grandmother stopped, hand on the newel

post. 'And who might that have been . . . I might not remember you know . . .' she warned her hurriedly.

'Joe . . . Joseph Somebodyorother . . . He's a fisherman . . . met him down on the quay . . . said he was at school with you . . .'

'And very probably he was,' said her grandmother quietly, but this time Theresa was sure she knew exactly who she meant.

'Lunchtime, I think,' the old lady continued. 'And I think it's a lunch-in-the-garden kind of day.'

The four of them sat in deck chairs on the lawn quietly munching on separate choices of salads and meats and cheeses. Grandmother had cold rice pudding, Naomi, a peach, Andrew some apple pie left over from the previous day, and Theresa, a giant orange.

At the end of the meal, Theresa stretched out on the grass, a tremendous sleepiness stealing over her as the sun beat down on her black T-shirt.

'Look Theresa, my little friend's come,' her grandma called her urgently.

'Who?' She sat up and there was a robin sitting on the back of the chair she'd just vacated.

'Run and get a bit of cheese, there's a dear. He likes Stilton best, don't you?' she cooed at him. He turned his black beady eye protruding from his head and looked at her trustingly.

'Mother,' Andrew protested. 'That bird is spoiled.'

Cuthbert lifted his head, seeming to agree entirely with Andrew's sentiments, but obviously he'd given up interfering long ago.

'Why Stilton?' Theresa inquired when she returned.

'Sshh!' Her grandmother held out her hand, the morsel of cheese obvious in her fingers. The robin took his time, eyeing each member of the group with a sideways look, before darting to her hand and scooping the prize away and flying off to the buddleia bush to eat it.

'Stilton cheese and fruit cake are his favourites,' she told Theresa.

'P'raps worms taste like Stilton cheese and vice versa,' suggested Theresa. Her grandmother laughed.

'Do I take it you're not partial to blue cheeses then? It's an older palate's taste. You'll grow into it,' she prophesied. 'Time for my nap,' she announced, folding her napkin and rolling it into a tube which she replaced in her silver napkin ring. 'Don't let me slumber past three,' she told Theresa. 'Perhaps we could take a walk together before tea.'

'OK. Let's do that.'

Theresa sank back into a semi-soporific state, only distantly aware of the voices around her. Naomi was telling Andrew about her visit to the doctor, the details of which Theresa did not want to hear. She blocked her ears and thought of those kids hanging out in the shelter.

'You're looking very pale,' she heard her father commenting.

'I'm not feeling one hundred per cent . . . could be the sun.'

'You've overdone it.'

'I'll have a rest . . . lie down properly.'

'Do that. We can manage, Theresa and I. Don't you think about supper . . . I'm only concerned about you.' That syrupy tone again which made Theresa feel like screaming. She wanted to be far away, asleep, not hearing, but she was awake, feeling cross and hot and prickly.

It was only after Andrew retired to his office and Naomi had gone for her lie down that Theresa reclaimed the peace of the garden. Gradually she became aware of the bird song, trilling and piping from the bushes and the hedges nearby and cutting across the sky above her. The bushes of wigelia and honeysuckle hummed with bees; she found herself breathing in time to Cuthbert's heavy snores until she felt herself sinking back into the grass and the sunlight and the warm air around her.

8

It was a clock striking three, very far away somewhere, which finally pulled Theresa back into the
hot afternoon. With a sudden panic she jumped to
her feet and stumbled towards the house feeling
clumsy and functioning in an unco-ordinated way.

She knocked quite loudly on her grandmother's
door and hearing no reply, she looked in. She wasn't
on the bed, nor immediately anywhere to be seen,
but then she heard a kind of scrabbling coming from
the other side of the bed.

'Grandma!' The old lady was on her knees searching through a small shoe box. As soon as she saw
Theresa she put the lid back on as though she'd
been discovered in the middle of a naughty act and
stood up. She didn't say anything.

'Are you looking for something? Can I help?'
Theresa offered.

The old lady hesitated, fingering the rope of
bright glass beads at her throat as though she were
going to decline the offer.

'Well, I'm sure I can trust you,' she said finally.
'Though I don't want them all poking their noses
into my business.' She sat down on the edge of her
bed and patted the quilt next to her. Theresa sat

down and the old lady grasped her hand, stroking its soft skin.

'When a person gets old, it gets increasingly hard to keep other people out of their business,' she told her and, without expanding the thought, she added suddenly: 'You bite your nails.'

Automatically Theresa curled up her hand and pulled it away.

'I used to myself,' her grandma confessed. 'Never seemed to matter to me. Better than many sins I always thought, but my mother painted my fingers with bitter tasting lotions and told me I'd live to regret it, which I never did. Losing your teeth, that's the best way of stopping biting your nails.' She laughed. 'Your grandfather made me wear gloves when we went out . . . it was the hands which gave me away he always told me . . . not that I cared . . . a fisherman's girl and proud of it.'

'Mum tried to make me wear gloves in bed once,' Theresa said. 'I always have a good chew last thing at night.'

'Terrible child! What's to be done with you, eh?'

They smiled at each other.

'Now, what are we looking for?'

Her grandmother wiped her cheek with the flat of her hand.

'Ah yes! I seem to have mislaid something. It's nothing . . . just important to me you see . . . a card, a greetings card . . . well, half a card in fact. Cut down the middle, and I have the one half and . . .' she hesitated '. . . this friend of mine, Gillie, has the other half. I need it you see, so that I can go and visit her again . . .'

They searched together through the boxes under her bed, through the little drawers in her dressing table, through the books by her bed, through her wallet, and even through the pockets of her dresses and coats.

'It'll turn up, Grandma. Why don't we go out for a bit now, while it's sunny, and we'll look again later?'

Rather reluctantly, the old lady was persuaded into her yellow coat and Theresa tied the laces of her stout ankle boots.

'I'll wait for you downstairs, Grandma, just put your hat on and I'll get my coat.'

As she stood in the hallway, waiting for her grandma to appear, another craving for some kind of quick drink swept over her, turning her legs weak and somersaulting her stomach.

A dry house was it? That's what her mother had said. Of course her grandma had that strange puritanical thing about alcohol which no one quite understood . . . something to do with some event long buried. And her father rarely touched the stuff either. His mother had done a good job on him! Theresa thought. She was certain, however, that she remembered the existence of a bottle of something 'for medicinal purposes only' that Grandma kept in the back of the larder . . . or at the back of a dusty cupboard somewhere.

There was nothing in the larder, even at the back of the top-most shelves where all the dusty bottles of preserves and homemade chutneys used to be stored. They had been freshly painted and lined in washable paper and contained delicacies such as Baxters Lobster Bisque and green olives.

It was like a tantalising game of Hunt the Thimble . . . if not in the kitchen, then where?

The corner cupboard in her father's office struck her immediately as a likely place. Readily available from the garden, the hall or anywhere on the ground floor, should faintness overtake a visitor, should an accident occur and should bad news be received . . . and yet inaccessible to the eyes of the visitors who might not have heard of the rules of the house and who might linger on after an invitation to afternoon tea.

The more she thought about it, the more she convinced herself that her hunch was right. Her whole body seemed to throb with certainty as she stood staring at the closed door.

She knocked hesitantly on her father's office door.

'Come!'

'Sorry Dad, it's me . . . just wondered if you'd been to the bank yet . . . I need some sun-cream . . . look, I'm burning already . . .' She lifted her sleeve to show him the rather vivid line dividing red from white.

Without further ado he reached into his back pocket and peeled off a five pound note.

'This should do it? We'll talk finances proper later on . . . I'm chasing a bit of a deadline at the moment.'

Theresa did manage to have a quick look round, however, and located a possible cupboard behind his desk, a corner antique piece which is where she'd have kept her decanter and glasses, had she been . . .

'See you later then . . .' she said as she opened the door.

'Hang on, Theresa, I've got you in charge of Grandma this afternoon, OK? Just till I've finished this thing and got it faxed off . . .'

'OK.'

That was all according to plan; they could toddle down to the harbour together, maybe have tea in one of the cafés and then she would slip into the off-licence, making some excuse; then she'd call at the chemist and get the smallest tube possible . . . and if she didn't have enough . . . well, then Grandma would surely oblige.

'Still dressed for a funeral! Don't you find it hot?' Her grandma was taking the stairs carefully one at a time.

'Not particularly.'

'I always thought black was meant to be the hottest colour, something about refraction . . . I don't remember . . . but then, when you think of it, all those Bedouins in the desert, they wear black, don't they? And they must know a thing or two . . . now where are we going to go? You choose.'

They walked, arm-in-arm, across the shady driveway. Above, the sky was a deep Cornwall-blue.

At the gate, however, her grandmother turned without any hesitation to the right.

'Oh, I thought we could go down to the harbour,

Grandma . . . I've got one or two errands . . .' she began to explain.

'Going down to the harbour is something I *never* do!' her grandmother told her emphatically.

'Oh come on Grandma, you and I . . .'

'Not any more I don't,' she cut in. 'I don't, I won't, I can't. Don't ask me, please.'

Seeing the look of confusion in Theresa's face, she continued quietly.

'I can't explain it all, my darling. It's something that happened a long time ago now . . . but then, you see, the past has a way of coming back to haunt you . . . and there's a reason why I can't go down that street any more. Let's just leave it at that. And now,' she said, forcing brightness into her voice, 'let's enjoy ourselves anyway . . . we'll go up to the fields and then we can look over to the sea.'

Theresa took a deep breath as the image of the bottle faded away in her mind.

'OK,' she said bravely. 'The fields it is.'

But when they got to the stile in the fields, Theresa could see by the pallor in the old lady's cheeks it might be unwise to continue.

'If I just rest here for a moment,' she said, sitting herself on the spur of wood, 'I might gather my strength and my wits. Poor Theresa. Not the companion I used to be.'

'Oh, you are,' Theresa protested hotly.

'And such fun we used to have in this field, didn't we . . . we used to steal up here nights when Old Nance had his cows to pasture here . . . and we used to dare each other to steal the milk from the cows . . . we had a little pail . . .

A field, wide and grassy, an abundance of clover and startling gold buttercups, bumble bees lifting and settling; red-bodied flies crusting cow pats . . . silence but for the swish, swish of the cows' tails, tongues wrenching lushness from the ground, teeth grinding and pulping the green.

A slow Fresian lifts her black head, ears like cups, and stares towards the empty lane. They come, the five of them, two in rough-woven skirts to mid-calf, and three with trousers from knee to chest, elongated by braces, with their shrieking and shoving, their teasing and squeezing, their giggles and gestures, their chippy chatter. They clamber over the rickety gate, never thinking of opening it and stand huddled yet restless, like young bullocks, weighing up the situation. One is pushed forward and sneaks towards the herd, milk pail in his hands. Four are left at the gate, arms hooked, stitches in a line of knitting.

But behind them, the other side of the gate, in the lane, near the dark hedge, is a movement, a fleeting shadow, or something like a shadow. A smudge of a boy, furtive, alone, adrift and longing not to be, watching the line and wanting to hook onto it, watching the game and wanting to be part of it. Silent, he is cut out of their laughter, but his eyes are watchful as a blackbird's. A bramble snatches at his bare arm, snatches and snags, leaving small beads of blood, a scarlet thread.

The thief is stealthy now and purposeful, his sights on a slow moving, doe-eyed, creamy dreamy Jersey, with a hide like bracken and udders so full, the pink tips of her teats tease the grasses and blue veins throb.

By the time she registers that the tweaking and teasing is no longer the grasses but the hands of this urchin, he already has a pailful, white and frothy, sweet and warm.

Suddenly the cow kicks out, electrocuted into action. She bellows a protest. Her tail flicks up like a whisk and she starts to run and jump free of those tickling hands. But it is a current which soon dies, and before the boy has picked himself up, coughing, one arm clasped over his bruised chest, his milk half wasted, sucked back thirstily into the grass roots, she is once more grazing peacefully, her tail swish-swishing, jaws pulping, tongue rasping.

... we thought he'd been kicked into Kingdom Come, poor George... laugh, how Gillie and I laughed! I don't know how we ever got him home!'

There were tears of laughter now in her grandma's eyes.

'I thought you meant us ... me and you,' Theresa said. 'We used to come up here too ... hide and seek in the hay bales ... jumping ... making daisy chains ...'

But when she looked at her grandma, although she was still smiling, she realised she was still further back, much further than she could go.

Theresa sighed. 'OK. Shall we go home now?'

'Home!' her grandmother repeated. 'I thought we'd come out for a walk! Now, I shall just need a little assistance over the stile ... silly old legs, just 'don't behave like they used to . . . put one hand in my back.'

Gamely, Theresa pushed hard and the old lady managed to pull herself up onto the bottom spur.

'If I sit here,' she said, placing herself on the top, 'perhaps you could just help me swing my legs over . . .'

But it wasn't as simple as that at all. They managed to get one leg over, so she sat astride the stile like a horse, but manoeuvring the second leg over was more problematical. She put her arms round Theresa's neck and leaned forward and though the leg rose slightly, by no means did it lift high enough.

She was heavier than Theresa had imagined and for one moment she thought she might collapse under her weight and then they both might tumble to the ground.

And then, just at the moment of greatest impasse, Theresa felt her grandma shaking in her arms. She was laughing.

'Oh my goodness . . . what a sight we must be,' she hooted into Theresa's neck. 'I am utterly stuck.'

Theresa started giggling, too.

'Now hold on. Look, if I turn round, then you can fall onto my back . . .'

'Piggy-back.'

'Yes, exactly, then try and pull the leg over when I walk forward.'

Somehow she wriggled round through forty-five degrees and she felt the old lady slump onto her back.

'Right? One . . . two . . . three . . . Go!'

She staggered forward three paces and somehow the old lady and the leg followed.

She was so exhausted, however, by the effort of getting over and laughing so much, all she could do was sit on the spur of the wood on the field side and catch her breath.

'Oh dear . . . and you've cut your leg!' said Theresa, seeing a thick, rather deep red trickle of blood seep down the leg exposed above the ankle.

'Oh, it's nothing. Old skin . . . just old skin . . .' she replied, dabbing at the grazed leg with a tissue from her pocket. 'But we made it . . . that's the point . . . and we had fun,' she said to Theresa who was standing by her leaning against the gate.

There were no cows in the field now, no hay bales either, but a wild rough pasture of long grasses and cornflowers and stray flashes of yellow rape.

'Oh no!' Theresa cried looking down. 'Would you believe it!' There was a simple lever-pull on the gate which opened it with no effort. 'We could have just opened the gate and saved the bother.'

Her grandmother just laughed again.

'But I wouldn't have missed it for anything,' she said.

Naomi, feeling unwell, possibly because of the heat, took to her bed before supper. Theresa and her father managed to cook the potatoes that Mary had prepared, put some cold chicken on plates, and prepare a healthy salad. Grandmother, once more revived by a rest, helped too. Hearing that Naomi was indisposed, she sat happily at the kitchen table chopping radishes, slicing cucumber and tomatoes, dicing avocado and green pepper.

'Anything except onions,' she told her son. 'I draw the line just before raw onions.'

At six o'clock, alerted by the hall clock striking, she announced she wanted to see the News and took herself off to the lounge.

That's when Theresa asked about George and Gillie.

'George and Gillie?' her father repeated. 'They're new ones on me. Don't ring any bells. Have to ask Pat about them.'

'Grandma called me Pat too, first thing this morning.'

Andrew laughed. 'She's coming over on Sunday by the way, Pat . . . she usually does . . . gives me a break.'

Theresa remembered her Aunty Pat only dimly, she having been working abroad for most of Theresa's young life. She was there one Christmas, wearing tight trousers and a lot of make-up, smoking black cheroots which Grandma had not approved of, telling her it would give her yellow teeth and bad breath. She was sure she remembered Aunty Pat with a glass in her hand . . .

'Did you get the sun-cream?' Andrew was asking.

Theresa shook her head.

'She simply refused point blank to go down Mariner Street . . . said she hasn't done it for ages.'

'Well, now you mention it, I think she's right there. She's got some bees in that bonnet of hers, as I said. Something happened, a few years back, can't remember quite what it was . . . an old enemy of hers moving back or something. Pat might remember . . . ask Pat. Something upset the old girl before we came down, sometime after your mother and I . . .' he trailed off. 'Talking of which, I think one of us ought to give your mother a ring, don't you? Tell her you arrived safe and all that.'

'She will be relieved.' Theresa couldn't help the sarcasm in her reply.

'Right, right . . . I'll do it . . . good thing Naomi's in bed.'

'What's that got to do with it?' Theresa asked, immediately hostile.

'Nothing, nothing. Forget I said anything. Look, just fill the water jug will you and get your grandmother in for supper.'

9

It was the sound of her father's car scuffing up the gravel as he backed out of the garage, of doors banging followed by a fresh flurry of gravel against gravel as he sped out of the drive which woke Theresa the next morning.

She noted the urgency but dismissed it from her mind. If she put her head under the bed clothes she might be able to get back into that dream . . . something about driving fast over the Downs . . . Debbie had been there and Sam, strangely enough, at the wheel . . . and he'd been crying.

She soon found that her eyes had sprung open, however, and she was staring at that glass dome filled with withered flies.

'How come *he* got into my dreams?'

She drew back the pink chintz curtains with hope. But it was a grey day with a wetness in the air which was clinging to the yew trees. Outside the window, there was a huge spider's web lined with clear droplets. How she used to love these 'fairy necklaces' as Grandma had told her they were. On days like this they would go together to the cornfield at the top of the hill to see them draped like treasures between the stalks. And you must *never* break one, at least not on purpose, because the glass beads are lost for ever, tumbling over the dark earth and the fairies get *ever so* cross and then they won't put money under your pillow when your teeth fall out.

One of her front teeth had fallen out here. It had been wobbling so much, she was able to bend it a complete right angle with her tongue and her father had said: 'Show me' and she had. Before she knew it he'd yanked it out and she'd cried and cried and he hadn't understood, and then Grandma had taken her away and solemnly wrapped the bloodied little tooth in a tissue and they'd placed it under her pillow.

'How will the tooth-fairy know?' she'd agitated.

'Don't you worry, my lamb, the tooth fairy always knows,' her grandmother had promised mysteriously, and she had. And not only had she woken to find 50p wrapped in the same tissue but the fairy had left the tooth so she could put it into her little Swiss chalet box when she got home. In London the tooth-fairy only left 10p, *and* she took the tooth away.

Theresa smiled at her memories as she washed her face and cleaned her teeth. A jeans day today and a sweat shirt and socks . . . and that was it . . . the rucksack was now empty, save for one extra pair of knickers and her swimming costume. She'd be forced to do some washing, she supposed. She'd ask Naomi and, with a bit of luck, it would be done for her.

Naomi, however, had gone.

Grandmother was waiting for her in the kitchen,

breakfast things not in evidence. Round her shoulders, she wore a paisley shawl, its scarlets and greens faded with age, and tiny moth holes picked a pattern over her back. She had a piece of paper in her hand.

'They've gone to the hospital,' she told her. 'Bit of an emergency. I don't know the details, Andrew says he'll ring.'

She passed Theresa the piece of paper, written in fountain pen of course, but scrawled in haste.

'Oh dear,' said Theresa.

They exchanged an anxious look.

'Nothing we can do by worrying,' Grandma said sensibly.

Just then Mary's cheerful voice came through the open window.

'Morning!' She stopped at the back door to take off her ankle boots and hang up her macintosh. 'Come on in, then. Wipe your feet, mind.'

There was someone behind her carrying a shopping bag. He came just into the entrance of the room and stood back, staring at his feet.

'Morning, Theresa. Morning, Mrs Bird. Come on then, what's up with you, not usually backward in coming forward!' She laughed at her own joke. 'My son,' she announced proudly. 'Paul! He has his uses, don't you my handsome?' She attempted to ruffle his hair.

Theresa looked down, embarrassed for him.

'Mum!'

'They grows up so fast, don't they. One minute they're clambering all over you all day long. Can't

84

get enough of you. Turn round and you can't see them for dust.'

'Good morning, Paul,' the old lady said, a smile of sympathy playing round her lips. 'Come in. Come in. Such a morning.'

'Mucky, that's what I call it. Mucky,' Mary repeated with emphasis.

'And you find us a depleted band,' Mrs Bird went on. 'Andrew has taken Naomi into the hospital.'

'No! It's not her time is it? Another six weeks by my reckoning.'

'I didn't press for details,' her grandmother repeated. 'Andrew will keep us in touch.'

'Oh my God, well let's keep our fingers crossed. Come on, Paul, cat got your tongue or what?' she asked her son. 'Plug the kettle in . . . they do wonderful things nowadays . . . where they gone . . . over Treliske?'

Grandmother's shoulders expressed she had no idea.

'That'll be it . . . Treliske . . . wonderful maternity place . . . I had my little Jenny there, didn't I, Paul. Had *him* at home in my own bed.' She indicated him with a jerk of her thumb. 'And what a time I had too!'

'Mum!' Paul protested.

'Don't like to hear this sort of talk, prefers to think he were found under a gooseberry bush, don't you?'

And as Paul was opening his mouth to protest again she said: 'Oh yes you do.'

For the first time Theresa caught Paul's eye.

There was something about the twitch of his eyebrows which made her giggle. She went over to reach for the cornflakes which were on a high shelf. She was conscious of her back view as she did so, almost seeing herself as Paul could have seen her.

Idly, she tried to tame her hair before she turned back round, aware that she hadn't wet it and combed it down as she usually did.

'Never mind, you won't starve at least . . .' She couldn't sit still for a minute, Theresa realised, watching her bustling round the table, unwrapping the pie she had brought with her and setting it on a plate from the rack.

'Now, what've we got today? . . . Oh, Library,' she answered herself before Mrs Bird had drawn breath. 'Have you got your books ready, Mrs Bird?'

'I haven't,' she confessed. 'I clean forgot . . . I'll go and get them sorted out.'

And so saying she got slowly up from the table, adjusted her shawl and took her time leaving the room, stopping for a word with Cuthbert who had taken up his position on the hall rug.

'Now,' said Mary, wiping her hands on a tea towel. 'I think I'd better have you two staying here while I just pop down with the books . . . keep an eye on her . . . Paul won't mind, will you, Paul?'

'Doesn't she go herself, then?' Theresa asked, surprised, remembering how fussy her grandmother used to be over her reading matter.

'No sir – she won't! Not since a certain someone moved into Mariner Street. Won't set foot on it, will she, Paul?'

Her grandma reappeared with three books in her hands.

'I enjoyed these two . . . but I haven't read the third one. I can tell from the cover that it is not my kind of book,' she announced with emphasis.

Immediately Paul and Theresa tried to see the title: *Born To Love*. Again they caught each other's eye and giggled.

Mary picked the books up from the table and stuffed them into a polythene bag, put her mac and galoshes back on and disappeared into the mist.

'And you used to tell me never to judge a book by its cover, Grandma,' Theresa reminded her, though her eyes were still on Paul.

'Ah, but this really was a *book*,' her grandma told her and they all three burst out laughing.

When Mary returned, she made lots of suggestions as to where Paul should take Theresa, who he should introduce her to, and it was Theresa who volunteered to be back at lunchtime to wait for the call from her father and to take charge of her grandma.

'What a good girl, isn't she, thoughtful I call that,' she heard Mary say to her grandma as they were scooting out of the back door.

It wasn't exactly raining, but there was wetness in the air sufficient to give Theresa's hair a covering of water droplets. They didn't say anything as they walked down the street side by side.

'Smoke?' offered Paul, handing her a crumpled Benson and Hedges from his inside pocket.

Theresa didn't often; but to be companionable,

she decided she would. They stopped outside the High Class greengrocer's to light their cigarettes from the one match he had left, a tricky operation in the damp. At the bottom of the hill, they passed the butcher's shop. It still had a very old-fashioned board hanging outside: *Spedding: Purveyors of Fine Meats.* And above the shop, the name was repeated in curly apple-green writing: *Arthur Spedding and Son.* Theresa read it out.

'Great sign,' she commented. 'I like the writing.'

Paul looked up as though he'd never really studied it.

'Yes . . . never took the sign down when they sold it . . . don't belong to the Speddings now . . . sold it ages ago, but they kept the name for some reason. I'd have thought they'd have changed it quick as they could, specially taken the "*and Son*" off, but there you go.'

'Why?' Inside the shop they could see the butcher, his apron stained with blood, trimming the fat off some bright red steak for a customer.

'Well, it's our one and only murder in the town in living memory,' Paul told her. 'Let's keep walking, eh? Don't seem right standing here talking about it.'

They threaded their way through the narrow lane, past the fudge shop, to the harbour.

'Shipwrecks, hauntings – plenty of those,' Paul continued, 'but that was our only killing, that we know about anyway . . .'

'Get on with it.'

'Happened a long time ago, when my grandad

was a lad. The old butcher, Spedding, had a son, William. Little Willie, Grandad says they used to call him . . .'

Theresa giggled.

'Yea, well, he was a bit slow like, you know, peculiar, always had been . . . but quiet and you'd never have thought he was dangerous, not according to Grandad anyway. They were all at school together and they all knew each other. Well, it turned out one night he got his father's meat cleaver and went after this boy, just another of the lads . . . lay in wait for him in Cobbs Lane near where he lived and then jumped out on top of him and hacked him to death.'

'Uk . . . that's gross!'

'Yea . . . and he didn't have a chance of getting away with it . . . still covered in that poor geezer's blood and he hadn't even wiped the cleaver . . . wasn't bright enough for that see . . . but anyway . . . got sent away . . . diminished responsibility or somat.'

'But why did he do it?' Theresa asked. They had reached the conical shelter which was empty, save for a couple of visitors with plastic macs over their shorts. They were looking gloomily at the low damp air which hung over the harbour.

'I don't know exactly, something about some girl or something . . . you'll have to ask my grandad. They used to live above the shop, the Speddings. He had a sister too, she was OK, and the parents. But when he got sent away, hardly anyone went into the shop any more, only the visitors, not the locals.

Then the old boy died and the sister sold up and put her old ma in a home. But they never changed the name. Strange that.'

Down the other end of the town, past the baked potato shop, the shell shop, the winkle stall, they came to a rather ugly grey shelter which had been built, so the slate notice said, to commemorate Her Majesty's Jubilee. They sat side by side at the far end and Paul lit another cigarette. Theresa shook her head.

'Maybe they didn't know the story,' Theresa pondered.

Paul leant back against the grey slate wall and stretched his legs in front of him.

'Don't suppose Esmie would have told 'em! That's the sister. She moved away for a bit, nearer Broadmoor so she could visit or something, but the funny thing is, she came back a few years ago ... got a cottage top of Mariner Street ... I should have showed you ... she just lives there all alone ... The Haven, I think it's called ... don't see her much ... always wears black, scuttles around like an old spider. Don't think she's got any friends.'

'That's awful,' Theresa said. 'I mean, it wasn't her fault was it?'

'Spose not,' Paul agreed. 'But that's the way it goes, don't it.'

They sat in silence for a moment, each mulling over the injustices of life. Reaching the end of his cigarette, Paul threw the stub onto the ground and crushed it slowly with the heel of his boot.

'Others'll be along soon,' Paul told her. 'We're always here or the other place,' he told her.

Theresa, feeling restless, jumped up and walked over to the harbour wall. She leaned over, watching the boats over the far side of the estuary bobbing about on their moorings. Not such a good sailing day with, unusually, practically no wind.

The tide was coming in but there was still a pale expanse of sand in the middle of the estuary. The ferry boat was already loading at the harbour steps and, as they watched, it came past them heading out to sea to avoid being grounded halfway across. Paul, having followed her over, waved at the man collecting tickets on deck who waved back at him and then made some expression of interest and pointed at Theresa. Paul laughed.

'Be all round town now! That's the trouble in a place like this. Everybody knows everybody else's business. He's my cousin too. That's the other trouble. We're all related some way or another.'

'I went on that ferry years ago. We got stuck at the other side and we had to wave a white flag.'

'Yes. There's always some visitors get stuck over there,' laughed Paul. 'Serve 'em right usually.'

'Would I be a visitor?' Theresa asked tentatively. 'Suppose I am really.'

'No, you don't count, you're family, cos of your grandma and your dad and that. I don't mean we're related to them at the top of the hill,' he explained hurriedly. 'You know, the big old families.'

'Maybe we could go across,' suggested Theresa

before she realised that going on a boat was no big deal for Paul.

'If you want,' he said politely. 'It was my grandad's boat, the ferry, my dad's dad, but he's dead now, so now my uncle's chief ferryman . . . but my dad's got a speed boat . . . *Jaws 2* . . . it's OK. Does a roaring trade in the season.'

'Oh that sounds good, can we go on it? I mean can *I* go on it?'

'Sure. I'll ask him tonight. He might let me take it out, but he's a bit funny about that boat of his.'

Theresa nodded sympathetically.

Looking back towards the shelter, leaning on the harbour wall, they could see that a small group had indeed gathered under the shelter. They were not visitors.

'Come on, meet the others.'

Theresa hated meeting people. Especially without a drink inside her. It was all right once you had met them, but the actual meeting, wondering what to say, what to do, feeling critical eyes on you, making your own assessments, was all a bore as far as she was concerned. Nevertheless, it had to be done. She stood shyly, hands deep in her now damp jacket, frowning slightly as Paul did the introductions.

'Tod! Bing – the Surfing King.'

Bing's blond curly hair and tanned face, not to mention his muscular arms, visible under his rather tight sweater, seemed to fit his name.

'Tod's a champ too. Just nothing good rhymes with Tod.'

'What about Cod,' suggested the rather stout girl

standing next to Tod and she screamed with laughter.

'Jill-the-Pill,' Tod said flipping her round the head with the red neckerchief he was holding. She screeched loudly.

Theresa noted her shoes, flat black leather shoes with rather pointed toes. She had white ankle socks on too.

'Hi,' she said.

'Theresa,' Paul said. He didn't add that old Mrs Bird was her grandma, that Andrew Bird the architect was her dad and she was staying in the house where his mother worked. For his omissions, Theresa was thankful.

'You surf?' Bing asked.

'Not yet,' she replied.

'We usually have a barbecue Saturdays on the beach . . . you could come along,' Tod suggested.

'OK.'

'I'll give you a lesson, Sunday morning, if there's a wave,' Bing promised.

'OK.'

'Where's Sue?' asked Paul suddenly.

Jill-the-Pill and Tod exchanged looks. Then Jill gave Paul a look which said: 'Well, really, you dummy, isn't it obvious?'

'What?' Paul asked. Suddenly he flushed. 'Don't be daft!' he said angrily.

Theresa had had every intention of going home via the off-licence and the chemist, making up for her failure to complete her errands from the day before, but she caught a glimpse of Tod's overlarge

Mickey-Mouse watch. It was much later than she had thought.

'I gotta go.'

It seemed strange to be flying back to meet an adult-imposed deadline.

'Mum, you wouldn't recognise me,' she muttered as she tore up Mariner Street, the air rasping in and out of her lungs because of her pace and the steep gradient.

'Hardly know myself.'

10

Mary was standing with her galoshes on, ready to get away.

'I'm sorry . . .' wheezed Theresa.

Upstairs she knocked at her grandma's door. She was sitting in the little velvet button-back chair by the window, in a purple crêpe-de-Chine dress, a rope of heavy amber-coloured beads round her neck, book in her hand, reading glasses on her nose.

'It's me.'

'Ah, Theresa! It's just us two, my dear. I wonder what kind of mischief we can get up to – a cream tea, up at Trenance's farm maybe. What do you say?'

'As long as we don't have to go over the stile, I say yes!'

Grandma appeared in the hall twenty minutes later looking like Sherlock Holmes, kitted out in a vast green macintosh complete with a hood.

'Are you coming like that?' she asked Theresa, but in a tone that only suggested a question. 'Haven't you got a coat?'

'Only this one.'

'Ridiculous! I shall speak to your father. The girl's got to have a proper coat in Cornwall.'

'It's OK,' said Theresa hurriedly. 'I like this one.'

'I can see that. You're never out of it,' the old lady laughed. She reached for the sleeve and pulled it towards her face.

'Pooh! Thought as much. Smells like a damp sheep in this weather. Well, I suppose it *is* a damp sheep.'

Arm in arm they went up the lane, avoiding the drips from the yew trees where they could. Just before the stile, they turned left away from the sea up a small rutted track to Trenance's farm. It was the way old Mr Trenance used to take his cows from the fields to the milking sheds. The road surface was muddy and splattered in crusted old cow pats.

'Impassable in winter,' her grandmother told her, picking her way delicately from stony patch to stony patch. 'Keeps the visitors away though, the cow doings. They seem to prefer those clean little places on the sea front with shop-bought scones and synthetic jam.'

'Grandma, you are such a snob!' Theresa told her cheerfully.

'I know it. I know it. Painful lessons, but I learnt them well.'

'What do you mean?'

'Well, coming up, a mermaid from the sea, to my prince on the hill ...' she laughed ironically. 'Smelling of fish, hands like barnacles, never having read a book in my life. There were more than a few rough corners to be smoothed off. But I did it well, and I left all the rest behind.'

The old farm buildings at the end of the lane looked sorry and dilapidated. The cow byres were empty and the gate was falling away from the stall where old Trenance had kept his prize bull. Theresa remembered her father lifting her up so she could see him, eyes rolling, snorting at that cruel ring which punctured his huge wet nostrils.

'Where are all the cows, then?' she asked.

But it was obvious her grandmother had no idea. She was standing in the deserted yard, mouth agape, looking utterly lost.

'We used to go round to the front,' she said, but Theresa held out little hope for the welcoming parlour, fresh scones and dishes of thick yellow cream.

She banged with her fist on the old front door and eventually a young girl came to the door, wiping red hands on her apron.

Theresa hesitated.

'Do you do cream teas?'

'Eh?'

'Cream teas!' her grandmother repeated loudly.

The girl shook her head at them as though they were mad.

'This is Trenance's farm, isn't it?'

'He's my grandpa,' the girl conceded.

'Where are all the cows, then,' the old lady persisted.

'Gone, while back now ... EEC ... milk quotas ... somat like that ... don't do teas no more ...'

'It is an abomination!' the old lady said, picking

97

her way back along the track. 'One of the finest herds around he had. His milk was the best . . . I told you about our escapades in the fields . . . and Bert used to bring some to school all those years ago, warm from the cow . . . he was one of our gang, was Bert Trenance.'

'Like Joe?'

Her grandma stopped and looked at her.

'You know, Joe, I met him at the harbour the other day, I told you.'

'Ah yes . . . and Joe, yes, and all the others . . .'

When they reached home, her grandma was pale and weary. She struggled out of her vast macintosh with Theresa's help, and went straight up the stairs to rest, breath labouring, and leaving muddy footprints in the deep red of the stair carpet.

She had reappeared for the evening News with enough energy to declare the pie and salad, eaten in front of the television, 'A real treat.' Fatigue had sent her slowly up the stairs again before nine o'clock, however, leaving Theresa with nothing to do.

It was during the opening, suspense-filled minutes of a film Theresa had seen before, that the idea of phoning Debbie struck her. A distraught woman who'd been bludgeoned half to death crawled, bloody, clothes ripped, to the phone and dialled for help.

As soon as she saw it, she made the connection and couldn't imagine why she hadn't thought of it before. Debbie would most probably be at home, bored out of her mind, even watching the same film as Theresa was now.

'Come on, Debs. Please be there.'

She sat in Andrew's swivel chair listening to the repeated ringing so far away.

But there was no reply and, as Theresa eventually replaced the receiver, she felt a weight of disappointment in her stomach. Almost the second she had put it down, however, it rang, sending a panic through her.

Andrew's voice on the other end was urgent. She picked up the tone before she heard the message.

'Things not so good this end . . . don't know what's happening . . . don't seem to have time to explain to me . . . something about losing blood, spotting . . . mustn't move . . . they've taken her away to do something to her right now . . . and well, quite frankly it's panic stations here, Trees . . . I'm not going to be able to get back tonight, I'm sorry love. Do you think you can hold the fort?'

'Yes, don't worry,' Theresa replied before she could think about it.

'Should I phone Pat or the vicar or someone? Maybe you could go round to Mary's . . . she's not on the phone unfortunately.'

'It's OK, Dad. Don't worry about us, we'll be fine. Just ring when you can.'

'I'm really sorry, love.'

'I'm sorry too, Dad.'

'Look, got to fly. I'll call you again as soon as there's anything to say.' She caught the catch in his voice.

'I'm sure it'll be OK,' she said, but before she'd finished she heard the distant click and the dialling tone.

To return to the film was now out of the question – all that tension, as the woman put her trust in the guy who turned out to be the serial killer and the one who'd attacked her in the beginning. She and Debs had watched most of it from behind the settee in her front room, clutching each other and screaming, which they'd enjoyed at the time. No way. It would have to be some sitcom, or a boring documentary, anything which would wrap her in sound, but not frighten her.

She thought of Paul. It would have been good if he could have come round and kept her company. But not being on the phone, how could she alert him? She tried beaming out telepathic thoughts, but he didn't arrive.

In fact, she fell asleep in front of a programme about the history of ballet shoes, and stumbling up to bed didn't wake her out of her soporific state. She drew the curtains, shutting out the moonlight and the dark shapes of the yew trees against the sky, and turned out her bedside lamp, all without thinking.

Quite what disturbed her, she had no idea. It must have been *something*. She sat bolt upright in bed. No time to come slowly to the surface. It was pitch black with the curtains drawn. She knew instantly that she was in charge. Some instinct had alerted her to danger. Straining her ears, she could hear nothing more than the ticking of the hall clock. She had left her door open, just in case.

Throwing back the duvet and without putting on the light, she tiptoed onto the top landing. At her grandma's door she stopped and gently opened the door a crack. In the moonlight, her drapes still looped back, she could see her grandma peacefully asleep, the sheets rising and falling across her chest.

Strangely, Cuthbert was standing at the foot of the stairs, his head cocked to one side and the hair on his back bristling. When she whispered his name, he flicked his tail once, but was not to be deflected from his concentration.

'What is it, Cuth? Did you hear something?'

He licked his jowls and whined softly.

Although her heart was beating loudly, she walked softly into the lounge.

Afterwards, when she thought about what might have happened, she was nearly sick at what she did, but at the time it was curiosity she felt more than personal danger.

She was sure she saw someone, just fleetingly, a small dark shape streaking across the lawn. She blinked and it was gone.

'I didn't imagine it, did I?' she asked Cuthbert.

He was panting and whining and licking his lips all at the same time.

'You saw it too, huh?'

What to do – that was the question. Phone the police? Surely not.

'Probably only a prowler. No harm done,' she reassured herself.

But to make sure, she patrolled the premises with Cuthbert, turning the lock in the back door, screwing the security lock on the kitchen window, shooting the bolt on the front door and checking the mortice lock on Andrew's office windows.

'While I'm here . . .' she said to herself tiptoeing over to the corner cabinet. 'Won't waste this opportunity.'

It was like finding Treasure, although there was only a small glass decanter, almost empty. Pulling the glass stopper out, she took a long inward breath.

'Ah!' she exhaled loudly. 'Sherry! To calm my nerves,' she explained to Cuthbert who was standing in the doorway eyeing her suspiciously.

No sooner had she poured a thimbleful in one of the miniature glasses next to the bottle than she heard a rattle at the back door. Cuthbert heard it too. He swung stiffly round, threw back his head and managed to produce one deep bark, like a sea lion.

'Oh no!'

This time Theresa armed herself with one of the walking sticks from the hall stand. Leaving the light on in the office, she crept into the kitchen, but before she reached the back door, there was a sound from behind her at the front door, someone was most definitely trying to get in.

She stifled a scream, just, and then noticed that Cuthbert's tail was wagging excitedly from side to side.

'Damn it!' she heard Andrew's voice coming through the letter box.

'Dad!'

So relieved was she, that she quickly threw back the bolt and flung her arms and the walking stick round his neck, forgetting completely the incriminating evidence she had left behind her in the office.

'What's going on?' he asked disentangling himself.

'I thought someone was trying to get in,' she explained.

'They were. *I* was!'

'No – before that . . . I saw someone running across the lawn, I think,' she ended lamely.

'Did they come in the house?'

She shook her head. 'Don't think so.'

'And did you call the police?'

Again she shook her head. 'Didn't seem worth it. I might have been seeing things . . . I got a bit spooked up,' she confessed.

'Come to think of it, I saw someone running across the street just now. Late, I thought, for a kid. I think it was just a kid. Odd.' He checked his watch. 'It's nearly one.'

'Perhaps it was someone from the caravans.'

'Lost their way home?' He wasn't buying that theory.

Theresa shrugged. 'Let's forget it, all's well, etcetera.'

'I'm sorry, Trees . . . leaving you like that . . .'

'Oh, sorry, Dad, I wasn't thinking – what's happened? How are things?'

'Oh, not too good, but there's nothing I can do. She's sleeping, wired up to all these machines . . .

they're going to phone me if there's any emergency . . . but they told me to come home and get some sleep . . . Why's the light on in the office?' he asked.

Theresa gulped. 'Oh, yes, I was just checking the windows . . . and . . . I came over a bit weak at the knees . . . and . . .'

A smile broke over his tired face.

'Go on, finish it then. You only have to ask you know!'

She knocked it back in one. It was very sweet and thick, almost like syrup.

'Not my favourite. I wonder if I should clean my teeth?' she thought as she snuggled back into bed and her last conscious thought was of all that sweet sherry rotting her teeth away to decayed stumps.

11

Unfortunately, on the Saturday morning Theresa woke to a distant yet persistent noise of drumming.

'Rain! We'll never have a bar-b in this!' she moaned.

She peeked between the curtains for confirmation, but knew what she would see: a sheet of water falling from the sky so dark it was nearly like night. She had to put the light on to see the time. Ten-thirty!

The clothes situation, she realised, as she smoothed her crumpled and stale T-shirt, was getting drastic. She'd just have to tackle the machine herself if she wasn't going to become a Health Hazard.

The whole house was strangely silent. Cuthbert, lying in his usual position on the hall rug, was the only sign of life. There was a note, written in fountain pen, lying on the kitchen table.

'Taken Gma over to Vicar's wife. Give you a break. Mary doesn't come at weekend. Have a good lie in. See you later. Dad.'

For some minutes Theresa just stood and stared at the rain cascading down the window panes.

Everything in the garden was bent over with the force of the water and the strength of the wind.

At least she found a radio and managed to tune it to Radio One until the signal kept fading away in such an annoying way that she returned it to a local station. The washing machine was in the utility room. Loading it took at the most two minutes, and she soon found herself back staring at the dark sky and the rain. She slumped down into Grandpa's chair and thumped the leather arm of the chair and only stopped crying when she saw the dark stains her tears had made on the soft brown leather. As her sobs subsided, she had a sudden and compelling urge to phone her mother up and speak to her. She bit her lip and clenched the arms of the chair.

'No!' she said emphatically. 'Let her stew! Why should I!'

And yet, beneath this strong voice, there was a little voice which kept on wanting to . . . She could chat, tell her about Grandma, and the failed cream tea, and Joe, the weather, and the fact that they'd never have a bar-b tonight which was the only thing keeping her going . . . and she'd tell her about last night . . . how she'd woken to find everyone gone . . . and that the house was empty and she had no clean clothes. She'd melt. Of course she would . . . she'd be so full of pity for her and full of guilt too, she'd get in the car and come racing down . . . Theresa checked her watch . . . she could be here by tea time . . . and then she could take her home again . . .

'Gotta get out of here!' she shouted suddenly, springing to her feet.

Of course she had no suitable clothes, only the old jacket, and by the time she'd reached the entrance to the road, she was soaking, rain dripping off her nose and hair plastered round her face. There were dark, uncomfortably tight patches on her jeans. Nevertheless, it was better than being a prisoner, and she still had the five pounds her father had given her. Not much point wasting it on sun block, she thought.

Down Mariner Street she went, with the water running in rivers down the sides of the road and gurgling into the drains in swirls and eddies like water down the plughole. The Haven, she noticed, was the dreariest cottage in the row, painted black. It was the one with the dead flies behind yellowed curtains. It seemed to have a blocked drain and the water was spilling over and crashing down over the front door like a waterfall.

Of course the harbour was nearly deserted. Just a sprinkling of visitors, bravely determined under sheets of bright coloured plastic, still eating ice-creams or fish and chips or pasties. Yumm! Irresistible, the smell of those pasties. She went into the bakery and in spite of the hostile looks from the ladies behind the counter as she dripped rain water onto their grey slate floor, she selected a good fat pasty and paid for it.

She took it to the conical shelter to devour.

Unfortunately there was nobody there who she was hoping to see, only the ever-present visitors, probably slung out of guest houses or B and Bs and not allowed back in till suppertime. Or maybe they'd come from the caravan site. Imagine being cooped up in a tin box on a day like this.

Halfway through the pasty, with flakes of pastry sticking to her damp jacket, Theresa began to feel slightly queasy. The first bites had been so good, oniony and succulent, peppery in parts, but now she felt the pastry lying heavily on her stomach.

'Seagulls!' she thought.

Up in Church Meadows, overlooking the grey estuary, there was no one. Just Theresa. But as soon as she started to unwrap the soggy half of her pasty and throw the bits into the air even against a strong wind, the sky filled with gulls, noisy, rude, seemingly unaffected by the wind and the rain. The way they wheeled overhead and swooped and dived, the way they opened their yellow beaks and screamed, was thrilling. She loved too, the way the scruffy grey juveniles, already of equal size to their parents, pestered them, moaned and whined and never let them forget their parental obligations.

'We didn't ask to be born, did we?' Theresa cried in sympathy, laughing at one youngster who had landed on the grass behind a parent and was circling it, mewing piteously, fluffing out its wings and pouting with its beak.

'Feed me! Feed me! I may look big but I'm only a baby at heart!' Theresa spoke the gull's feelings. The parent stood seemingly impervious to this display, its eyes cold and emotionless and fixed on Theresa.

'I haven't got any more!' she told it. 'Honestly!'

She shook the paper bag out to demonstrate the point and the gull stretched out its wings, ready on the off-chance that a crumb might fall.

The Jubilee shelter was empty too, and there was no sign of the pleasure-craft or the ferry as she rounded the harbour. Her eyes flickered over the distant fishing quays. There were no boats moored up in the left hand side.

'Must be off fishing.'

It wasn't until she reached the warmth of home, until she was down in front of the gas fire in the front room which she'd lit to dry her hair, that she remembered the off-licence.

'I don't believe it! How could I have forgotten!'

Cuthbert, who assumed the fire had been lit for his comfort had no answer.

'Well I'm not going out again,' she determined. She was in fact in her T-shirt, her jeans and jacket were steaming on a chair pulled up near the flames.

At that moment, the phone started to ring in Andrew's office. Could it be Debs? She picked up the receiver.

'Naomi? It's Pat . . . I'm awfully sorry but as you can probably hear . . . I've lost my voice . . . got the flu I think . . . can't risk giving it to the old girl . . . how is she by the by? . . . is Andrew there?'

She didn't pause for breath so Theresa was almost hopping with agitation by the time she managed to break in.

'It's not Naomi!'

That silenced her.

'Have I got the wrong number? I'm so sorry.'

'No, no. Naomi's in hospital . . . there's only me here.'

'Oh my God! What's happened . . . is everything all right? Who am I speaking to?'

'Theresa. And no, not really. Dad's there now.'

'Oh my God . . . poor old Andrew. Makes me feel twice as useless . . . but I've got this absolute stinker . . . I wouldn't be any help . . . hindrance rather than a help . . . what timing. I'm so sorry, Theresa . . . and what a surprise . . . haven't seen you for ages . . . are you down on holidays?'

'Sort of.'

'Well, thank heavens for that . . . how could he manage without you . . . what a blessing . . . terrible weather too if you're having the same as we're having up here.'

'Yes, it's hammering down.'

'God, how gloomy . . . poor you . . . look, I'm so sorry to be so useless . . . I've got a fever of God knows what . . . do you think you can manage? Keep me posted . . . tell Mum I'll see her soon as poss . . . God, I'd feel so guilty if I could feel anything at all except bloody ill.'

Theresa hardly had time to replace the receiver when she felt a presence behind her.

She whipped round.

'Dad!'

'Who was that?' Always that edge of suspicion in his voice.

'It was Pat . . . she's got a sore throat and she's not going to make it tomorrow.'

'Oh great!' he ran his hands through his hair.

'That's all I need. Not sneaking another sherry while you had the chance, were you?'

'No I wasn't!' she replied, hurt. 'I don't even like sherry!'

Andrew sniffed as though not quite believing her. 'What's that funny smell?'

'My jacket!' she screamed.

Theresa raced out of the room. The living room door was shut. She closed her eyes and taking a deep breath, turned the handle, imagining an inferno of orange flames. As it was there were only thick curls of acrid smoke rising from the sleeve of her jacket.

'No!'

She raced across but already there was a large brown hole, though her jeans, steaming, were unscathed.

With the jacket still smouldering, she raced into the kitchen and plunged the whole thing under the kitchen tap.

'What's going on?' Her father appeared behind her at the kitchen door.

'It's my jacket!' Theresa was close to sobbing.

'What on earth were you thinking of Theresa! You could have burnt the house down. I'm beginning to see what your mother was talking about!'

'Is something burning?' Her grandma's voice came tremulously from the top of the stairs.

'It's all right, Mother . . . something Theresa was drying . . . but it's all all right. Nothing to worry about!'

'There is!' Theresa sobbed. 'This is *my jacket* we're talking about!'

She was folded over the sink, her shoulders heaving against the unfairness of his anger, against the whole unfeeling, uncaring world.

Seeing her so agonized, miserably pulling at the sodden brown sleeve, the smell of dampness and burning mingling strangely in the air, Andrew felt suddenly guilty.

'Here! Come here! Come on! Stop crying! There's no real harm done.' He put his arms round her shoulders and pulled her towards him. Reluctant at first, she finally allowed his strength to win, and she buried her head in the warmth of his chest and threw her sopping arms round his neck. He patted her head.

'Come on cheer up. We'll get you another jacket, but what were you doing trying to dry things by the fire? Could have been a lot worse.'

'It couldn't.'

'Anyway, we've got a perfectly good drier.'

'I didn't know how to use it.'

Andrew sagged suddenly. 'I'm sorry Theresa, I've been too preoccupied. I never thought to show you the ropes – mea culpa – I'm sorry.' He stroked her hair and immediately Theresa stopped crying.

'But I can't think what possessed you to go out in this weather anyway,' he added.

'I wanted a pasty.'

12

Full of good intentions, Theresa leaped out of bed the following day, only to find the house deserted again and the clock in the hall already chiming eleven. How could she be sleeping so long? She never meant to. Must be something to do with the rain which was still pouring down the window panes like glue.

A note on the table merely stated that Andrew had taken Grandma to the garden centre, there having been no change to report when he'd phoned the hospital. They'd be back for lunch. Could she do veg?

She was just scraping the last carrot when there was a knock at the back door. It was Paul, completely covered in a huge yellow oilskin and thick green thigh boots.

'Morning!' he said cheerfully, the water actually dripping off the end of his nose.

He took his gear off in the porch and hung it to drip from the pegs on the back of the door then he padded into the kitchen in his thick socks to where Theresa had the kettle on.

'What happened to you, then?' he asked.

'What do you mean?'

'Barbecue . . . Rave! Mad it were!'

For a moment Theresa was genuinely grief-struck but then she saw the smile in Paul's eyes.

'You!' She flipped the tea towel at him.

'Had you there, I reckon, for a moment.'

'I just thought you might be mad enough,' she countered.

'Nearly,' he conceded. 'Reckon the lads will be out surfing today. Want to go and see this afternoon?'

'You bet.'

'May not be the best day for a lesson, up to you.'

'Maybe not.'

The wind was throwing handfuls of water at the windows and bending the tops of the yew trees in the lane until they seemed in danger of breaking.

'It's a bit rough, but the boys are good, know what they're doing. We'll pick you up at the top of Mariner Street at about two. OK?'

Suddenly everything was wonderful. It was as though the sun had come out.

'Can't stop now,' he told her. 'Mum'd do her nut if I were late for Sunday lunch. See you at two. Right?'

'Right.'

Unfortunately, it wasn't all right as far as Andrew was concerned.

'I'm sorry, Theresa,' he said when she brought the subject up over lunch. 'I really don't think that's on.'

'Why not?'

'Well, I've got to go over to see Naomi, visiting

starts at two-thirty. That means leaving here at one-thirty and someone's got to look after Grandma.'

'Can't she go with you?' Theresa knew it was an unreasonable idea. She stabbed a carrot savagely.

The old lady took her arm. 'My dear, don't stay on my account.'

'There'll be other days,' Andrew said meekly. 'And normally Pat is here.'

'Yes, where is Pat?' asked Mrs Bird.

'I told you, Mother,' Andrew said wearily. 'She's got the flu. She'll be here next week.'

'Ah yes, of course,' she said firmly.

Andrew cleared the dishes away and began to stack them in the dishwasher. He sighed, seeing his daughter's face set heavily against the world.

'I'll have to go and meet the van at two.'

'That's all right. Just slip out. I just don't want her left alone for longer stretches, Theresa, you must see that.'

'But what would you do if I weren't here?' she asked angrily.

'Well, you are, aren't you,' he answered.

At a quarter to two, Theresa jumped up and switched off the racing she was watching, and slipped on her jacket. In spite of its scorched sleeve, she would rather wear that than anything hanging up behind the door. It pleased her somehow to hold her head up and let the rain slam into her face and, with the speed of blotting paper, spread over her jumper and the legs of her jeans.

At the top of the hill she stood at the side of the road, looking to left and right, unsure which direction they would be coming from. A few cars passed with a hiss of spray. Water was snaking its way down the side of the road and gurgling into the drains.

By the time the old van pulled up, hand painted, white on blue, curling waves and seagulls, she was on the point of giving up. The side door pulled open and Paul leaned out.

'Jump in!'

Theresa shook her head.

'Can't. Grandma.'

She didn't need to say anything else.

Paul just nodded his head, though Tod, driving, was protesting, and Jill the Pill and Bing were gesticulating from the back.

Theresa put her hands into her pockets and hunched her shoulders as she turned round and went back down the hill.

'I don't believe I'm doing this,' she thought to herself. 'What's happening to me? What's going on?'

But it wasn't anger she was feeling, not any more. As she crunched back over the gravel drive, she had the sudden image of Grandma, a younger woman, standing in the doorway, with herself, a tiny tot, winding round her skirts, and waving as her mother and father walked over the drive toward the roadway, huddled together under a huge striped golfing umbrella.

She hung her dripping coat with its singed sleeve over the back of a chair in the kitchen. Even her T-shirt was damp. As she pulled it over her head, it snagged on her bracelet, leaving her entangled in dark dampness.

'Damn!' she said, extricating one arm and feeling up under the material for the clasp of her bracelet. With a combination of delicate finger work and brutal tugging, she freed herself. Only a few threads pulled! She stretched them back into position, sniffed the armpits, rolled the shirt up into a ball and shied it through the open door of the utility room. Finally, she kicked off her sodden shoes and pulled off her jeans.

Upstairs she found another pair of socks and her knee shorts, and although it was cold and there was a gap of goose-bumps between where her shorts ended and her socks began, she couldn't bring herself to accept the offer of rooting through Naomi's wardrobe.

Passing her grandma's room, she saw the door ajar.

'Theresa! That you?' her grandma called out. 'Come and see what I've found!'

'What?'

She was sitting on her bed, surrounded by old papers and photographs.

'See?' She was holding an old calendar which stirred a vague memory in Theresa's mind.

'1983 . . . Let me see . . . I was three.'

A rather badly cut out basket of appealing kittens had been stuck crookedly onto a piece of dingy sugar paper and the tiny calendar stapled firmly to the bottom.

Her grandma smiled.

'A treasure, my darling!'

Theresa handed it back. Her grandma fingered the lumpy paper, the result of over-enthusiastic gluing, a wistful expression on her face.

Visible, lying at an angle in the box was an old photo, snaggle-toothed grinning children in school uniforms, their stony-faced but incredibly young looking teacher at their side.

'Is this your school photo?' asked Theresa.

Her grandmother smiled and shook her head.

'That's me! Unbelievable isn't it, that that little wretch should grow into an old woman like me!'

She took the photo and looked at it for a long moment.

They sit in a row at their wooden desks, tops grooved for pencils, glass ink wells stopped up with broken corks. The girl and the boy, inseparable as they were when their arms clasped round each other in the womb, sit side by side in a double desk. She is pale as the morning sky, he has the blood for both of them, coloured where she is waxen, rounded where she is pinched and hollowed. And next to her is the wild one, hair dark and tangled as bladderwrack, eyes as sparkling as salt. Next to her is the ferryman's son, who smells of the sea and whose hair is thick with brine and salt spray. Beside him, at the end of the row, in the dark corner where the sun barely reaches with its warming fingers, hunches the strange boy who everyone shuns, smelling of fresh blood from his father's shop. The teacher does not see him, nor ventures often near his desk, the pages of his book so agonized and impenetrable. The children do not play with him, do not

*include him in their games, but his shadow darkens the
edges of their worlds, for he watches them and he sees
them when they do not see him, and he hears them,
though he is silent. Should he venture too near, someone
will turn and spit at him:*

*'There's a bad smell near here,' and turn up a cruel
nose.*

'Ox heart . . .' one will suggest.

'Sausages,' another.

'Sheep's liver . . .'

'Offal.'

'Mutton bones.'

*And he will shrink back, rage and pain in his cheeks.
He tries calling back: 'Fish heads . . . fish tails . . . fish
guts . . .' But his slow, spluttering speech makes them
laugh and mock the more.*

*'Fish heads!' they call after him, their mouths con-
torted and tongues rolling.*

With Grandma's eyes misted in reverie, Theresa's
attention was taken by the point of a little card protruding between two faded envelopes. She drew it
out and examined it more closely. It was an old-
fashioned greetings card decorated with a looped
garland of tiny faded flowers. A small blue bird was
holding up a bow of pink ribbon. The writing, ornate
and slanting, was gold and raised from the card.

> *'Friendship
> Glad days – sad days
> Are all the brighter made
> With . . .'*

119

And then came the clean cut. The bottom half of the card and its verse was missing.

'Is this what you were looking for the other day, Grandma?' she asked.

Immediately, the old lady snapped back to the present and snatched it from her granddaughter and clamped it to her breast.

'Mislaid! That's all you were. Temporarily mislaid!'

She beamed at Theresa in gratitude.

'Now, all is well, I can visit my friend again and she will know me. It's a reminder, don't you see. And an identification. Something to hang on to! For both of us,' she laughed.

There were also two medals lying on the gold eiderdown, in front of Theresa, which she had never seen before.

'Were these Grandpa's?' she asked, holding them up and showing them to her grandma. One was a scarlet cross edged in gold, the other, smaller, seemed to be some regimental insignia.

Her grandma looked at them distantly. Then, quite suddenly, she put the card down in her lap and broke into a smile.

'That's right . . . your grandfather's . . . his decorations . . . they sent them to me after . . . after the war. I've got his watch too, somewhere . . . they sent me that.'

It was lying half-hidden under a pile of faded letters, but the heavy gold strap was protruding. Theresa picked it up. It was thick and heavy and very tarnished. The face of the watch was buckled and burned and there was no glass in it.

Her grandma appeared unmoved, but Theresa felt a sudden sadness.

'I wish I could have known him, Grandma.'

'I know,' she said quietly. 'I wish you could have known him too.' Later, down in the lounge, sitting watching Songs of Praise and sipping a late cup of Earl Grey and eating toast, her grandma said to Theresa:

'He was a good man your grandfather. He took me, warts and all, never mind what had happened . . . and married me. Gave me two beautiful babies too and he only knew Pat for a month before he got sent away to war. He was always good and kind to me, although he was so much older, we got along. He was devoted you see . . . and I was just so grateful, I think that's the word, grateful.'

Theresa was sitting in Grandpa's leather chair.

'And this was his favourite chair. I often imagine him sitting in it, watching television.'

'Heavens, child, no! No television . . . it was the wireless! That's what he liked. The six o'clock news. Five to six he would settle down with a whisky and soda and sit there until six-thirty. I never got to listen to the news until after he was gone. This house was my world.'

'What about all your friends in the town?' asked Theresa.

A slightly pained look flushed across her face.

'I left them all behind when I came up the hill and married Francis Bird. He picked me up and carried me away and I might as well have been on the moon.'

'They still know you, in the town, don't they? They know who you are, they even know who I am,' Theresa told her. 'People say I look just like you when you were young.'

The old lady smiled a fond smile.

'It was after what had happened, I didn't even want to show my face down there again. Responsible, I felt, though perhaps I didn't need to. And it's how I still feel.'

She saw the baffled look on Theresa's face.

'Never mind, my precious. It was all long ago. All forgotten. *Nearly* forgotten anyway,' she added with a laugh.

13

The barbecue was only postponed until the Wednesday. It was now universal school holidays and although most of the kids, according to Mary, seemed to have part-time jobs connected with the visitors in some way or another – washing up at the hotel, serving coffee in the cafés, sweeping up at the Chippy on the front, or helping with the boats – it seemed that everything stopped for surfing. The tide was right, the waves were good, and the sun shone from a cloudless sky.

There was nothing washed or faded or tentative in the scene which greeted Theresa as she pulled back the curtains. Everything was defined in high colour.

'Kodak Gold!' she said to herself and her heart leapt. At last, the beaches, the cliffs, the sea – freedom! Gulls were thundering on the slate roof above her head, calling out warnings to rival gangs already on the wing.

Pulling herself out of the window as far as she could, and twisting her body round, she could see a gull sitting on the crest of the roof, sleek and pure, white and grey with that cold menacing look in its eye.

'I don't know what you're doing here, buddy! Get off to the beach! It's such a great day!' She waved her arms at the gull who eyed her disdainfully and then lazily spread his wings and took off over the fields towards the headland.

Mary was already in the kitchen by the time Theresa got there for her breakfast.

'Morning! And what a beauty, eh? Message from Paul before I forgets: Bar-b-que's on – he'll call around lunchtime.'

'But what about Grandma?' Theresa asked.

'Love her, her first thought! No, I'll stay with her. There's nothing I've got to do can't wait and I can get ahead with some baking and whatnot. You go. Get off and enjoy yourself.'

Theresa wanted to leap up and hug her. Perhaps she should have done so. Instead she just said, 'If you're sure,' and hoped her eyes shone out some of the brilliance she was feeling inside.

When Andrew came into the kitchen jangling his keys and carrying a jar of stuffed olives in the other hand, Mary was just putting the finishing touches to the frills on a nightdress with the iron.

'There we are.' She held up her work for her own inspection. 'And how is she?'

'Well, hanging on, I think is the best way to put it, fingers crossed. They're keeping her flat on her back and monitoring every thing you can think of and a few other things besides . . . touch and go still, I gather, but she's being very brave.' He turned to Theresa. 'You're off to the beach I gather.' He got his wallet out of his back pocket and peeled off a £5 which he handed to her.

'What's this for?' she asked.

'It's a barbecue, isn't it? Food! Good of Mary to stay.'

'Yes, I said so,' Theresa answered and then felt guilty at the hurt on his face as he nodded, folded the nightdress over his arm and left with a deep sigh.

'Thanks, Dad,' she added.

'There goes a worried man and one with far too much on his plate,' said Mary.

'I know,' said Theresa.

Upstairs Theresa pulled her old black swimming costume from the bottom of her rucksack, the only remaining garment. Quickly she took off her shorts and T-shirt, stepped out of her pants and bra and pulled the swimming costume over her body. It was cold, dampish and smelt of last year's chlorine. The shorts and T-shirt she put back on and stuffed her undies into the rucksack. She took a large towel from the airing cupboard, pale blue, covered in darker blue, leaping dolphins, put it in her sack and added a hair brush and a band for her hair. If she went surfing, her hair would hang over her face like seaweed and she'd never be able to see which way to swim to shore.

She waited for Paul in the garden. She had only closed her eyes for a second when he appeared round the side of the house.

'Ready?'

Theresa sprang to her feet, picked up the sack,

gave Cuthbert a brief rub on his head and walked after him.

'Got anything?' Paul inquired.

'Howd'ya mean?'

'Can't have a bar-b without food and drink!'

'Dad gave me some money.'

'Great! We'll get some meat from the butcher's then . . . the others are doing buns and drink and that.'

Theresa bit her tongue, wanting to ask what he meant by 'drink', but she'd find another way.

Just by the row of little cottages, Paul grabbed her arm. 'That's it,' he said.

'I know – Esmie Spedding's house. Could do with a lick of paint, I'd say.'

The black paint was indeed cracking and peeling round the front door and the window frames. All the windows were firmly shut and an angry old bluebottle was beating himself to death against the bottom window pane.

'Things don't look good for him,' Paul remarked pointing at the crizzled corpses littering the window ledge.

Inside the butcher's, they chose two pounds of pork sausages and as the butcher wrapped them in shiny white paper, Theresa nudged Paul.

'What?'

She motioned towards the big meat cleaver that lay on the worn butcher's block.

'What do you reckon?' she asked as soon as they emerged into the street. 'Same one?'

By the time they got to the coast path, Theresa

was pouring with sweat, and her legs and arms were as red as a lobster.

'I'm dying!' she said. 'I'll never make it.'

'You will. Only over the next headland. We'll get a lift back. The others came straight from work, that's the trouble.'

'All I want to do,' said Theresa, looking down at the huge spread of ocean, as bright as a metal sheet under the glare of the sun, 'is to strip off and dive in.'

'Don't mind me!' Paul laughed.

'Wish we'd got something to drink... I'm parched.'

'Quarter of an hour and we'll be there,' Paul promised her.

They found the two girls, Sue and Jill, in the van in the car park. Why they weren't in the sea, Theresa could not imagine. But they had the side of the van open and a big sound system was blaring out some ancient sixties music. Sue was sitting in the passenger seat smoking.

'Where you bin?' she asked Paul crossly.

'Getting here!' he replied. 'What do you think?'

'Oh yea!'

She turned away. Paul stood looking uncomfortable.

Theresa cut through the awkwardness by ignoring it.

'Hi, I'm Theresa.'

Sue turned slowly. 'Hello,' she said quietly.

And although they hadn't met before, Theresa

had a strange feeling that Sue was familiar to her somehow.

'Hi,' Jill said in a friendlier manner, distracting her from her thoughts.

'I've got some sausages . . . where shall I put them?'

'Give it to me, we've got a cool box.'

'Got anything to drink? I'm parched,' Theresa asked.

Jill took the lid off the cool box.

'Coke, Diet Coke, Lilt, Tango . . .' she looked up.

'Go on.'

'Oh, I get it, you want a beer?'

She tossed a can of Heineken to her and she pulled the tab back as quickly as she could and poured it down her throat, head, gas, liquid and all.

'That's better! I needed that. Right, next thing, got to get in that sea!' She began to take off her shorts and shirt.

'Coming?' she asked Paul.

He glanced at Sue nervously.

'Nah. Go ahead,' he told her. Theresa threw Sue what she hoped was a withering look. But Sue turned away and stared out over the car park.

'Suit yourself!' Theresa said lightly, feeling anger tensing her muscles.

She ran off down the beach like a sprinter from the blocks. Over the loose sand rarely washed by the sea, she tore, through the river which felt like ice, across the pits and bumps of the middle section to where the sand levelled out to a smooth flat and firm surface. Between the flags, there were plenty of others in the water, but mostly near the edge, standing with surfboards at the ready, crouched nervously, heads twisted round watching for a suitable wave.

Theresa never stopped or even eased her pace, but straddled the waves like a hurdler, until her feet wouldn't break the surface, then with a leap and a gulp of air she dived under a huge wave as it thundered towards her, white and wild but surging with power.

Under the wave all was calm, whilst over her head a passion of water raged. She surfaced and sure enough, her hair clung round her face in a suffocating curtain.

'Damn it!' she called out as she attempted to pull it back behind her head; but as she did so another volume of water seemed to rise out of nowhere, tower over her in a terrifying, heart-stopping way before smashing itself on her head. Too late to dive, she felt as though her neck was going to break and then she felt herself being turned and tumbled like clothes in a washing machine. For a second she had no idea which way was up. Under the water, she opened her eyes to a world of murky blue with white bubbles of trapped air everywhere. Even this gave her no instant clue. Her lungs were bursting. Her limbs were tensing.

'Relax!' she told herself and as she did so, turning her struggling limbs to jelly, she rose up like a cork and broke the surface like a whale, blowing water from her mouth before she gulped in the air as though her lungs would fill for ever.

'My God!' she thought. '*Well*, powerful!'

With a little more caution, a little more respect, she turned again and watched the big waves rising and crashing down just where she had been standing. It was the timing. If you could just catch that moment before it curled over and burst its power upon you, you were safe, you could take your energy through the water as easily as a knife through butter, but a split second too late, if that terrific force was unleashed, you were helpless.

She didn't intend to get caught out again.

Gently, wave by wave, Theresa inched her way further out until again she was at the point where the waves were breaking.

And then suddenly she was out beyond that point. If she turned towards the shore the surfers were a long way off, and the vans in the car park were only dots. Further out to sea, she could see the black insect-like Malabu surfers patiently bobbing up and down, waiting always for the perfect wave. Letting her feet dangle beneath her, she felt for the bottom which wasn't there, though just how great a depth of water there was beneath her she had no idea. The void sent a shock through her system.

She struck out for shore, swimming with an intensity borne of increasing panic and though she was swimming straight for the shore, swimming with all her strength, she didn't seem to be making progress. The opposite in fact. With a shock of fear, she felt the water pulling against her legs, sucking her greedily from behind.

'No! Let me go, please!' Instantly, she heard her grandma's words of warning:

'The sea is a monster!'

'It is! It is! Let me go!' She was shrieking the words in her head as she pulled and pulled against the water, mustering all the strength she could.

'I told you, the sea is full of little boys and girls who paid no heed to their grandmas!'

And suddenly she was cold too, and, though she tried not to, she kept gulping the water until she felt as though her body was filling up, like an old dinghy with a leak, and the salt dried her mouth and scratched at her throat.

'And they won't even be watching me,' she thought. 'So many people and I'll just disappear and they won't even notice.' And although the other surfers were dots on the distant shore, she tried to wave, and although she could still hear the crashing of the waves, she tried to cry out, 'Help!'

It was no good. No good.

'Poor Dad!' she thought, 'Poor Mum!' and then 'Poor me!'

She was so tired it was as though the panic had broken free from her body and now she was floating, a piece of flotsam, a mermaid with bladderwrack for her hair.

'Hold on!' She heard the words as though from a great distance. 'Quick! I'll hold the board. Get her head up. Tod! Get the guard – fast! I'll keep her up!'

There were arms round her and big shark-like shapes bobbing around in the water near her, colliding, bumping. Someone was hauling her over one. Its surface was waxy and pitted. It felt like cheese.

Then came the crescendoing roar of an outboard motor which was cut suddenly, and she felt herself being pulled backwards into a cushion of rubber. Someone put thick fingers in her mouth until she choked and spewed up seawater, salty and hot from her stomach. And then amid shouts and confusions, she heard the words:

'She's OK.'

And she realised she was. But she hadn't been. And then she cried.

For some while she sat in the guard's hut, a towel and a blanket round her shoulders. They gave her hot tea but her hands were shaking so much she couldn't hold the cup. Paul appeared and held it for her, and she was ashamed to be blubbering so much in front of him and all the others.

'Not quite the lesson I was intending!' Bing in a bright pink wet suit knelt beside her and put his arm round her shoulders.

'It was Tod who got to you,' Paul informed her.

'And Bing. We saw you waving,' Tod said. 'Didn't know it was you, though. So nothing personal!' he laughed.

Theresa felt herself beginning to sob again.

'I'm so sorry,' she apologised. 'I feel so stupid!'

'Yes – you were a bit stupid,' the lifeguard said bluntly. He was an older, more grizzled man, without the gentleness of the younger boys. 'You were out too deep. Nasty rip currents. And you should never try to swim against a rip, always across it. Remember that next time.'

'There won't be a next time!' Theresa vowed. 'I'm never going in the sea again!'

'No, you'll feel different tomorrow,' Tod said.

'I did the same thing once,' Bing told her. 'Hot day. Big waves. I just jumped in . . . outgoing tide . . . thought I knew better . . . won't do it again, though. We're the lucky ones,' he said cheerfully.

Paul led her back to the van when she had recovered enough to walk. He had his arms round her shoulders and she was leaning against him. Theresa was only dimly aware of someone jumping out of the van with hostility blazing in her eyes. And as she lay down, knees curled under her chin, she could smell a musty dampness mixed with rubber and tar and the gritty smell of charcoal. She could hear angry voices outside the van – 'But we've got the fire going . . . and what about all the sausages?' – before she sank into a deep and dreamless sleep.

She heard the door opening and closing, and eventually felt the van pull out of the car park. Before the van stopped, there came a clear sensation of gravel scrunching under the wheels and she knew she must be home. Paul offered his shoulders for her to lean against as she pulled herself upright.

'She's had a bit of a misfortune, Mr Bird. Got pulled out on a rip current. Got her back, no sweat. But she's feeling a bit knackered, I'd say.'

But before Paul could even pass her over to her father on the front porch, she had dissolved into heaving sobs again. She felt her father's arms round her and she allowed him to carry her, like a little child, into the lounge, where he lay her tenderly on the settee.

'My poor old thing,' he said. 'What a thing to happen. What a fright!' He wrapped her in the rug Grandma put over her knees in the winter and snapped the gas fire on.

'Just lie quiet for a minute. I'll phone the doctor.' Theresa shook her head vigorously.

'Of course! Whatever would your mother say if I didn't take every precaution.'

When he came back, he had a little glass of sherry in his hand.

'Do you think this would do any good? Haven't got any brandy, I'm afraid.'

Theresa's weak smile turned into another sob. But the sweet liquid felt warming, although she only took a couple of sips before there was a sound of someone walking through the kitchen.

'May I come in? Hello, Cuth! Now, young lady, what have you been up to, eh?'

It didn't take Dr McCloud long to pronounce her shaken but undamaged which, Theresa assured him, she could have told him.

'Your dad was right. Better safe, eh?'

And although offered sustenance, he departed immediately with another call to attend.

'Now,' said Andrew. 'Better get you up and into your bed, missus.'

14

Theresa slept deeply, quietly, after all the struggle of the previous day. It wasn't until she was coming to that she recalled the sensation of rising desperately, snatching and gulping at the precious air above her head. When she got out of bed she found her legs were shaking.

It was another glorious day, and she sat quietly in a deckchair enjoying its warmth as she drank a glass of milk. The air felt dry and the breeze wafting across her upturned face was soft. She could even feel the sun's power penetrating through to her bones.

Her grandma appeared at the french windows, a large straw hat on her head. She was trying to hurry, but the speed exaggerated her rather stiff-jointed movements.

'My precious child,' she was saying, 'I have just heard . . . how dare it . . . even for a moment . . .'

Theresa jumped up and they stood hugging each other. She felt the tension in her grandma's squeeze as she clutched her.

'That sea *is* a monster,' Theresa said.

'A greedy monster,' Grandma agreed. 'I have seen

it take so many. I have learned to be always in awe of it – and I thought I had taught you as well.'

'You had. It was my stupid fault – just showing off – not thinking. But I won't do it again,' she promised, breaking away and collapsing in her chair again.

'But go down for a paddle again today,' her grandma advised. 'Make friends with it again. After all, you won. And it's best not to fear it. Always go through fear, that's my advice.'

Later in the morning, Mary came out into the garden where she was lying, reading her book.

'How you feeling, my duck? Paul told me all about it.'

'Oh, I'm fine now, thanks to all of them. Just glad to be here.'

'Aren't we all glad of that! Now this is his idea – Paul's – I can't think you'd want to do any such thing – but he said to tell you the boat trip's all arranged for tomorrow evening. I told him – give her a chance – ' she shrugged her shoulders. 'Still, if you want to go, he said he'd meet you at the quay about six . . . or when your dad gets back. He'll understand if you're late. OK?'

'Oh, that's great,' said Theresa. 'Tell him yes and thanks.'

She had just found her place in the book when she was interrupted again.

'Ah, my little mermaid! Feeling better are you?' Andrew asked, a mug of coffee in his hand. 'How would you like to come over with me and see Naomi this afternoon?'

Theresa did not reply but picked the head off a daisy.

'I'm aware that we haven't done much, haven't managed to get out in the boat, not even had a walk together. Circumstances have rather taken over . . . but I thought we could go into Marks and Sparks in Truro and pick you up a few clothes.'

'Oh, it's OK Dad. I don't need anything.'

'Well, you're a bit short, aren't you? I've never seen you in anything else since you arrived.'

'I only wear this kind of stuff,' Theresa assured him. 'Just grey, white, black . . . you could pick me up a couple of T-shirts if you like, but it doesn't matter.'

Andrew drew a deep breath.

'So the answer's no then I take it.'

Theresa bit her lip guiltily. 'I'll come if you like, Dad.'

'No, no, it's not if *I* like . . .'

'And what about Grandma?'

'I thought I could ask the Vicar's wife. Well, never mind.'

'I'm not too good in hospitals anyway. And I just want to take it easy today.'

'Yes, of course, I understand.' He paused. 'So all right if I leave you in charge of Grandma this afternoon, then? You know, just keep an eye on her.'

After lunch, Theresa moved into the lounge and switched the TV on. It was hard to see the black and white pictures, even with the curtains drawn. She must have fallen asleep, because as she opened her eyes the credits were rolling.

The house felt ominously quiet.

'Grandma!'

There was no response. A quick glance out of the french windows and to the garden beyond showed it was empty. She ran to the bottom of the stairs.

'Grandma!'

Cuthbert appeared in the doorway to the kitchen, wagging his tail. If he knew anything, he certainly wasn't saying.

She took the stairs two at a time. Grandma's door was open but she was not inside.

'Oh no!'

She tried the bathroom door. Empty. She flew down the stairs again, ran through the kitchen, glancing at the table as she went to see if there were any clues. The back door stood open.

'If only you were a bloodhound, Cuth! Stay!' she told him unnecessarily as she struck off across the gravel drive.

She stood hesitating at the entrance to the road. Left or right? And where after that? Right only went to the farm track and the fields; surely she wouldn't go that way by herself, although she might, why not? Left led down Mariner Street to the town and she knew her grandma wouldn't go down there. But perhaps she'd gone up the pathway between the houses opposite and taken herself up to the main road.

'Oh no!' Theresa thought again, remembering with a sinking feeling her first day she'd arrived, when she'd been found stumbling along the grass verge – no, waiting at the bus stop, she had insisted.

On the far side of the road there was a bus-shelter. No one there, and the traffic both ways on the main road filled Theresa with fear.

At that moment, she saw a bus approaching from the right.

Without thinking, she waved her arms at the bus and then, unconvinced that the bus-driver would take any notice of her, she ran out into the road, a fair distance in front of it, forcing it to a halt. The bus-driver was not so much angry as dumbstruck and utterly bewildered. He sat staring at Theresa and she had to beat on the glass doors before he would open them.

'Is there an old lady on this bus?' she asked.

'Plenty,' he answered slowly, still not sure whether this interruption to his routine was some kind of hoax or something more serious.

Theresa pulled herself up the first step from where she could easily see the passengers. Her grandma was not on the bus.

'Right!' she said decisively. 'Will you take me on to the next stop, please? I think my grandma will be there.'

'I shouldn't be doing this,' he said as the doors hissed shut behind her.

'No, I know ... it's really nice of you,' Theresa gushed. 'She shouldn't be alone. But I fell asleep and I'm meant to be looking after her.'

Of course she did not know for certain that Grandma would be at the next stop, but she shared none of her doubts with the driver, and as it turned out that would have been unnecessary. As they chugged up the hill, the driver changed down a gear and they swung round the corner, and she could see her, a lone figure in a brick-red long-sleeved dress, a paisley shawl round her shoulders, and a straw hat pulled well down to shade her face.

'That her?' the driver asked.

'Yes.'

The bus pulled up and the old lady was about to get on when she saw Theresa and stepped back, a look of astonishment on her face.

'Theresa! What are you doing here?'

'I was going to ask you that? I'm meant to be looking after you! I promised Dad. I'll get into all kinds of trouble.'

'No you won't. I didn't want to disturb you and I'm quite capable of visiting my friend unchaperoned you know.'

'But where are you going, Grandma?' asked Theresa.

'I'm visiting, just visiting a friend ... I've been a visitor for years,' she addressed her comments to the driver.

'Yes, but where, M'am? If you can tell me where, I'll let you both on!'

The old lady fiddled with the fringed edge of her shawl. She cast a sidelong glance at Theresa.

'Oh, I know I can trust you to keep a secret ... I'm going to the hospital ... to The Hawthorns.'

'The Hawthorns?' the driver scratched his chin.

Someone called out from the back of the bus. 'Closed that down a year ago now ... Care in the

Community and all that . . . mis-management . . .
something like that . . .'

The driver looked at his watch. 'Look, I'm sorry,
love, but I've got a schedule to keep . . . you'll have
to make your minds up.'

'Come on then, Grandma – nothing ventured . . .'
Theresa helped her up the steep steps.

She said nothing during the journey; she just sat
and stared out of the window, frowning slightly as
though trying very hard to concentrate on something so that it would not disappear.

'It's the next stop!' called the helpful voice from
the back of the bus. 'Up that drive, dear, The Hawthorns. Don't know what it is now.'

The driver stopped and Theresa helped her
grandmother from the bus. She waved and yelled
her thankyous as the bus pulled away in a cloud of
diesel, leaving them suddenly miles from anywhere,
two lone figures on a grass verge, surrounded by
bird song.

'Come on then, Grandma! Let's cross the road
and go and have a look.'

At the entrance to the driveway, her grandma
stopped suddenly and fumbled in her bag. She
pulled out the little card Theresa had found the
previous day.

'I haven't been for some months, you see. I mislaid the card. It helps her remember who I am. Poor
Gillie. It's a link . . . something she can hold on
to . . . she doesn't remember much.'

'Was Gillie a special friend, Grandma? You mentioned her name before.'

'Gillie is my best friend,' she answered simply.

'Another member of the gang?'

'That's right.'

'With Joe and Bert Trenance, and Willie Stebbings, the butcher's son?'

Her grandma stopped suddenly, her face blanched, her hands agitating with her shawl.

'I'm sorry Grandma, I didn't mean to upset you.'

'Please . . . please, don't mention that . . . him . . . again . . . do you understand me?'

She only whispered the words but there was something so urgent in her tone the words pierced Theresa's heart. For a second her eyes met with her grandma's. Behind the faded blue a deeper shadow lurked. Theresa looked away.

'Sorry, Grandma,' she whispered.

Her grandma adjusted the brim of her hat, cleared her throat and resumed their progress up the tarmacked driveway, lined on either side with huge rhododendron bushes, now, of course, deep green and glossy and somewhat forbidding.

'Simply beautiful in May,' her grandma said softly. 'Foreign interlopers, I know, and they ruin the soil and I don't know what . . . but I love them.'

The old house was obviously deserted. Before they even reached the padlocked front door, Theresa had noted the absence of curtains in the windows, and round the side of the old house, she had caught sight of the broken glass of a conservatory.

'Strange! And sad!' her grandma commented. 'Why would they want to do that? A beautiful home it was.' She tugged at Theresa's sleeve. 'Round the back. Let me show you... the lawn... the garden... beautiful.'

Of course the grass was overgrown and the flower beds seemed to have merged their edges with the straggle of couch grass and weeds, but it did not require too much imagination to visualise it as it must have been.

'It breaks my heart,' the old lady was saying. 'To see it like this... neglected... what a waste! We used to sit out here on hot days and drink our tea. We even went for walks together. There's a pond behind the hedges at the end of the garden. We used to sit and watch the dragonflies. Wonderful camellias they have there too. You should have seen it.'

They stood for a moment, looking out over the deserted garden before Theresa gently guided her grandma back round to the front of the house and the driveway.

'Might as well get back, Grandma. Hope you've got some money for the bus. Otherwise we'll just have to hitch.'

Her grandma passed her purse to her. There were plenty of coins in it; Theresa could feel them weighty and bulging without even opening it.

Turning through the gate at the end of the drive, the old lady stopped and peered up at the old board which was still visible though rather overgrown by the rhododendron leaves: The Hawthorns. But a vulgar red sticker – *For Sale: Bunt and Coker* – obliterated the rest of the information.

Waiting by the bus stop, the sun beating down on them, made her grandma wilt and fade.

'Do you want to sit in the shade, Grandma, it could be hours. We passed some logs just inside the gates. Wait a mo!'

Theresa wheeled out two blocks of wood. They were a bit damp and she'd had to disturb assorted woodlice and an odd centipede. She set them one on top of the other in the shade by the wall of The Hawthorns so her grandma could sit quite comfortably. She sat at her side because from there she had good visibility and would be able to see any bus approaching in good time to stop it.

'The thing is,' her grandma said thoughtfully, 'if Gillie's not here, where is she? That's what's puzzling me.'

'Well, I'll tell you what we can do, Grandma, you see the notice: Bunt and Coker's. I could go and ask them if they know anything – or if it was a hospital. Someone might know at Treliske . . . Dad could ask.'

'No!' she said adamantly. 'I don't want Andrew to know. I have kept this from them for all these years; I don't want them to know now.'

'OK. Whatever you say. But I just meant someone must know and, if someone knows, you can find it out.'

Theresa's eyes were fixed on the blank road. She was still mulling over the situation when a car came into sight, pulling up the hill towards them. Without thinking or stopping to ask her grandmother her opinion, she just ran to the side of the road and put out her thumb.

The approaching car was a big estate, the kind which had its lights perpetually on. There was a lone woman driver.

'No chance,' Theresa had just said as the car passed her, when she saw its brake lights flashing red and it came to a halt.

'Is she with you?' The woman indicated the old lady, still sitting on her logs like a gnome.

'Yes.'

'Well, get in then. She looks all in, poor thing. I'm only going as far as the town.'

'So are we,' Theresa told her. 'Come on, Grandma,' she called. 'We've got a lift.'

She struggled to her feet, holding on to Theresa's arm and closing her eyes for a second to gain strength before she walked across to the waiting car.

'It's very kind,' she said easing herself slowly into the front seat.

'No problem; you looked so tired sitting there and there won't be another bus until this evening. They've cut our country bus service down to the bone,' she said.

'Thanks for stopping,' Theresa said to the woman as the car drew up outside the house. 'Don't know what we'd have done otherwise,' she added truthfully.

15

Theresa was lying on her stomach in the hot sun, idly turning the pages of her book the next day, when Grandma called from the french windows. Mary had opened them earlier in the morning to clean them and let the fresh air into the rather sunless room.

'Theresa! There's a letter for you.'

She was waving the white envelope in the air like a flag.

Theresa was excited until she recognised her mother's writing with a sinking heart and almost threw it away, unread.

'I don't have to read it, you know,' she comforted herself, settling back on the rug.

Picking up her book, she pretended to resume reading but the letter throbbed away, tucked as it was in the back of the book.

'Oh God!' Theresa moaned. 'Well, here goes.'

There was only a single sheet, which relieved her, with writing as neat and controlled as ever.

Dear Theresa,
Hope you are enjoying this lovely weather and are managing to relax and perhaps think about things. I am

sorry it came to this. I am not happy with the way I handled everything. I miss you.

Mum.

'No, no, no!' Theresa laid her head down on the prickly wool rug and beat her legs up and down, like a two-year-old having a tantrum.

She couldn't read any more. Up she jumped restless, but unable to find anything to occupy her. Then the image of Joe sitting among his nylon fishing nets and lobster pots came into her mind.

'Just going down to the harbour OK?' she called out to her father and without waiting for permission, she flew off across the forecourt and turned left down Mariner Street.

This time Joe was standing on the quayside leaning against a pile of empty fish trays. He was talking to another fisherman who, seeing Theresa approach along the quayside, slid away punching Joe on the arm in a friendly gesture and nodding in her direction.

'Heh up, Missie! Come to cheer a poor old man up, eh?' His eyes twinkled mischievously.

Theresa smiled. 'Well, actually, just wanted to ask you a couple of things, Joe, if you've got the time.'

'Time!' he laughed. 'Time I have got, specially if you was to see your way to lending me a hand while we talk. What say?'

Theresa nodded.

He led the way down the iron ladder on the wall of the quay and down onto the boat.

'Just got to sort out the nets for this evening.

Keep your eyes peeled for rips or tears and pull out the bits of weed and whatnot and sort out the tangles. Then we'll fold it up, concertina-like, see? You take that side now.'

The wooden deck was bleached and whitened with salt and the rails round the decks were nearly rusted through.

'Wish the nets weren't made of this nylon stuff,' she commented, pulling the first swathe through her fingers.

'Why's that, then?'

'Doesn't look very nice, does it? Horrible colour.'

Joe snorted with laughter.

'Just like your grandmother! Only she used to help with the nets when we had the old rope kind. Prettier colour maybe, but this stuff lasts twice the time and costs half the price; and it takes a quarter of the time to sort it through so the colour don't bother me none.'

Theresa pulled at a small piece of bladderwrack caught in the netting. She took a deep breath: 'Joe, tell me about Gillie.'

Joe didn't look at her, he merely repeated the name: 'Gillie.'

'We went to see her this afternoon. Well, we didn't actually get to see her . . . it was some hospital or something. Grandma doesn't know where she is now. Do you know?'

'That I don't. I haven't heard. But I could ask around. Well, what you want to know about poor Gillie then?'

'I don't know. Just who she was. Grandma said she was one of the gang.'

'Aye, she was. Along with the rest of us. Funny little thing was Gillie Meredith. Skin as pale as milk. Always had to wear a bonnet and this long smock to keep the sun off her arms.

'Followed your grandma like a shadow, she did. Best friends for all those years – that's until she got fonder of boys than girls, your grandmother I'm talking about, then I think young Gillie was a bit put out. She weren't the only one.'

Theresa looked up quickly.

'There were plenty of us had a soft spot for Tilda May, but she only had eyes for the one, and that weren't me. Thank the Lord, as it turned out.'

'What do you mean?'

They had reached the end of the net. The last section was folded on to the top of the huge green mound which reached higher than the cabin roof.

'No, that's your lot today, missie. Said more than I should have done maybe.'

Theresa sniffed at her hands which smelt of seaweed and the sea. 'Spose I better get back and have a wash. I'm going out on *Jaws* later on.'

'Are you now. There's a thrill for you.'

It was hard to tell when Joe was being serious. His eyes gave nothing away.

'Come on then, you get up that ladder and you can help me up this time,' he told her.

The hand which she took hold of was so hard it felt like old gardening gloves, stiff and dry.

Finding, on her return, that her grandma had

already retired for her rest and Andrew on the point of leaving, Theresa took a sandwich into the garden. She was just wondering how to plan the afternoon, but was saved the bother by the arrival of a visitor.

'Yoohoo!' came the call round the side of the house. 'May I?'

It was the Vicar's wife, small and dumpy and wearing a white dress, belted at the waist and full-skirted and covered in large purple blooms. Her shoes were flat, comfortable walking shoes with laces and she wore white gloves.

She came towards Theresa in a rush as though she was going to hug her, but at the last moment she stopped and extended a gloved hand.

'So pleased to have a chance of meeting you at last. Heard so much about you. Known your dear grandmother for years. Old friends. Is she up yet?'

'I don't know, she might be. I'll go and see.'

'Don't think of waking her. I can quite well return. I was only passing and I try to pop in for a chat on a regular basis.'

Unbidden she settled herself in a chair and was surveying the garden as Theresa disappeared into the house to alert her grandma.

'Hope I'm not interrupting,' the Vicar's wife continued as soon as Theresa reappeared. 'I was just up seeing old Mrs Baxter. Do you know her? Top of Mariner Street . . . in trouble with her feet . . . can't get out at all . . . breaks your heart . . . stuck in the one room . . . can't do the stairs . . . all on her own . . . appreciates someone to talk to . . . tell her what we're up to at the church . . . keeping in touch ... like your grandma ... she used to be a regular attender too ... but not for the last little while ... can't persuade her ... maybe you could ... it would be joy ... Ah!' She sprang to her feet as Grandma appeared, impressive in her brick-red dress with the amber beads round her neck. On her head was the wide-brimmed blue straw hat.

'Mrs Bird! How lovely! As ever, such style,' she whispered to Theresa. She charged at her in the same way she had charged at Theresa. Her grandma, obviously used to it, did not flinch but stood her ground, and Mrs Appleyard shuddered to a halt just before she knocked her to the ground, and clutched her hand in her own gloved one.

'Come, my dear. Let's sit down ... take the weight off our feet. Such an enjoyable chat with your granddaughter. Now, how's dear Naomi?'

Theresa left them at that point and retired to the kitchen to prepare the tea.

'Angel,' Mrs Appleyard enthused as Theresa appeared. 'Read my mind.' She turned back to Mrs Bird. 'Just saying ... been to Mabel Baxter's ... not good ...'

Andrew returned a good half an hour earlier than he usually did. Mrs Appleyard had not long since departed and her grandma was looking exhausted. She was sitting in the lounge next to Theresa watching *Home and Away*.

'What on earth are you two doing in here on a day like this?' he began.

'I'm saving my skin, and grandma's saving her life

after an afternoon with the Vicar's wife,' Theresa told him.

'Oh dear ... say no more,' he sympathized. 'Though I must say she has a heart of gold. Looks after all the old dears with never a word of complaint. Come on then, Trees. You can go now. Boat trip, isn't it? Off duty.' And she was about to rush off to pick up her pouch from the hall table where she had left it when he caught her arm.

'Want any money?' He took a five pound note and pressed it into her hand. 'Have a good time!' he called after her.

Halfway down an empty Mariner Street Theresa wished she'd remembered to ask how Naomi was.

The area round the harbour was as full and busy as the area round the church was deserted. Visitors, mostly lobster red with over-doses of sun, sat about on the few benches round the harbour as though their brains had melted. The streets were thick with people and so, Theresa noticed, were the shops; not just the shell shops and the souvenir shops, but the strange little dress shop on the corner, and the nautical shop which sold everything a fisherman could want; even the china shop was packed.

'When in doubt, go shopping!' Theresa muttered aloud.

She walked slowly along the arm of the harbour. Ahead of her she could see the Jubilee shelter. A lone figure stood in its shadows. Strange on a day like this, Theresa thought. But by the time she drew level with it, the figure had gone.

Of Paul, there was no sign. Over the harbour wall

Theresa could see the sailing boats flitting about the estuary like colourful butterflies, and the windsurfers, and then the small dart-like shape of the speed boat, its front lifted clear of the water, trawling a mass of boiling water, and sending out waves, upsetting the windsurfers and causing the fishing boats to bob up and down on their moorings.

No sand bar was visible. Must be nearly high tide. The boats would be plying their trade from these steps. *Jaws 2* came gently to the bottom of the steps and the passengers disembarked. One of the women, wearing a clear plastic raincoat through which her pink shorts were visible, was flushed in the face from excitement. The couple who had been sitting in the back of the boat had wet hair. There were more people waiting, four of them, not quite a full load. Perhaps this would be the last scheduled trip of the day.

As the speed boat set off, a larger pleasure boat came pulsing up the estuary, packed with people who had been out along the coast, past the little islands. Music was blaring from the green speakers near the funnel.

'Hi!' said a voice behind her. It was Paul.

They watched the speed boat weaving a slim but slow track out into the estuary and then saw it gather speed and rise up torpedo-like out of the water. As it sped out of sight, Paul put his hand into the inside pocket of his jacket and produced a tin of lager. It wasn't cold, but Theresa gulped thirstily before passing it back to Paul. He finished it quickly and crushed the can in his hand before putting it into the litter bin near them.

There were still a few people, as there always were, standing watching the boats come in and out. A shark-fishing expedition had recently arrived back from a day at sea. On a long wooden trolley lay the body of a small shark, very heavy-looking and dead. Theresa went over to take a closer look. It was a beautiful blue colour on its body and pure white on its belly. Gently, she stroked the skin: smooth one way like silk, as rough as a cat's tongue the other. Shockingly, there was a great gash down its stomach where someone had ripped out its entrails. She peered into its eye which was open and surprisingly alert-looking and then she touched its head, tipping it slightly so she could catch a glimpse of its amazing shearing teeth, set in a perfect crescent in the white of its lower jaw in a weird and irregular pattern.

'My orthodontist would have a fit,' she told Paul who was standing behind her, more interested in her inspection than the shark itself.

Carefully, she put a finger to the pin-like end of one tooth. It felt like the tip of a dagger.

'Wow!'

It was as she touched the tooth that she had a sudden sense of someone focusing on her, some one wishing her ill.

She drew back quickly, looking behind her quickly for some clue.

'Heh!' came a voice. Along the quay a middle-aged man was hurrying towards her waving his arms.

'Get away! It's dangerous! He'll have your hand off!'

The man came puffing up and took hold of the long handles of the barrow and started to wheel his victim away. But it wasn't him.

'It's dead!' she called after him and then turned back, scrutinising the faces in the crowd. She scanned the far quayside, the shelter, and the path above it which lead up to Church Meadows, trying to find something that connected.

'What are you looking at?' Paul asked.

She shook her head dismissively. 'Nothing – it doesn't matter.'

Jaws 2 appeared again. Its engine was chugging and little clouds of grey diesel were coming out of its rear end. The four passengers disembarked, helped up the ladder by Paul from above and his father below.

'Come on.'

Just for a second Theresa hesitated, seeing the green depth of the water and recalling the way her legs had dangled into nothingness. But once on deck, with her feet anchored on its substantial wooden planks, she felt safe again.

Paul's father had a round and weather-beaten face which was exactly the same shape as Paul's face. It had just seen more years, experienced seasons of sun and wind and salt. He wore a huge grey sweater, in spite of the sun, and a blue woolly cap over his head.

'Theresa – Dad!'

He nodded to her and spun the wheel round in his hands.

They seemed to spin round sharply and without much of the gentle passage they had watched on the previous trip, they were off, speeding round the estuary. As he put his foot down on the accelerator, the boat reared up and roared off, skimming over the chopped blue surface, cutting a V-shape which spread out behind them, causing havoc with the windsurfers and giving the few seagulls swimming there a fairground experience.

Theresa screamed at the speed and, as they slapped into the waves, screwed her eyes up. Spray covered her hair and face. It felt cool and delicious. Paul's dad flipped the wheel recklessly, cutting an erratic path through the water for maximum excitement. Paul stood unmoved as he had been when Theresa was looking at the shark, but he was smiling at her enjoyment.

By the time he cut the speed, when the harbour wall was visible again, Theresa was not only wet but breathless.

'I've forgotten to breathe!' she shouted at Paul. 'Ace!' she said to Paul's dad who nodded again.

It was a beautiful boat with three bench seats across the back, seating for at least ten. There were seats along the sides at the front too but Paul told her the effect of the speed was not so satisfactory there.

'Don't get so wet.'

In the front, Paul's dad had a high screen protecting him from the spray and the wind. All the brass was shining and the paint was new and fresh.

'Great boat,' Theresa admired.

He smiled and nodded again.

'Spends all his spare time polishing it. You should hear my mum on the subject.'

'I can imagine.'

He took them back to the steps. His hand, like Joe's, felt as hard as leather when he helped Theresa from the boat.

'Do you want any help, Dad?'

He shook his head.

'See you later then.'

He nodded.

'And thanks,' Theresa called after him.

'You coming home to tea?' Paul asked her. 'Mum said to ask.'

'Yeah – oh, what about Dad?' She felt stupid having to say things like that. 'I know, I'll phone from the phone box.'

'We could go up and tell him if you like.'

'No, I'll phone.' There was a box behind the Jubilee shelter. It smelt like a gents' lavatory, so Paul held the door open for her as she punched in the number.

'Dad? It's me. Just down in the town. Great, thanks. Look, I'm going to eat at Mary's, OK? Yes . . . yes . . . no, I won't.' She made a mocking face at Paul who laughed.

'Come on – let's go. Shall I get something to drink?' Theresa asked.

'Na! Mum don't like it,' Paul told her.

16

It was a long haul up the other side of the town, to a newish estate of ugly concrete-fronted council houses.

'Used to live further down, one of those cottages near the front, but it got too small and then me mum found out how much it was worth and that was that! It was my grandad's house. He don't like it up here much.'

Inside, the kitchen was full of the smell of food cooking. Never mind the weather. The pots were boiling and the oven was on. Mary was standing at the stove, spiking the potatoes with a skewer.

'Good timing,' she told them. 'Paul call the others. How did you like it?' she asked Theresa.

'Great.'

'Glad you thought so, you wouldn't catch me doing it, not for anything, but there you go. Takes all tastes, thank goodness, or we'd not be eating tonight,' she added, opening the oven. A great wave of sizzling hot fat wafted out to mingle with the smells of cooking vegetables.

'Hope you like pork,' she said, hefting the vast leg out onto the meat dish to drain.

Its skin was juicy with crisp crackling.

'Yum! I love the crackling,' Theresa told her.

'So do I, best part I reckon! Nothing worse in this world than crackling that's lost its crackle, that's what I say. Where's that girl? I called her twice!' she muttered to herself.

Suddenly and quite unexpectedly, Mary rushed out of the room, leaving Theresa and the joint of pork alone.

'Turn that bloody thing off!' she heard Mary yelling. 'If I've told you once, I've told you a hundred times. When I say off, I mean off. Now you, get out and see to the vegetables! You get out and scrub those finger nails. I'll not have you sit down with guests like that. And wipe that look off your face if you know what's good for you!'

The door swung open and a sulky-looking girl in floral knee-shorts and a vast pink T-shirt scuffed into the room, followed by Mary who resumed her moderate tone as though nothing had happened.

'You introduced yourself?' she asked the fat girl. 'Don't imagine so for a moment. This is Jenny, this is Theresa Bird! Mrs Bird's granddaughter.'

Jenny nodded in her direction before straining a huge cauliflower through a metal colander.

'Can I help?' Theresa volunteered.

'Now there's manners for you,' Mary said in her daughter's direction. 'You can take this apple sauce in for me and sit yourself down.'

There were already four children sitting around the huge dining table which took up most of the room. There was just enough space for a television on the window sill, an enormous one which flickered

159

and distorted the familiar faces of the officers of *The Bill*.

All the children were exactly the same shape, like Russian dolls. Their attentions were riveted on the screen until Mary burst through the door behind the huge joint of meat. A smaller version of Paul rose immediately to his feet and switched the set off.

'I should think so, where's your manners? Have you introduced yourselves?'

The four pairs of eyes swung towards Theresa. They obviously hadn't realised she was there.

'No, I thought as much. This is Theresa . . . Mark, Sharon, Eileen . . . Lily . . . and where's that Paul got to?' She squeezed herself behind the chairs on the far side of the table and went to the door.

'Paul! Dad!'

To and fro, to and fro Jenny scuttled bringing dish after dish which she set down on the mats in the centre of the table.

'Looks like I'm carving!' Mary said. 'That man of mine never gets here till after we've eaten.'

She wiped her steel knife up and down the steel sharpener. The blade of the knife was eaten away to the shape of a scimitar. She plunged it into the meat where it cut its way with ease.

'Now, come back later for your crackling. Help yourself. If you can't reach, get one of the kids to shovel something on for you. OK?'

It was a huge portion covering the entire plate, white and thick. By the time Theresa had piled on cauliflower, carrots, parsnips, roast potatoes, boiled potatoes, apple sauce and gravy, there was a mountain of food, the like of which she had never had to tackle before.

Paul came into the room just as she'd taken her crackling from the dish that was being passed round. He snapped a bit off and put it into his mouth.

'Paul! Mind your manners!' Mary bellowed. 'Where's your grandpa got to?'

She was about to give another yell when an old man appeared at the door. It was Old Joseph with his pipe in his mouth.

'Not in here, Dad! How many times have I told you! Tobacco and food don't mix! Well, not in my house they don't anyway.'

Slowly, he took it out of his mouth and rested the bowl in his other hand. He caught Theresa's eye and winked. Having established there was no tobacco in the bowl anyway, he slipped it carefully into his waistcoat pocket before joining his grandchildren at the table.

'Do you know Theresa, Dad? I told you she was coming, you know Mrs Bird's granddaughter.'

He winked at her again.

'*Dynergh dheugh-why*![1]' he said, inclining his head.

'Oh Dad!' Mary said exasperated. 'Don't you go on with all that nonsense now, it's rude!'

'*Dynergh dh'agan chy*![2]' he said.

Mary sighed. 'Don't mind him,' she told Theresa.

[1] *Dynergh dheugh-why*! – Greetings!
[2] *Dynergh dh'agan chy*! – Welcome to our house.

The old man turned to Mark who was sitting next to him. '*Gorthewer da*!'[3] he said.

Mark blinked at him. 'What?'

'*Gorthewer da*!' the old man bellowed.

'*Gorthewer da*!' mumbled his grandson.

'It's Cornish,' Paul explained to Theresa. 'He's a member of the Gorsaid and all that.'

'What?'

'Don't take any notice, it's a dead language and I don't hold with it,' Mary said.

'*Bew*![4] Living, not dead, girl!'

'He only does it to wind my mum up,' Paul whispered to her.

Theresa smiled and caught the old man's eye. There was a naughty twinkle in it.

Having filled his plate, but before he put the first mouthful into his mouth, he raised his glass of water into the air.

'*Yeghes da!*[5] *Myghtern Arthur a-vew*!'[6] he said.

Mary sniffed loudly.

'Silly old man,' she whispered to Theresa.

'Theresa Bird and I are old friends,' he announced suddenly in English.

Mary nearly choked on her cauliflower.

'How come?'

'We met at the quayside. Spitting image of her grandmother. I knew her at once.'

Paul sniggered.

[3] *Gorthewer da*! – Good evening.
[4] *Bew* – Living!
[5] *Yeghes da*! – Good health!
[6] *Myghtern Arthur a-vew*! – King Arthur lives!

'Her grandmother as she used to be,' the old man told Paul gravely.

'Well, why didn't you say you'd met her?'

'You never asked me,' the old man replied mildly.

And that was his contribution. Having cleared his plate, he stood up and pushed back his chair.

'Where you off to?' Mary asked.

He merely pulled the pipe out of his pocket.

'Oh all right then! Don't expect me to save you any pudding though!' she called after his retreating figure.

'Tobacco addict,' she whispered to Theresa. 'Clear your plate, Lily! We're all waiting for you!'

Amazingly, all the plates had been practically licked clean.

'Good job I put a plate by for my old man, I reckon we've cleared the lot! Now then, who's for some pie and cream?'

'Me!' they all chorused in unison.

Theresa was about to say she simply couldn't, but when she saw it was treacle tart, she knew she had to.

The cream was clotted of course, great bowls of it, thick and yellowy, pitted and crusted on the top.

'I get this straight from the farm . . . proper job,' she told Theresa. 'Go on! Have more than that! You'll be making us all feel greedy if you don't.'

After the meal, all the girls rose and started to collect the dishes. Mark turned on the television and Paul slumped on his chair like a beached whale.

Theresa was shocked. 'Don't you help, then?' she asked.

He grinned at her. 'That's the advantage of having all those sisters,' he said.

17

On the Saturday morning Theresa met her father in the hall sorting out the post.

'Expecting something?'

'Well, hoping, rather than expecting,' he said lightly.

Theresa thought no more of it until the phone rang in the office. Andrew had just slipped out to get a paper.

'Hello!' Theresa picked up the receiver.

'Theresa? It's Naomi.'

'Naomi!' she said in surprise. 'Where are you?'

'Flat on my back . . . plugged in to the National Grid. Still, every day that passes . . . just keep your fingers crossed for us, won't you?'

'Yes, of course,' promised Theresa, blushing guiltily. The reality of this drama hadn't impinged somehow before hearing Naomi's voice.

'Is your dad there? I just want to surprise him.'

'Dad! No . . . he's just gone for the paper.'

'Just my luck. You know what today is, don't you?'

'No.'

'Theresa! It's his birthday.'

Theresa's blood ran cold. How could she have

forgotten? What was worse, Naomi had found her out in such neglect.

'Don't tell him I phoned. I'll try and get the phone brought back in about an hour . . . try to keep him in, OK?'

She heard the click at the other end of the line and carefully replaced the receiver. For a moment she stood thinking. What to do?

Before he arrived back, she had wandered out into the garden and picked a little bunch of honeysuckle. She put it in a milk bottle and scrawled on a piece of kitchen towel:

'Happy Birthday, Dad.'

She'd just managed to slip into the lounge when she heard him return. The car engine cut, the door opened and slammed and she heard his footsteps crunching across the gravel and into the kitchen entrance. He stopped. She found herself smiling as he read the note.

'Not much I'm afraid, but what can you expect if you won't give me any money.'

He turned to her, smiling broadly.

'And there was me thinking the whole world had forgotten.'

'Forgotten what?' Mrs Bird appeared in the kitchen, a long multi-coloured scarf wound round her neck and wafting round her waist.

'Dad's birthday, Grandma . . . it's August 2nd.'

She clapped her hand to her forehead. 'Of course it is. How could I have failed to think of it. With Mrs Appleyard here to remind me just yesterday!'

'Mrs Appleyard! To remind you of your own son's birthday!' Andrew said in surprise.

She patted her scarf distractedly. 'Not in so many words.'

'Never mind, Grandma . . . I'll be going out shopping later on . . . I could get you a card or something if you like,' Theresa offered.

'Did Pat remember?' Grandma asked, sitting herself on one of the slat-backed kitchen chairs.

'No,' he replied pretending not to mind.

'Oh dear. We're all in your bad books. Poor Andrew!'

'Not to worry. I'm a big boy now.'

'Nobody is ever too big not to mind a birthday being forgotten,' his mother said. 'I can't think how I failed to make the connection.'

'I thought I'd just pop over to Hasset's and pick up the baby bath Naomi ordered. I had a note to say it was in during the week. Would you mind staying with Grandma?' Andrew asked Theresa.

'There's no need . . .' her grandma said impatiently.

'Um . . . yes . . .' Theresa blushed. 'I mean couldn't you go later? There's something very urgent that I've got to do now.'

She blushed awkwardly as she went to the washing-up machine and slotted in her cereal bowl and cup.

'Oh?' Andrew sounded peeved.

Before he could remonstrate Theresa hit upon the ultimate excuse, one she'd had occasion to use most successfully before.

'It's personal. I have to go to the chemist. I must go now, I'm afraid. It's urgent.'

Andrew fumbled in his pocket in some confusion and brought out his wallet.

'Oh, sorry, love, of course. And I'm sorry I haven't sorted this money thing out properly. I'll give you this for now,' he peeled off a ten pound note, 'and then perhaps we can sort something out tonight. By the by, I was sort of hoping that we might have a little celebration tonight, just the three of us. I've got the good woman at the fish restaurant to cook us a seafood platter and I thought I'd pick up some frozen profiteroles from Marks and Sparks when I go over this afternoon. And I imagine a glass of wine would be acceptable.'

Theresa nodded nonchalantly.

'Well, they do a very nice Chablis which I indulge in on special occasions.'

'OK, Dad. That would be great. I won't be long now . . .' She tucked the money into her pouch.

'Shall I get you anything, Grandma? I could get you a card . . . or some socks or something . . .'

'Get me some chocolates, why don't you? I'm very partial to chocolates, but I can't eat the hard centres, I like something soft. And don't get milk chocolate, I like the plain.'

'But I thought these were for Dad,' laughed Theresa.

Perhaps it was the ten pounds in her pouch which made her feel lighter, or the success of her ploy to keep her father all unsuspecting in the house, or perhaps it was the idea she had for a present. She'd make him a cake. A proper birthday cake. She could do it in the afternoon when he was visiting. A chocolate cake. And she'd fill it with strawberries and cream and smother it in icing and decorate it with smarties and candles . . . and they'd all sing Happy Birthday and he would be so pleased.

As she had the money, she did go into the chemist and buy her supplies. Next door, she bought a big box of Black Magic and two cards, one with a posy of flowers on it which Grandma could give, and another for herself to give, saying:

'Another birthday but don't worry. AGE is a case of mind over matter . . . if you don't mind, it doesn't matter!'

In the grocer's she bought all the ingredients for the cake, even the flour in case there was none at home. But of course, they didn't sell candles, so back she had to go to the newsagents for those and the smarties, and, as she was right there, a copy of *19* for herself.

She found a packet of candles, the kind you light and then they light right back up again. That would surprise him.

'Someone's birthday, is it?' said a voice behind her.

'Paul! My dad's actually. What are you doing?'

Paul winked and showed her the cigarettes in his coat pocket. For a moment she thought he'd taken them.

'You paid for them?'

'Of course!' he replied hotly. 'Saturday, isn't it. What you doing? Come down the shelter this evening . . . we'll all be hanging out there. Might be a party, who knows.'

Theresa bit her lip. 'Can't I'm afraid. Dad's going to have a bit of a do. Sorry.'

'After then . . . come down about eleven. Won't go off before that, promise.'

As Theresa stood at the till, she added a further packet of Benson and Hedges. They might come in handy.

That gave her something else to think about as she walked back up the hill. How was she going to get her father to agree to her going out at eleven after the birthday do. It would only spoil it all . . . there would be some kind of row . . . best not ask . . . just go . . . slip out . . . he'd never know . . . no harm. The excitement lightened her step and as she arrived home she found she was singing:

'Oh I do like to be beside the sea-side . . .'

The kitchen was deserted, apart from Cuthbert who was lying in a shaft of sunlight, panting.

'Cuth, you're too hot. Why don't you move, you stupid animal?'

She bent to stroke his head affectionately and his tail thumped the floor.

Unpacking her shopping hastily, she secreted all the incriminating evidence in cupboards, leaving out only the things she had purchased in the chemist discreetly wrapped in paper bags. As Andrew came into the room, she quickly swept them off the table and made as if to take them upstairs. He averted his eyes.

'Thanks Theresa, you're a good girl. That was Naomi on the phone.'

'She told you, then?'

'I didn't think she'd forget, but I didn't think she'd be able to do anything about it.' He was grinning from ear to ear.

'Like a big kid you are, Dad! OK, now you can go and get the bath. Where's Grandma, by the by?'

'I think she's in the garden. Last seen setting off with the secateurs and that trug over her arm.'

Theresa wandered out into the sunlight.

'Shall I help, Grandma? What are these flowers for? The lounge?'

'They're not for us, dear,' her grandma said. 'They're for the church.'

'The church! But I thought you didn't go any more.'

Her grandma smiled.

'There will still be flowers in the church dear, whether I am there to see them or not. I always arrange for flowers to be put in church on August 2nd – Andrew's birthday as it happens. Mrs Appleyard came to remind me yesterday, she's taking them for me; she's done it for some years now.'

Theresa pulled down a branch of pittosporum and held it at a height convenient for her grandma to cut.

'Who are they for then, Grandma, if not for Dad?'

'A friend,' her grandma said quietly. 'A friend who died on August 2nd. A long time ago now. There,' she opened her basket and examined the contents,

171

'I think that will do. Aren't they lovely!' She sunk her nose into the centre of the bunch and drew a long and lingering breath.

Mrs Appleyard came for the flowers just as Mrs Bird had retired for her rest, Andrew having driven off for his afternoon visit, and Theresa having moved into the garden with a cup of tea and her book.

'Yoohoo!' She appeared round the back of the house. 'Come for the flowers. Is she resting?' Her eyes quickly scanned the garden. 'Don't disturb her . . . routines are so important to old people.'

Theresa hesitated before she asked: 'Grandma said they were for a friend who died a long time ago. Who was it? Do you know?'

'Name is George Meredith, I believe. He's buried in the graveyard . . . many years ago . . . apparently your grandma has never forgotten. Used to do the flowers herself. Bit of a story attached I think, but I don't pry. Does the name mean anything to you, dear?'

Theresa shook her head.

'No well, don't suppose it would. Ah well, would be lovely to stay and chat, but must be about my business.'

It was time to start the cake. First Theresa put all the ingredients on the table, rescuing them from their scattered hiding places.

She found a large white bowl at the back of a cupboard and as the butter was rock hard from the fridge, she filled the basin with hot water and stood the bowl in it, until the butter started to seep yellow into the surrounding sugar.

So mesmerised was she by the infinitesimal process of grains succumbing to the staining spread that she didn't realise she was no longer alone.

'What are you doing?'

She spun round.

'Oh you gave me a fright, Grandma! I didn't hear you coming.'

'I'll ring a bell next time,' she said. 'What are you doing? I thought you were being sick, hanging over the sink.'

'I'm making a cake, a birthday cake for Dad. I got the chocs for you.'

She had hidden them in the mat drawer. Her grandma fingered the card dubiously.

'Not much choice, I'm afraid. I got some paper and I'll get scissors and Sellotape for you. OK?'

The butter was completely melted into a yellow lake when she returned. Of course when she added the eggs, it curdled.

'Looks like scrambled eggs!' she wailed.

Her grandma looked up from her parcel.

'Add flour, child – add a little flour. It will be fine.'

Theresa followed this advice and soon the mixture had lost its curdled appearance. It was flopping creamily from side to side of the bowl in a very satisfactory way.

'Now, the chocolate.'

'A chocolate cake! My favourite!' Her grandma clasped her hands under her chin.

'Oh, I forgot – haven't greased the tins. I hate greasing tins.'

'That, I take it, is a thinly disguised hint,' her grandma said.

As Theresa stirred the dark cocoa into the cake, watching it streak and marble and then eventually darken the whole mixture, her grandma greased the tins with butter until their surfaces glistened.

'But you haven't lit the oven!' She was shocked.

'Don't have to. It's a . . . well, one of these electric ones, fan-assisted or something. Don't ask me how it works but I know you don't have to. Mum's got one at home.'

She slipped the tins in, turned on the dial and set the timer before turning her attention to the bowl.

'Still the best bit,' she said, licking the rough wooden spoon.

'You always liked this bit best. You told me it was a waste of time cooking them. If I turned my back for an instant, you'd scooped a whole spoonful out. It was touch and go whether there was anything left for the tins,' Mrs Bird laughed. 'And we may not have had fan-assisted ovens in those days, but we made pretty good cakes, didn't we?'

'We did.'

'And how is your mother?' her grandma asked suddenly and quite unexpectedly.

Theresa concentrated on eradicating the tiny brown smears from the inside of the bowl.

'She's all right, I think.'

'You had that one letter from her.'

'Yes.'

'You could write to her you know, send her a card. She's probably feeling as bad as you are.'

'I'm not feeling . . .' but she caught her grandma's eye and didn't bother to finish the denial.

She wrote the card before the pinger went. Andrew always kept plain postcards on his desk. Perhaps it should have been a picture of the sea or something. Theresa stared at the two blank sides. Impulsively, on one she drew the outline of a seagull in flight with a bubble coming out of its mouth saying 'Caw! Caw! and then on the other she wrote quickly:

Dear Mum – Just made a chocolate cake with Grandma for Dad's birthday. Lovely and sunny. Peeling nicely. Love Trees.

There was a book of stamps by the pad of paper and she stuck one on and placed in it Andrew's pending tray. He'd post it for her and see that she'd written.

The pinger went.

'Done,' she told her grandma who was just sealing the envelope, her lips pursed with distaste.

'How do you know, you haven't looked?'

'No, I mean the card to Mum.'

They *were* done, the centres, cracked open slightly like a mountain outcrop, sprang back as she touched them, and the kitchen was filled with the delicious smell of cake. Even Cuthbert lifted his head and twitched his nose.

'Do you want to help me decorate the cake later?

Better wait for it to cool. I've got strawberries and cream and smarties for the top and candles. Ah, that's a point, no idea how many I'll need.'

'Fifty-three,' her grandma said immediately.

'Fifty-three! Well, I haven't got that many. He can have ten cos there's ten in the packet. There, what do you think?'

'I think that's fine,' her grandma smiled.

18

After all the seafood platter, the profiteroles and then great slabs of rich cake on top, Theresa felt decidedly sick. At the end of the meal, her father had been on the point of placing his suction stopper back in the end of the wine.

'Dad!' Theresa had remonstrated. 'It is your birthday!'

So pleased he'd been with the cake, delighted by the way the candles reignited just as he was on the point of cutting, he relented and half-filled her glass, and poured the remaining glassful into his own.

Grandma had been provided with a bottle of Elderflower cordial. She sat now with two pink spots glowing on her cheeks, like a doll.

'Isn't it past your bedtime, Mother? I don't remember the last time you were up this late!'

But she had her eyes on the chocolates. Theresa nudged him and giggled.

'No, I can't believe it. Do you want a chocolate, Mother? I was going to keep them.'

'Keep them – whatever for? It's your birthday, dear boy. Eat, drink and be merry!' she continued.

'Well, if you think it's wise.' He offered her the box.

'I said nothing about it being wise . . .' Her eyes flickered over the contents until she spotted the orange cream.

'Orange cream!' Andrew moaned in mock agony. His mother looked startled for a second. Theresa biffed her father on the arm.

'No, no, Mother, only joking, can't stand them,' he teased.

'Perfection!' she murmured. 'A perfect end to another August 2nd.' She picked up her glass of cordial and drained the last remaining mouthful. 'Lest we forget!' she said, kissing her son on the forehead before leaving the room.

'Don't suppose you want one?' Andrew asked Theresa.

'I think I could force one down.'

'Not the brazil nut, that I forbid, and it's my birthday,' he added.

'I thought you were too full,' Theresa reminded him.

'Don't want to offend my own mother, do I?' he said, hooking out the Brazil nut. 'And now *my* perfect end to a perfect day . . . a bit of Wagner, I think.'

'Goodnight,' Theresa said at once. She carried three trays of dirty crockery out to the kitchen and parked them on the kitchen table.

'Leave them! Leave them!' Andrew called from the depths of the sofa. He was shouting rather because he already had his head phones on and was deep into Siegfried. He blew her a kiss and then remembered, pulled off his ear phones and called her over.

'Thank you, Trees,' he said, 'for making my birthday so good,' and he pulled her to him and kissed her rather wetly on the cheek. His breath smelt of wine. Theresa smiled.

She didn't have to climb out of an upstairs window and shimmy down a drain pipe, which in view of the large meal, Theresa was quite happy about. No, Andrew always left the back door unlocked; often he left it open so that Cuthbert could wander in and out, his bladder control being somewhat unreliable.

It was a quarter to eleven when Theresa slipped out of the kitchen, carrying her scorched coat across her shoulders.

She didn't even worry about the way the gravel crunched, neither had she pushed the pillows down the bed in case her father looked in. He wouldn't. She knew it would be all right.

The quayside was buzzing. There were still the never-ending procession of visitors walking round the harbour. There were concentrations of noise and hubbub outside the pubs, although it was still not closing time, and there was a queue at the chip shop, although some of the other cafés seemed to have shut up shop. Had she wanted to, Theresa could still have bought a shell, or a box of fudge, or an ice-cream, but she didn't.

There was a moon out which was reflecting a rippling white light over in the estuary. The harbour water itself was filled with the loops of festive lights which laced the quayside. There was no difficulty in making out Paul's shape as he stood looking over the far wall to where the boats bobbed up and down on their moorings.

Although there was a group of other kids in the Jubilee shelter, the tips of their cigarettes glowing like fireflies in the dark interior, Theresa ignored them and went straight to Paul. As she approached, she began to tread softly, finally rushing up on him and clapping her hands over his eyes.

'Sue!' he said with irritation in his voice. He pulled her arm away roughly.

'Wrong!' Theresa laughed, more at his discomfort than anything. 'It's little ole me.'

'Didn't hear you coming,' he said defensively.

'They don't call me cat woman for nothing.'

'Do they?'

Theresa laughed at him again.

But before he could really feel uncomfortable, she produced the packet of cigarettes from her coat pocket and handed them to him.

'For me?'

'Yeah! Dad was in a good mood. His birthday wasn't it . . . like a big kid.' She burped crudely. 'Pardon me! Ate like pigs!'

'You tipsy?' Paul asked.

'Not enough,' she said. 'Got anything?'

Paul pulled his coat round his body.

'Might have,' he teased.

She grabbed hold of him, body searching her way round the great folds of material.

'Give over.' He stood back and opened his coat either side like a flasher.

The lining of his coat was heavy with lager cans.

'What are we waiting for.' He took two out and pulled back the tabs presenting one to Theresa as though it were roses.

They stood side by side, staring out over the water. Occasionally a seagull flew past, or a fishing boat slipped into the dark waters of the estuary. A man in thigh-length boots and a woollen hat walked past giving Paul a friendly thump in the back as he did so.

'Evening, young Paul,' he said.

'Heh, Jack.'

'Don't let him try anything, love . . . break his mother's heart.' He winked at Theresa who laughed. Paul gave him a rabbit punch and they tussled a minute until the man turned and with a wave continued his way.

'Is there a party or what?' Theresa asked.

Paul shook his head.

'Well, might be something up at the caravans but I don't fancy it much, do you?' he asked anxiously.

'Not bothered,' said Theresa which was the truth.

'I thought we could row out to the boat maybe . . . have a drink. What say?'

'Sounds good.'

'Better wait till the lights go off. They switch 'em off about midnight . . . bit bright now.'

'Can't turn the moon out though.' Theresa gazed up at its round soulful face.

'True! Well, who'll be watching anyway?'

It was surprisingly dark when the lights went out, though. Theresa felt like a shadow as they moved round the quayside. There was a slipway which ran down into the water right opposite the Jubilee shelter. There were no more orange tips illuminating the darkness there. Paul went down first.

'Watch your feet,' he hissed. 'Bit slippery on the seaweed.'

At the bottom was a small rowing boat tied by a rope to a metal ring in the wall. He untied it and pushed it back down the slipway. For a couple of feet, there was the noise of terrible scraping and then a faint lapping as it slid into the water.

'OK. Get in.'

Paul handed her in, holding the boat as steady as he could, but it wobbled and Theresa had to put her hand over her mouth to stop screaming. In spite of his efforts, one of her feet was sopping.

Paul stood in the back of the boat and paddled with one oar.

'Just one Cornetto!' Theresa sang softly.

It wasn't far to the speed boat and Paul pulled alongside, holding the boat steady as Theresa pulled herself up and over. She fell onto the softer plastic seat. Having fastened the boat securely, Paul joined her. They sat side by side and silently sipped at their lager.

'It's good,' Theresa told him. 'I like it, the rocking, the way the water just slaps into the side, you know, the smell . . .'

'Can't stand that smell myself . . . diesel . . . gives me a headache.'

'Not diesel! I meant fishy smells, seaweedy smells, sea smells.'

'Reading too many books, I reckon,' Paul laughed.

In spite of it being August, in spite of it being in the middle of a heat wave, Theresa began to feel cold. Her foot particularly felt like a block of ice. The last of the bodywarm lager had been downed. There had been some lapse of time since either had said anything. The moon, though still bright, was moving slowly across the night sky.

'Spose we better get back then,' Paul said stifling a yawn.

'Yea, all right.'

Just before she closed her eyes, snuggled deeply under the feather warmth of her duvet, Theresa wondered had she been expecting anything more.

'No it was OK,' she thought. 'He's OK.'

She felt comfortable, deeply comfortable and the alcohol eased her into an untroubled sleep.

19

The muffled sound of church bells moved Theresa from her dreams to the morning light, and fixed the day as Sunday. They were particularly indistinct because she was snuggled under her blankets, a winter position in spite of the glorious summer weather.

For a while she lay quietly in bed, allowing the joyous peals to ring in her ears, the runs and somewhat irregular patterns giving way eventually to a single toll. At this point she could imagine all the front doors opening and the women in their Sunday hats and the men in their tight collars dragging unwilling families to the little church behind the yew tree hedge, snug in its hollowed earth.

Strange, Grandma not attending church any more. Theresa remembered so well going off with her when she was little, willingly, no reluctant worshipper she. She would skip along by her grandmother's side, wearing her little red coat with the velvet collar – down Mariner Street – through the lych-gate, which she didn't like because ghouls and ghosties lived there under the eaves, perched on the rafters, waiting to swoop down and pluck your eyes out if you looked up at them.

'That's why no one has ever seen them!' she told her sceptical grandma, who laughed and told her what a lot of nonsense she talked.

She remembered the way the man handed her a hymn book and how important she felt. It had a hard red cover and smelt like mushrooms. They would always sit in the same pew. It was shiny but dark wood and there was a strange dragon carved on the end. Hanging on those little hooks were the kneelers. She liked the cross-stitched butterfly. Grandma always swopped if she could. She absolutely refused to kneel on the Cornish chough with its savage red beak. And she enjoyed it, standing on the seat while Grandma found her the right page in her book; always someone to watch, a misbehaving boy, the choir lady whose chins wobbled as she sang, the bald head of the organist which you could see in the little mirror above the organ if you twisted round, and the Vicar himself in his wonderful clothes, gold and glittery.

And now no suggestion even . . . strange. Briefly, the image of that dark little house, inappropriately named The Haven, came into her mind, with its cracked paint, its shuttered windows, the flies battering themselves to death on the grimy panes of glass. Then there was Mrs Appleyard and the bunches of sweet peas and roses and soft trails of gypsophila and pittosporum which she had taken to the church the day before. And who were these Gillie and George Meredith? Perhaps Aunty Pat would be able to shed some light on all this.

Before she had even finished dressing, Theresa

heard the car in the gravel driveway. A cheerful greeting came from downstairs as she was spitting toothpaste into the basin.

Outside the kitchen door, she suddenly felt overcome with shyness, hearing voices the other side of the door. Taking a deep breath, she peeped round and saw a tall rather slim figure, auburn hair tied back in a loose bun, standing leaning against the Aga, a cigarette in her hand.

'Theresa! Good heavens how you've grown. Well, of course you have . . . and thank goodness for that.' She laughed. 'Not at all what I expected!'

'What did you expect?' asked Andrew who was also standing, leaning against the sink. The chairs round the table were unoccupied.

'Oh, you know . . . neat, glamorous . . . like her mother, I suppose.'

Theresa flushed. 'Not exactly, I'm afraid.'

Andrew stared into his coffee cup.

Pat took a final gasp at her cigarette, a kind of double puff, and then she looked around for an ashtray. Not finding one, she reached for a saucer.

'Pat!' Andrew remonstrated. 'If Naomi could see you now!'

'Well she can't. Anyway, if you don't provide a guest with an ashtray, what do you expect?'

'Ashtrays are forbidden in this house,' he reminded her.

'Well then, you get what you deserve.'

This was obviously an old battle ground. Pat didn't appear the sort who lost battles.

'Now before you knock off completely, bro, give us a hand bringing the lunch in from the car.'

'I'll help,' Theresa offered, gulping down a half pint glass of orange juice.

'Feeling strong?' asked Aunty Pat.

'Reasonably.'

She too had a large estate car and in the back there was a big cool-box which Theresa had to take two hands to, to lug into the kitchen.

'Heave it up on the table, there's a love. Next to my bag!'

As Theresa did so, she noticed sticking out of the bag a large bottle of brandy.

'I'm off – see you later!' Andrew picked his car keys from the hook by the door. 'Remember, it's your day off too,' he told Theresa.

'Any plans?' Aunty Pat asked, picking up her pack of cigarettes and lighting another as soon as her brother had disappeared. She followed Theresa's stare to the brandy bottle.

'Help yourself! Go on! I won't tell on you, I know what Andrew's like, chip off the old block. Aptly named "Mother's ruin" or is that strictly gin? Can't stand it myself, utterly depressing drink but this stuff just hits the spot I always think.'

Theresa laughed shyly and surprised herself by saying: 'No, thanks anyway.'

Pat shrugged. 'Suit yourself, I won't push you. Don't mind if I do though!'

She poured a generous measure into a glass, swooshed it twice round the glass before downing it. Theresa saw every movement, saw the way the liquor swirled its treacly light and then poured its fire down her throat. She gulped hard and, to take her mind off the brandy, asked quickly:

'Do the names Gillie and George Meredith mean anything?'

'George Meredith? Gillie Meredith? No, I don't think so. Should they? Were they in that film on the tele last night?'

'No. It doesn't matter. Just some people Grandma knew long ago. He's dead. She sent flowers to the church yesterday, but she won't go near the church any more.'

'I know it. Just told me not to meddle . . . so I didn't. Anything for a quiet life, is my motto!'

Grandma's tread on the stairs put an end to the conversation. She quickly swigged her last gulp of brandy and put the tell-tale glass into the sink.

'You here, Pat?'

Pat stubbed her cigarette out hastily and fanned away the smoke. Theresa smiled.

'Hates me smoking! Always has!' Pat whispered. 'In here, Mother!'

'I thought I heard the car.'

Her nose wrinkled as she came in contact with the smoke but she said nothing but stood and closed her eyes as Pat planted a light kiss on her cheek.

'I missed you last week,' said Pat. 'Had a real stinker of a cold. Still, better now.'

'Not looking after yourself, Pat. It's all that smoking and sitting in dark rooms. What you need is some good sea air.'

'I'm sure you're right, Mother. You usually are,' replied Pat cheerfully.

She started to unpack the boxes on the kitchen table.

'What treats have you bought for me today then?' her mother asked peering into the cold box.

'Lamb,' Pat announced, heaving a rather bloody joint out of the box. 'Slam in the lamb! Thought we could go and get some rosemary from the garden . . . then there's spuds and carrots . . . I've got some beans as well.'

'And have you left those ridiculous animals behind?' Mrs Bird asked suspiciously.

'Yes, Mother! You have made your feelings about my beloved boys quite plain, as has my brother. I have left them languishing at home, to be fed and exercised by the doctor's son for a rather astronomical embursement. Now,' she went on, wiping her hands on a tea towel, 'I need you to show me the rosemary, Mother . . . you can show me your prize blooms at the same time.'

It was still warm and summery, but the wind was much stronger, battering the tops of the trees at the bottom of the garden. The roses were in a protected area, but the wind whistled round the side of the house and round the garden furniture.

Theresa took her rug to the other side of the lawn, to the lee of a privet hedge. All was peaceful, apart from the gusting wind which was shaking the plants and lifting the pages of the book, when suddenly, as though thrown by a sudden rush of wind, Mary appeared round the side of the house.

'I want a word with you, young lady!' she said.

Theresa looked up in surprise.

'A word? What about?'

'Coming down here with all your city ways, I was warned, can't say I wasn't warned, but I thought I'd make my own mind up, thank you. Well, and I've paid for it . . . and so will you my girl, you can be sure of that. You will not get away with this!'

Theresa felt that familiar but almost forgotten sensation of anger rising up like a volcano.

She sprang to her feet.

'What are you on about, Mary? What are you talking about?'

'Don't you raise your voice with me, madam. You come down here with a reputation as long as I don't know what and we show you a bit of kindness and this is how you repay us!'

'I don't know what you're on about,' repeated Theresa helplessly.

Pat alerted by the shouting, came striding over from the rose bed. 'Can I help?' she asked. 'What's going on?'

'Don't ask me!' said Theresa. 'I'm in the dark. She just came into the garden like a demented hen and attacked me!'

'You see?' Mary appealed to Pat. 'How rude she is. Demented hen!'

'Yes, now, that doesn't help,' remonstrated Pat quietly.

Theresa bit her lip.

'Now, just explain what's happened, Mary. I'm

sure there's been some misunderstanding that we can clear up. Would you care to sit down?'

'No I wouldn't, I thank you,' she added.

Grandma, looking as bewildered as Theresa felt, had joined the group.

'Mary!' she cried. 'It's Sunday! Did you make a mistake?'

Mary laughed.

'I think that's exactly what I did Mrs Bird, a mistake believing the best of your granddaughter.'

Theresa shrugged her shoulders and appealed to Pat and her grandmother. 'You see? She keeps saying that, but I don't know what she's on about.'

'Right,' said Pat seizing control. 'Mary, tell us clearly what the problem is.'

'My husband's boat has been wrecked, Miss Bird, vandalised, seats slashed and I don't know what. And it's quite obvious to all who's done it . . .'

'Now come, Mary, really, you can't go round accusing people. Why should you suppose Theresa knows anything about this?'

'She was seen in the town by at least three people near where the boat was moored . . .'

'Oh no,' Theresa breathed deeply.

'Is this possible, Theresa? Surely not!'

'I was down town late, I just went down for a walk . . . I couldn't sleep . . . yes, I did meet a couple of people but it has nothing to do with me, I swear!'

'And this!' From behind her back Mary produced a bracelet and held it aloft in triumph. 'I suppose you'll deny this is yours now!'

Theresa bit her lip.

'Oh and how strange, cos it's got Theresa Bird engraved on it!'

'I gave that to you, Theresa,' said her grandmother.

'And guess where it was found?'

Pat cleared her throat and looked at Theresa.

'On the boat! Scene of the crime! Gave yourself away, my dear!'

'This is ridiculous. There's been some mistake, I'd never do anything like that!' Theresa cried. She was almost tearful now.

'So see if you can wriggle out of this one, cos I don't think so. And let me tell you, you'll not be seeing my Paul again. I will not have him mixing with the likes of you, and until this matter has been settled, Miss Bird, you can tell your brother that he will not be seeing me in this house!'

And with that Mary turned on her heel and left.

20

Theresa didn't have a very clear sense of where she was going, but the turbulence that Mary had brought with her into the peaceful garden had got inside her head. Grandma would have believed her, so would Pat probably, but she couldn't stay, couldn't talk about it. She just wanted to get away, be on the move, let that anger fuel a walk somewhere, anywhere.

She couldn't very well go and see Joe, though, thinking about it, he might well have been on her side. Had Paul been on the phone, she'd have called him. She wanted to see him but couldn't think of a way of getting him a message. Unless . . . she could check out the shelters. The shelters . . . as Theresa had the thought, she recalled the red cigarette ends, those glow-worm tips burning in the dark . . . the fullest of moons. They must have been seen; of course they were, Jack in his waders was only one . . . there had been lots of people around.

'It was *her* . . . Sue . . . stupid bitch! I know it!' Theresa said. 'But I can't tell Paul. He has to find it out himself.'

She hunched her shoulders under her scorched jacket. It was much too hot to be wearing it and it felt good to be hot and scruffy and black when everyone else in the world was in the minimum of cotton pastels.

So engrossed was she in her thoughts, she was only dimly aware of the front door of the dark little cottage, The Haven, opening. The shock of the scream froze Theresa into stone. It came from the house, she knew it did. There was no time, however, to even think, before the front door shot open and someone was thrown out, landing on the pavement at her feet. The door slammed shut with a terrible crash.

The figure lay completely still, like a marionette with slack strings. She was dressed in black, with thick black stockings, and the feet, which were almost touching Theresa's own, were in large carpet slippers, old and frayed, the rubber soles worn to a lethal shine.

'Esmie.'

Theresa looked round wildly. There was absolutely no one in sight. As she swallowed hard and started to kneel, the figure moved her head and a tiny groan escaped her lips. Her face was old, lined and pale; her hair was thin and quite white.

'Are you all right?' Theresa heard herself say although the words were so inadequate.

Surprisingly, the sound of the voice was enough to activate the woman. Her eyes shot open and she pulled herself immediately to her feet.

She had a nasty graze on her forehead and tiny rivulets of dark blood were beginning to ooze down the furrows on her brow.

'You've cut your head,' Theresa told her. 'Should I get some help?'

The woman shook her head emphatically, dabbing at herself with a handkerchief she had pulled from her sleeve. The blood stained the white quickly and then began to seep over the woman's pale fingers.

'It's bleeding,' Theresa told her unnecessarily.

'It's nothing,' the woman said in a rather irritated tone.

But immediately, she started shaking.

'You'd better sit down.'

'I've got to get in . . . he can't be left . . . he can't be left for a moment . . . he's a danger to himself, see . . . he's got to open the door . . . make him!' she pleaded to Theresa. 'Don't fuss about me!'

There was such force in the woman's voice that Theresa did turn to the door. She lifted the heavy knocker which was stiff with paint and lack of use. She gave one dull thud before trying the door knob. To her surprise it turned and the door swung open. In the dark hallway beyond, she could just make out a chair. Not wanting to set foot in the gloomy house herself, she turned to beckon the woman in. She limped past her, one hand on her forehead, the other on her hip.

At the doorstep she stopped and seemed to peer through the gloom ahead of her. Turning quickly to Theresa, she said:

'That's all right now. Please go! We'll be all right now.'

'Are you sure?' Theresa hesitated but as she did

so, she followed the woman's gaze and at the far end of the hallway, in the dark shadow of the house, she could just make out the silhouette of a man standing there.

She ran.

It wasn't until she reached Church Meadows that she finally stopped. She was panting for breath and her chest felt like a cave. At least there was a breeze up here. She closed her eyes and shook her head, trying to toss away the image of the blood and the dark shape of the man. She snorted in huge lungfuls of salty air trying to scour and clean herself through and through.

The normality of the scene when she opened her eyes was a huge relief. A man was strolling along the path in front of her. He wore cream slacks and had a jaunty red scarf round his neck and a blue denim cap on his head. A lead dangled from his hands. Round and round the field an Irish Setter streaked, with feathered legs and coat the colour of glossed chestnuts.

Theresa watched his flight – all that energy and zest just for running, bunching and stretching those limbs, reaching out over the green grass for the pure hell of it. It was mad and wonderful.

No birds though, they had sensibly removed themselves until this young intruder flopped to the ground exhausted and slavering, then they would calmly reclaim their space. There was plenty more space though, up there in the infinite blue.

How utterly enviable to just soar lazily up and across the width of the estuary to the far coves, to have the ability to remove yourself without fuss from hot spots and trouble.

A cormorant flew low to the water along the length of the estuary. It followed its line so clearly Theresa could almost see it: a black wire over the water.

She thought of Mary again, but now her fury was spent, superseded. She jumped to her feet. Had to see Paul, though. Sort it all out, and then tell him about Esmie and the figure at the end of the hall.

From the path above the surfers' beach, Theresa scanned the car park for the van. It was easy to spot with its blue and white swirls, and today it was definitely empty. It was low tide and the sea was thick with surfers, clustering at the shoreline and again out in the deeper part of the bay. Quickly she ran down to the van. The side door was open. Inside she found an old advertisement for some new night spot in Truro and under the seat she found a felt tip pen.

Message for Paul from Theresa.
Meet me – Harbour wall – Eightish.

She stuck it under the windscreen and wrote *Urgent* on it in huge letters. It would be impossible to drive away without seeing it. She was about to leave when she saw the cool-box and, with a quick glance to right and left, she opened it and took out a can of Budweiser.

She walked back, completing the circle, and by the time she reached the house, her clothes were drenched with sweat, she had blisters on her feet, and the sun had turned her face flame-red. Her head, however, was clear as crystal and her eyes sparkled.

There was an ominous quiet that hung over the house. Andrew's car was in the driveway, as was Pat's, but there was a mood which oozed out from the open windows like an early warning system.

Some kind of council of war was proceeding in the kitchen where Pat and Andrew were sitting either side of the pine table. Pat was smoking and the saucer in front of her had three butts in it already. From the lounge came the sound of *Songs of Praise*.

'At last.' Andrew's voice was cool.

Pat shot him an anxious glance and cast a weak smile at Theresa.

Sensing prejudgment, she threw her jacket down on a chair, and sauntered over to the sink and turning the taps on full blast, put her head straight under the flow of water.

'Do you mind . . . what do you think you're doing?' Andrew jumped up angrily brushing a few stray pearls of water from his shirt.

'Sorry. It's only water. I'm so hot.'

'In hot water certainly,' Andrew agreed through pursed lips. 'I have just had Mary on the phone. She will not be coming round here any more while you are in the house. She doesn't wish to let your grandmother or I down, but feels that, in the circumstances, she would rather not be here.'

There was a pause.

Theresa felt her heart beating in anger. 'And what circumstances are those?' she asked lightly.

'Ah, I was hoping you might be able to shed some light on that subject myself.'

'Mean cow!' Theresa said vehemently, dissecting a crumb which had been left on the table in front of her. 'She knows Grandma needs her, you need her . . . what a cow!'

'Perhaps you should have thought about that earlier,' said Andrew.

Theresa wheeled on him, her anger targeted clearly at him now.

'What do you mean there, Dad? Could you explain. I'm a bit lost here!'

Pat lowered her eyes.

'Look, I only know what I've been told.'

'Yea, and what have you been told?'

'Well, that you went out last night, when I thought you were asleep upstairs of course, and persuaded Paul to take you out to his father's boat. And then he went home and you returned later and damaged the boat.'

And as Theresa drew breath to protest, he added hurriedly:

'There were witnesses, Theresa – people saw you, more than one, and they found evidence.'

'That's crazy!' she exploded. 'And you believe all that, do you?'

She was standing now and shouting at him, she could feel herself brittle with fury.

'I'm not staying here . . . I don't need to hear this . . . think what you want . . . I'm a real credit to you, aren't I, Dad? You all want me to be as bad as my reputation . . . right all along . . . that's me . . .

bad . . . bad . . . bad . . . juvenile delinquent . . . hooligan . . . leading others astray . . . I've heard it all before . . . Oh no, boat wrecker . . . that's a new one! You can think what you like, do what you like, I've had it!'

Words would not have stopped her this time. Andrew jumped up and intercepted her, holding her arms awkwardly but as she struggled, he tightened his grip.

'Listen to me Theresa! Don't just explode at me like this. I'm sorry, I haven't heard your side of it. It's just that I'm worried sick quite frankly, about Grandma, about Naomi . . . I admit I wasn't really thinking about the truth, what happened, I was just so caught up in the consequences. Now calm down please and tell me your side of the story.'

She could not but draw back under the look in his eyes. He relaxed his hands as he felt the tension drain out of her body.

'OK.'

She sat heavily on the chair, drew a deep breath, and began. 'OK. The truth. Cross my heart.' She made the childlike gesture without smiling and related the events simply, clearly, pausing only when she told him that they had rowed out to the boat.

'And what did you do there?'

Theresa flushed.

'Nothing, if that's what you mean. He's just a friend, he's got a girlfriend. We just drank a couple of cans of lager . . .'

'On top of that wine?'

Theresa smiled. 'And then I rolled home, singing

and hiccoughing and sitting under lamp posts and being sick.'

Pat smiled.

'All right, all right!' Andrew said. 'And you didn't go back alone?'

'No, I did not! I don't care how many witnesses there were, I did not . . . and no, I did not vandalise the boat and yes, I know my bracelet was found on the scene of the crime but it might have dropped off when I was on the boat the other day, or . . .' she hesitated, 'it might have been planted.'

'Oh, come on, Theresa, who would plant it?'

'Plenty of people, people who want to get me into trouble. It happens, Dad!'

'You've been watching too many police programmes on television.'

Theresa made a face of weariness.

'Is that the expression your mother finds so irritating?' he asked mildly.

Theresa flushed.

'Anyway,' Andrew continued, 'let's get down to the practicalities, rights and wrongs aside.'

'I don't want them to be asides!' Theresa said. 'You've got to believe me, I've got to know you know I'm telling the truth here!'

'OK. OK,' Andrew said. 'But you weren't in the right to go sneaking out of the house late at night . . . What if something had happened to you?'

'But it didn't. And anyway, I didn't sneak, I just went.'

'But you didn't tell me!' Andrew was peeved.

'OK,' Theresa conceded. 'I'll tell you next time, OK.'

'I meant, ask me.'

'If you say yes, I'll ask you,' said Theresa reasonably.

'Look,' Pat intervened, checking her watch. 'I'm sorry to butt in, but can we get on to the practical issues. I've got a pile of work two feet high and two desperate and neglected dogs to attend to . . . sorry! I simply can't offer much extra, but I'll do what I can.' She put in front of her an overstuffed filofax and started at the week ahead. The pages were covered in different coloured inks.

'OK. Let's assume that Mary carries out her threat. Can you cope, Theresa? Or rather can we cope between us? I'll have to get my visits to the hospital in and who knows when some emergency is going to crop up, but can we manage for the meanwhile?'

'I suppose we'll have to,' Theresa said.

'I'm choc-a-block with meetings, but nothing that can't be moved or cancelled if necessary,' Pat told them. 'And I'll come over on Friday night and stay through the weekend. How's that?'

'That sounds good,' said Andrew a trifle more optimistically.

Pat stood up, stubbed out her cigarette and straightened her skirt.

'I simply must make a move.'

'Before you go, I need a witness. Dad, I must tell you, I'm going out at about eight,' Theresa said quickly.

'Where?'

'To meet Paul.'

He frowned. 'But I thought Mary said . . .'

'I don't care what Mary said, she can't tell him what he can and can't do: he's sixteen!'

Andrew and Pat looked at each other.

'What are all these raised voices for?' Grandma appeared in the doorway, magnificent in her Sunday best, a peacock coloured dress, a purple shawl round her shoulders.

'I had to turn the volume up on *All Things Bright and Beautiful* – not a quiet one, though one of my favourites.'

She looked quickly from one to the other.

'In trouble again? Leave the girl, Andrew, believe in her a little. I know what it's like, my darling!' she sympathized, laying her hand on Theresa's arm: 'Suffocation.'

'It's OK, Grandma.' Theresa came to her father's defence. 'All over and done with. Friends again, eh Dad?'

Slowly, Andrew nodded his head.

21

Strange how ideas come into your head, rising like bubbles, and if you see them and don't like what you see and try to push them back down, as soon as you've relaxed your guard up they come again.

It wasn't really a plan. Not premeditated because the details weren't worked out. She hadn't sat on the edge of her bed and thought it through, stage by stage. Yet somewhere during the day, one of those bubbles had turned into a bottle of whisky; and then another had turned into the money to buy it with. Theresa had pushed the thought away several times, trying to convince herself they could make do with lager. But it hadn't seemed to work somehow and the idea of the whisky got stronger and stronger in her mind.

After supper she checked the small change in her pouch from the money her dad had given her, nearly two pounds, that was a start. She remembered her grandma hadn't paid her for the chocolates, but that idea she dismissed quickly. After their plain talking she could have asked Andrew directly, but there were lines, she thought, over which it would be stupid to step. There was a clear line here. Then she remembered, clear as a vision, that little stash in the pot-pourri dish in the drawer by Naomi's bed. When she'd fetched that book, what seemed like an aeon ago, she had seen it sitting there like a temptation, and she'd risen above it and felt really virtuous.

It hadn't been a temptation after all! It had been a sign, something for the future, and she'd mis-read it, that was all.

Quickly, stealthily as a cat, she crept into the bedroom. A lone evening blackbird was singing right outside the window and the room was still bathed in warm evening light. There was still sufficient to see the table, the pile of paperbacks and the little silver-framed picture of their wedding. Theresa slipped open the drawer and helped herself to a few coins. By their feel she rejected some, letting them slip through her fingers, but retained the heavier thick ones, the pound coins and the fifty pence pieces.

She stuck her head briefly round the lounge door where Andrew and his mother were involved in another case for Hercules Poirot.

'See you later!'

'Not much later, I trust,' Andrew called after her.

Down Mariner Street, she crossed the road before the cottages. Over the dark front door of The Haven, she noticed a dim glow in an upstairs window. There was a heavy net curtain diffusing the light which had a deep yellow quality, like the lighting from old gas lamps. As she passed she saw a heavy curtain being pulled across, sealing the inside more emphatically from the world outside. She shuddered remembering the blood on the handker-chief, the dark figure in the hall.

Paul wasn't leaning against the wall, even from the far side of the harbour she could see that. Never-theless, she dropped past the off-licence for the Bell's and, though the man behind the counter gave her a suspicious look, he took her money and she tucked the bottle in her inside pocket.

In the time it had taken her to buy the bottle, Paul had appeared. Even by the way he was stand-ing, pacing from side to side, not leaning and look-ing out across the estuary, she knew he was on edge.

'Come on!' was all she said to him and he fell in behind her without a word.

Quickly she led him up the steps behind the shel-ter to the Church Meadows. They walked in single file past the War Memorial, through the iron gate and out onto the broader fields beyond. It wasn't until they reached Estuary Cove that he came along-side her.

Past the ruined concrete bunker, they veered off the path, and at the edge of the steep sand dunes, she took a deep breath and challenged.

'Race you!'

Then she jumped and ran down the steep bank roaring like a mad person.

Not surprisingly, the beach was deserted. The tide was half-out, coming in, and the moon was turning the breaking waves to silver. They cast long shadows on the sand as they walked.

Theresa kicked off her shoes; the sand felt cold under her feet.

They sat, eventually, side by side in the dunes, protected on either side by two little spars of rock where the sand was loose and still warm from the sun. Theresa buried her feet as she drew the bottle out from her coat, taking a slug before passing it to Paul.

'OK. This is all I know,' she began suddenly '. . . here I was sitting in the garden minding my own business when your mum comes charging in and tells me I've vandalised your father's boat . . . she's got hundreds of first-hand witnesses . . . she always thought I was a bad lot anyway . . . and I'm never to lay eyes on her dear little son either in case I contaminate him . . . and that's about it really. Oh no, and then my dad tells me she's been on the phone and she's not coming round to help my grandma; in fact she'll never darken our doors again so long as I'm in the house!'

Silence followed her speech.

'So, what do you know?' she prompted.

Paul took another gulp of whisky, lit a cigarette and started:

'Well, I was asleep, and then I heard this great row going on. Dad had found the boat, seats slashed, you know, done over . . . and then these people said they'd seen you rowing out about 1 o'clock. And then he found your bracelet . . . and that's all I heard. And then me mum went mad and she said I wasn't to see you or she'd get the police and I don't know what.'

A sudden chill ran through Theresa's body.

'Now hold on Paul, let's get one thing straight

here . . . you don't think for a single minute . . . you don't, do you . . . you couldn't . . .'

She rounded on him in a fury.

'You *couldn't* . . .'

He shifted. ' I don't know what to think,' he said.

But that wasn't what she wanted to hear.

She leapt to her feet.

'You do . . . you do! Paul, for God's sake! You know I wouldn't do anything like that. Why on earth . . . what do you think . . . oh, sod the lot of you!' she said suddenly and turned and started walking away towards the silver sea.

'Hold on, Theresa!' Paul called after her. 'Come back! I didn't say . . . Oh don't be so touchy.'

'*Touchy*!' she repeated and snorted although she didn't stop nor turn back. At the edge of the water she stood and let the waves run up to her toes, sniff, tickle, probe and then retreat like a suspicious dog. The water left the sand so liquid under her feet, they sunk beneath the surface leaving her standing there in the moonlight on only her stumps.

'Hold on,' Paul had joined her, 'I didn't say . . . I just don't know what's going on.'

'Well, you're a fool Paul. If you don't know what's going on right in front of your face, that's your problem, not mine!'

'Sounds like it is yours!' he said mildly.

He was right. 'OK. So it is, but it's nothing I can't handle so that's OK. I know what's going on and that's all that matters really, isn't it?'

Paul still had the bottle, he offered it back to Theresa who took one more warming gulp of fire.

208

It felt strangely in conflict with the mercurial light their bodies were drenched in.

'What did you mean, anyway? Tell me Theresa, if it wasn't you, what is going on here?'

Theresa sighed. She paddled along the edge of the water to where a small tongue of rock poked out of the beach and into the sea. Up she clambered and sat on its summit. To her right, from this vantage point, she could see the distant fairy lights of the harbour. Paul settled himself next to her.

'All I'm saying is, it wasn't me Paul . . . and either you believe me or you don't and, if you don't, there's nothing I can do about that.' She hesitated: 'I may have done things other people think are bad – my mum, for instance, the school – but nothing much, just bunking off school, shop lifting *once*, but that was ages ago. I never did anything like stupid vandalism or anything, nothing that would hurt someone, specially if they'd been good to me, that's not me at all and it's hard when people just think the worst. Still,' she concluded with a sigh, 'that's the way it seems to be.'

'But if you didn't, someone did.'

Theresa laughed. 'Brilliant Paul . . . Hercules Poirot eat your bowler hat.'

Paul looked confused. He took another gulp of whisky.

'I'm not pointing the finger,' Theresa said. 'I don't know anything, do I . . . but someone went out, after we'd gone home . . . someone who'd seen us earlier on, maybe . . . someone who wanted to cause trouble . . . for me . . . oh, come on Paul . . . use your grey matter!'

'But what about your bracelet?'

'Give us a break. I could have dropped it earlier on or maybe I lost it, I can't remember when I last saw it. All I'm saying is, it wasn't me, it was somebody else . . . and someone else can work out who it was.'

Paul took another swig of whisky.

'Heh! You've nearly drunk the lot!'

'Want some?' His speech was getting rather thick. She shook her head.

Idly, she pulled a cockle from out of a crevice in the rock and threw it into the water. It fell with a small plip.

'My bum's getting wet. We'd better go.'

She got to her feet.

'Come on.' She put out a hand to pull Paul to an upright position.

'Just a minute . . . hang on a second . . . I want to say something . . .'

'You're drunk, Paul,' she said. 'You've drunk nearly a whole bottle. Here give us it . . .' She went to snatch it from him, but he jerked his arm back and held it out of her reach.

'I don't want it, you pig, I'm not in the mood, but I'm not carrying you home.'

'I'm fine,' he told her, swaying slightly. 'Look, I just want to say . . . I know it wasn't you . . . you had nothing to do with it, am I right?'

'Yes, you are right,' she affirmed. 'Now let's get back.'

But once started, Paul was not to be hurried.

'Hang on a minute . . . I just want to say something . . .'

'OK.'

'I always knew it had nothing *whatsoever* to do with you . . . I told my mum, I said, it has nothing *whatsoever* to do with Theresa . . . she's a nice girl . . . she wouldn't do that kind of thing . . .'

'Well, you didn't do a very good job of convincing her,' Theresa laughed.

Paul was serious. 'No I didn't,' he agreed. 'But I shall go now and tell her straight . . . Theresa had *nothing* to do with it, I know that for a fact.'

'Don't try and convince her tonight, that's my advice,' said Theresa. 'Wait till the morning. Now, come on. Let's get going.'

'Hang on!' Paul said, 'I haven't finished! I just want to assure you, Theresa, that I believe you and . . .' he emphasised the importance of what he was saying with a gesture from the bottle, 'I'm going to get to the bottom of this, Theresa . . . and I am going to clear your name!'

With that final statement he rose to his feet again and the two of them set off up the rocks.

Paul was impeded by the bottle in one hand, so he stopped swigged back the contents and only then would he give it to Theresa who stowed it away in her inside pocket again.

Their passage was somewhat more hazardous than the terrain warranted, Paul lurching and unsteady, but together, giggling and slipping they finally reached the path. Paul sat heavily on the path.

'Where are my shoes?'

'Oh no.'

Back they had to go to the place where they had begun their leaping. Together they jumped and rolled their way down to the bottom screaming and laughing. They landed in a heap of sandy limbs, tangled and giddy at the bottom. For one minute they lay silently. Theresa knew Paul was looking at her.

She went to get up but he pulled her down.

'I want to kiss you,' he said thickly.

'That wouldn't be a good idea at all,' she said.

'I do,' he repeated. 'I do.'

'Come on,' she put out her hand and pulled him up still muttering protestations.

They found the shoes where they had been sitting and held them until they reached the top of the cliff again. It was hard work struggling up the loose sand banks and at the top they were sweating and exhausted. Paul fell on his face on the grass and closed his eyes while Theresa put her shoes on.

'Come on, Paul,' she told him. 'Don't pass out on me now.'

With a degree of punching and shaking she managed to rouse him. She tied his laces for him as his fingers seemed to have become mutinous somehow, refusing to do what he told them to. Finally she hauled him to his feet, and only by allowing him to fling an arm round her shoulders, did they manage to begin the walk back.

It hadn't seemed very far going, but the journey back seemed interminable.

At the benches on Church Meadows, she sat him down.

'Now come on, Paul!' she said crossly. 'Sober up for God's sake! I'm not taking you home!'

'It's all right,' he assured her. 'I'm quite capable.'

'Quite incapable, more like,' she said.

To her horror, he proceeded to slip sideways and put his feet up on the bench, tucking his hands under his chin as though he were in bed.

'Paul!' She shook him roughly. 'You can't go to sleep here. Now just sober up, can't you. You only had a bit of whisky for God's sake!'

Paul's head slumped forward.

'Just let me have a bit of kip,' he moaned. 'I'll be fine then.'

'No!' she wailed. 'You can't go to sleep here.'

Theresa, without another thought slapped him hard on both cheeks. His eyes shot open and he sat bolt upright as though he'd been electrocuted.

'Right! Now get up!' she ordered and he did so.

Together they staggered down the slope into the town. Outside the Wheatsheaf pub, she propped him on the wall.

'Sit there,' she told him.

Inside, the Last Orders bell was just being rung. The pub was thick with smoke and people and loud with bright holiday chatter. She squeezed her way to the bar where the barmaids were flying about pulling pints, ringing the tills, washing glasses. It wasn't her turn but she asked urgently:

'Do you serve coffee?' The woman shook her head.

'Could I have a pint of water, then?'

She hadn't appeared to have heard but with some bad grace a pint of water appeared on the counter in front of her.

'Time please, Ladies and Gentlemen!' the publican was yelling as she left the mob-scene inside.

The courtyard was packed too. Paul was still sitting on the wall but slumped forward like an old tramp.

'Wake up Paul!' She shook him and pulled his head up roughly by the hair.

'They don't do coffee in there, so I got you some water. Now drink this.' He took a few sips before pushing it aside and belching loudly.

'I feel like throwing up.'

'Don't you bloody dare!' she threatened him. 'Look I'll light you a fag.'

She did and stuck it between his lips, where it hung, sagging as he sagged.

The pub was emptying quickly.

'This is getting ridiculous,' Theresa said out loud.

With sudden resolve she picked up the half full glass of water.

'You asked for this Paul. Now wake up, will you!'

The water struck him hard in the face and had much the same affect as the slap except that this time he woke in a blind fury and somehow managed to grab hold of her neck in his two hands and start to throttle her. His eyes were mad with anger and his hands were strong.

'Let go!' she managed to croak. 'Let go!'

It didn't take long for a party of stragglers to come to her assistance. Two men held Paul back while a woman pulled Theresa clear.

'You OK?' she asked.

Theresa nodded.

'It's OK! He's just a bit pissed that's all. It's all right,' she said to the two men. 'It was my own fault, I threw a glass of water over him to sober him up, he didn't mean anything.'

'Oh well,' one said uncertainly, 'if you're sure . . .'

They were about to back away when the publican appeared with a policeman.

'It's all right, lads . . . called for back up! They're fast around these parts. He was round the back actually! PC49 here will sort it.'

'Oh no,' Theresa groaned inwardly.

'It's OK officer . . . I can handle it . . . he's just a bit . . . had a bit much . . . he'll be fine now.'

But already the policeman was peering closely at Paul who was back slumped on the wall.

'Paul!' he said. 'Good Lord, it's Paul Mullins, my nephew!' he explained to the publican who was busy clearing the white plastic tables of glasses, piling them into a tall glass tower.

'Mary's lad. Does she know you're here?' he asked.

'Not exactly,' Theresa intervened. Oh, what the hell, it was all going to come out now. She was utterly resigned.

'Look, it was my fault . . . I bought the whisky . . . and he drank too much of it . . . I wasn't in the mood for it myself . . . and then he didn't seem to be able to handle it . . . and anyway, we've blown it now . . . but maybe you can get him home and then you can tell his mum it was all Theresa's fault and she'll believe you, I can promise you that.'

Paul's uncle, ignoring most of what Theresa was saying, was concerned with the practicalities.

'Frank!' he called. 'I couldn't ask a favour could I?'

'I'll call it in Terry, I'll call it in!' he was warned jocularly.

'You couldn't run my sister's lad back home, he's in no fit state to be out at all. And I just want him safe for the time being. Leave her to deal with the rest of it,' he added with a meaningful look at Theresa.

'Course I will, I've got the van out the back. Neil'll run him up, he won't mind. Better than clearing up eh? Neil!'

A young clone appeared in the doorway, he had the same cheery cheeks and gingery hair.

'Run this lad up the Estate would you, see him safely delivered.'

'My nephew,' explained the policeman.

'Paul Mullins. I know him. Shall I bring the van round?' he suggested, seeing that Paul had slipped forward off the wall and was lying comatose at its base.

'I'll be getting off then,' said Theresa. 'Don't need me any more.'

The policeman hesitated.

'Have you far to go, would you like Neil to give

you a lift? Though this place is pretty safe, I don't like to see young girls alone at night.'

'It's OK. I'm just up the hill. I'll be home before Paul,' she said. 'Thanks,' she added.

As Theresa walked quickly up the steep hill, walking in the road which was quiet and car-less at this hour, the tarmac was still like a silver path. But as she neared the church, the road became as dark as earth. Glancing up, she saw the moon had been swallowed in a thick bank of cloud. Taking a deep breath, she hurried past The Haven which was black and sinister to her eyes. The image of Esmie, lying like a rag doll at her feet, flashed through her mind.

'Never even told him the best bit,' she thought.

22

Theresa sat in the kitchen the next morning munching her cornflakes and wincing as she replayed the previous evening.

'Oh no . . . stupid . . . why didn't I . . . if only . . . oh what the hell . . . sod them all.' Resolutely putting all further recriminations out of her head, she sipped at her tea.

'Pat! Pat! Is anybody there?' Her grandma's voice, though faint, sounded urgent.

Theresa shot out of the kitchen and took the stairs two at a time. The old lady was standing at the head of the stairs, clutching the bannisters with one hand and holding her dressing gown together at her throat with the other. She hadn't combed her hair, which was wispy and tangled and stood away from her head in an unusually dishevelled way. Her face looked as though it had caved in and her speech was mumbled and indistinct.

'You OK, Grandma? What's the matter?'

The eyes were misty, confused. When she saw Theresa, she muttered something, released her hold on the bannisters and started to stroke vaguely at her hair.

'Where's Mary?' she asked.

'She's not coming today, remember? She can't come today, got to make do with me I'm afraid.'

There was something in the trembling of her grandma's hands, the pallor of her face, which struck a chill of fear into Theresa.

'You sure you're all right, Grandma?'

The old lady smiled resolutely. 'I'm perfectly fine my dear . . . nothing to worry about . . . we'll get along just fine you and I . . . I'll go and put my glad rags on.'

Theresa hesitated as she watched her grandma turn slowly and return to her room.

The sound of the letter box opening and shutting and Cuthbert's customary two ineffectual barks switched her mind to the letters on the mat.

There were the usual batch of business letters for Andrew: New York, Milan, Sydney, Australia, but at the bottom of the pile there was one for her in Debbie's writing.

She retired to the kitchen and sat at the table, greedily devouring the news.

'Dear Trees,

Sorry I haven't written before but I didn't have your address and I didn't like to ask your mum. We've just been away for a week to Mum's cousin who lives in Norfolk . . . it was O.K. Bit boring. Nothing much to do. We went to the beach a couple of times, but it's all stones and you can't really lie and get a suntan. Mum's back at work now . . . it's really boring without you. I've got a job at McDonald's . . . hard work but the pay's O.K. and you get lots to eat . . . it makes a change from

Pasta and tomato sauce. Take care, When are you coming back?

Lots of love Debbie.

Thoughtfully, Theresa folded the letter and placed it under her book on her bedside table. After reading it, she felt miserable all of a sudden, wanting to talk to Debs, be with her, hell, she'd even fry burgers or whatever, it sounded OK. It was lonesome being all this way away, with all these difficult things surrounding her.

She heard the phone ringing twice before it stopped. Presumably Andrew had answered it. And then before she had time to formulate another thought she heard an almost familiar:

'Yoohoo! May I come in!' from outside the kitchen door.

It was Mrs Appleyard. She came into the room talking.

'It's all right, dear, I know. It has been explained. And I'm not taking sides, I'm not saying anything. My concern is with Mrs Bird and with you to see you are managing. It's a big responsibility, that's what I said to my husband, for a sixteen-year-old girl whatever she may have done . . .'

'I haven't done anything,' Theresa told her mildly.

'Well, as I said, I am not here to judge or to take sides. Is she upstairs?'

'Yes, she's not dressed but she seemed a bit dithery this morning.'

Theresa felt surprisingly relieved to be able to draw an adult into the situation.

'I'll go on up, I'm used to all of this, don't you worry. Why don't you put the kettle on and make us a nice pot of tea.'

'Tea, tea, tea! I'm sick of tea!' Theresa thought as she plugged in the kettle but Mrs Appleyard was still speaking.

'I can't stay long, I've got to go over to the Barnstables at Lower Harptree. He's had another fit and they've got the twins, only two months old and how they are managing with the cows to milk and I don't know what, only the good Lord knows!'

Barely had she disappeared than Andrew's office door burst open.

'This is too much!' he began in a voice tense with anger. Theresa was just putting three tea-bags in the pot.

She looked up, a question on her face.

'That was Mary . . . *again*!'

She looked away. 'Oh dear.'

'Oh dear indeed! What on earth were you thinking of Theresa? Talk about making bad matters worse, I should never have let you go. And I did think, after our talk, that I could trust you. Well, I should have listened to my own better judgement, not yours! Taking him out and getting him drunk . . . rescued by the police . . . this is a small town, Theresa! I don't think you understand this! Everybody's related to everybody else, anything one person does affects everybody else!'

'I'm beginning to realise that,' she said.

'Well, is that all you have to say?' he blazed at her.

'No,' she set the cloth on the tray and put the Rich Tea out on a china plate.

'Who's that for?' he asked suspiciously.

'Mrs Appleyard. She's upstairs.'

He groaned.

'Do you want to hear about last night?' she asked.

'Not really.'

'OK.'

'No, no, I do, I suppose.'

'I wanted to see Paul, find out what he knew, clear my name if you like. And I thought a bit of whisky might break the ice . . . bad idea, OK. I admit it. I didn't want more than a mouthful. He drank the lot . . . couldn't handle it . . . end of story . . . well, not really the end . . . met a policeman who turned out to be his uncle . . . said he'd get him home.'

'God, Theresa, I must say, you have some kind of flair for making difficult situations worse,' he said.

'Thanks,' she replied.

There were sounds of movement from upstairs.

'Look, I don't want to get caught up with Mrs Appleyard if I can help it. I'm right in the middle of some important work . . . expecting a fax from New York any minute. I'll talk to you later.'

Mrs Appleyard and her grandma were deep in conversation as they came into the room; at least, Mrs Appleyard was talking and her grandma appeared to be in thought. She looked better in a purple dress, the paisley shawl over her shoulders, in spite of the oppressive heat of the day.

'I have told Mrs Bird that there is no point in

visiting The Hawthornes today, because it's been shut down. Mrs Bird had set her heart on visiting an old friend. Well, I told her, if she gave me the name, I'd find out what has happened to her friend. And that's just what I'm going to do, isn't it dear?'

She leant across and gave the old lady a squeeze of the hand.

Theresa pushed the tray of tea things towards them.

'Oh lovely, I'm gasping. I told Mrs Bird, I put the flowers out as we arranged, and beautiful they looked too.'

Theresa noticed her grandma's hands were still trembling.

'If it's any help,' Theresa said, 'you could try Bunt and Coker's. It's their board up outside The Hawthornes. We went there last week. Grandma wanted to go.'

'Well, that's a good starting point. Just you leave it to me, dear, I'll soon sort this one out!' Mrs Appleyard said confidently to the old lady again laying her hand on her arm.

Theresa left the two of them sipping their tea and wandered out into the garden. There was a heaviness in the air, an indistinct haze in the sky which made her wonder if it was really blue or really grey. But high above, the disc of the sun still burned gold, but with a strange copperish rim to it.

'It's going to break,' she told Cuthbert who had wandered out beside her. Too lazy, or too unsteady to cock his leg any longer, he squatted to relieve himself. After he'd done so, with stiff legs, he tried to scuff the grass.

Throughout the afternoon the heat built up like a furnace in the world outside the window. The grey clouds thickened, the air thickened, and there was an oppressive stillness in the garden. Even the birds seemed crushed by the weight in the air. All was strangely silent.

Theresa sat inside, in Grandpa's chair, with the french windows open behind her. She tried to read *The Camomile Lawn*, then she switched on the television and watched some afternoon Game Show which had a lot of screaming in it and some unbelievably easy questions.

'The things people do for one lousy microwave,' she thought.

Theresa again strained her ears and tilted her head towards the open door.

Not a sound.

She got up, stretched and yawned, turned off the TV.

Outside her grandmother's room, she stopped and bent down, listening at the keyhole. Gently she turned the handle. She was not in the bed though the bedclothes had been turned back. The purple dress and the shawl were lying across the button-backed chair. Theresa took two steps inside the room.

Then she heard the tiny moan.

She was lying on the far side of the bed almost across the bay window. She was on her front, her petticoat hitched up to reveal two very white legs.

'Grandma!' Theresa gasped springing round the bed. She knelt quickly by her side. Her eyelids were fluttering and she was breathing, although in a rather quick and rasping way.

'Don't move!' Theresa said unnecessarily. 'I'll call the doctor!'

She never thought of the 'medicinal' at all.

'Oh God!' she thought as she tore down the stairs. 'Please don't let her . . .'

The number was, fortunately, in the first place she looked, D for Doctor in Andrew's flip-up telephone directory.

A receptionist answered immediately.

'Doctor's surgery . . . how can I help you?'

'It's my grandma. She's had a fall . . . she's still breathing . . . but I don't know how serious . . .' Her voice gave a little wobble on that word.

'It's all right, my dear, I'll send the duty doctor right away. Can I have your name and address?'

'It's Mrs Bird, that's my grandmother . . .'

The receptionist cut in:

'Mrs Bird, Chillcott Lodge . . .?'

'Yes.'

'Doctor knows her . . . he'll be there in five minutes . . . just go and stay with her, my love, and don't worry.'

As though she could do otherwise, she returned to the room instantly and was almost surprised to see her grandmother hadn't moved an inch.

'Stay there, Grandma, the doctor's on his way . . . I'll just cover you up . . . don't want you to catch cold.'

She knew it was a silly thing to say as she said it; the very sound of her voice sounded false in this silent scene, but she looked more normal somehow, covered in her shawl.

Sitting down on the Turkish rug, Theresa took her grandma's hand in her own. It was cold and dry, the skin a thin covering over bone. But there was a pulse, she felt it, and saw also a little throbbing of a blue vein in her neck. She smoothed the old lady's hair which felt as fine as baby's hair. It was a shock to notice how thin it was. Her skull was clearly visible.

It wasn't long before she heard a confident voice in the hall:

'Hello, Dr McCloud. On my way up!'

The relief when he strode into the room was so immense, Theresa nearly burst into tears at the sight of him.

'You haven't moved her? Found her like this?'

Theresa nodded. He got down on the floor quickly and spoke to her in a loud voice.

'Hello Mrs Bird, it's Doctor McCloud here . . . what have you been up to, taken a tumble have you . . . don't you worry about a thing, my love, just give you a bit of an examination.'

Theresa, standing back at the foot of the bed, saw the eyes flicker and try to open.

'Can you hear me?'

There was the faintest movement of the head.

'Good, that's my girl, now you'll be able to help me . . . tell me where it hurts.'

He turned to Theresa.

'Could you be a love and get me a cup of tea . . . I've been dashing about all afternoon.'

At first she was appalled that he could be thinking of himself at such a time, but as she stood waiting impatiently for the kettle to boil, another thought occurred:

'Wanted me out of the way, I expect.'

And in a way she was glad, though all the time she stood there, she was wondering what he was doing to her, what he was discovering.

As the steam from the kettle began to rise, the first drops of rain hit the window pane with such force she thought for a second that someone was throwing something at the window. They plinked like pieces of gravel and splatted on the paving stones like ink blots.

By the time she returned, he had moved her to the bed; her legs were crooked over his arm and he was tapping her knees with a little wooden hammer. Laying her legs flat, he scratched along the soles of her feet with his nails.

'Hmmm . . . I think you've had a little stroke, Mrs Bird!' He turned to Theresa. 'Not getting much reflex reaction here. . . . but the great news is there don't seem to be any broken bones, do there?'

The old lady's eyes opened again and she smiled a weak lopsided sort of smile.

'A stroke!' Theresa's blood ran cold. 'A stroke!' she repeated.

'Only a little one, as far as I can judge . . . you can hear what I'm saying, can't you love?'

There was a faint movement of the head.

227

'And you can move your limbs can't you . . . show us again!' The fingers of her hands moved slightly on the bedclothes, as though she were playing a ghostly piano.

'Can you lift your hand at all, Mrs Bird?'

She did, unsteadily, like a marionette, up and down again, both sides.

'And your legs?'

Slowly, the knees bent and the legs moved, first one then the other.

'You'll be up and pedalling your bike again in no time!' he said jovially.

He turned to Theresa. 'Is this my tea? . . . that's great . . . Now, let's go outside for a little chat.' He turned back to the old lady.

'Stay there for now, Mrs Bird, don't you go falling out of bed again! I don't want you to move . . . and I'll send the district nurse round this evening to make sure your comfortable. OK? And I'll come back later on to make sure you're behaving. How's that?'

Again, there was a weak smile on her face.

Outside the bedroom door and out of earshot, the doctor sipped his tea and talked, between slurps.

'I gather you're here on your own . . . Theresa, isn't it?'

She nodded.

'Bad luck that . . . tell Dad to give me a ring when he gets back. I'll make all the arrangements, district nurse and so on.'

'Not hospital, then?'

'I think she's better off here, it was only a little

stroke. We'll keep an eye on her, try not to worry! Silly thing to say, isn't it? I don't like you being here on your own though . . . who can we get to come over? Wasn't Mary Mullins helping your grandma?'

Theresa shook her head. The doctor looked questioningly.

'Long story.'

'Well, what about Mrs Appleyard, she's a good sort, only lives up the road at the Vicarage. Why don't I give her a ring?'

He walked through to the office, as though he was familiar with the house and reappeared a few seconds later.

'On her way.'

He picked up his bag which he'd left at the foot of the stairs, passed his empty cup to Theresa, knelt to give Cuthbert a rub.

'Hello, old chap. How are you?'

A crack of thunder and a simultaneous flash of lightning dropped from the sky and the heavens opened. The doctor stood at the backdoor surveying the sheet of water he would have to breach to get to his car.

'I'll take you with the brolly,' Theresa offered.

Together they ran, his arm round her shoulders. The rain was cold against the flesh of her legs.

As he was fumbling with his door, another flash lit up the black sky and a shattering crack broke out of the heavens and enveloped them all.

The doctor slammed his door and lifted his hand to wave. Theresa turned and ran back to the house.

Cuthbert was sitting at the foot of the stairs panting, his back legs trembling. She took the stairs two at a time and tiptoed into her grandma's room. Her head was turned towards the window, and her eyes were open and quite alert. A further flash of light lit up the room but the gap between the lightning and the thunder was slightly longer.

'Moving away,' Theresa told her.

She nodded.

Theresa sat on the bed next to her.

The white light flashed across the room, across their eyeballs, across their brains with its electric power and the groaning of the sky was in their bones.

As she sat there Theresa felt her grandmother place her hand over her own. It was warm.

Mrs Appleyard arrived as the storm was subsiding; they heard her calling from the hall and then her tread on the stairs.

'My, look at you two sitting in the dark!'

'How is she?' she whispered to Theresa.

'I don't know . . . you OK, Grandma?'

Her lips twitched slightly and then opened. Slowly, experimentally, she moved them from side to side and then she whispered hoarsely: 'I'm perfectly fine!'

Theresa didn't want Mrs Appleyard to see her crying, but those words of her grandma's made the sobs burst out instantly. Once as a child, she'd been sick in her bedroom. She hadn't been feeling ill. There were no advance warnings. She just opened her mouth and was violently sick, so sick that she remembered her mother having to clean the far walls of her room.

It was like that.

She ran from the room, hiccoughing and spluttering, and buried herself in her maroon eiderdown, crying into her pillow until slowly the sobs subsided and she realised how hot she was. Gradually she became aware of the thrumming of the rain on the window and then the louder and nearer sound of a small plip plip plip, insistent, ominous. In the corner of the room a drip was forming on a yellowed patch of ceiling paper and was falling onto the floor below.

By the time she returned to her grandma's room, having placed a bucket under her leaking ceiling, the light by the bed was on and Mrs Appleyard was helping her to drink by means of a baby's beaker.

'Here she is, Mrs Bird! She was worried about you,' she told Theresa. 'I said, it was all a shock for the poor child . . . better now?' she asked.

Theresa nodded.

'We've had a cup of tea . . . always have a few gadgets at the ready. I do a lot of this,' she told Theresa. 'The beaker is among one of my most useful items.'

She beamed.

'And your father will be back soon, I told her, and the nurse is coming, and the doctor. It will be quite an eventful evening.'

Theresa glanced at the tiny clock on her grandma's dressing table, twenty to seven.

'He's a bit late . . . I hope he's alright . . . I mean I hope nothing's happened . . .'

Already there was a watery feeling in her legs and although Mrs Appleyard was saying, 'Oh now, I'm sure there's some logical explanation,' Theresa felt suddenly sick. Oh no, not that, not now, it would be too cruel; but before she had time to finish the thought, she heard the sound of his car on the gravel drive.

She met him at the foot of the stairs.

'Sorry I'm late . . .' he was beginning, '. . . she had a false alarm . . . you know . . . felt I should hang on . . . but . . . what's the matter?'

He had noticed Theresa's expression.

'What's up?'

'It's Grandma, she's had a stroke . . . only a little one,' she called after him as he leapt up the stairs.

Without even pausing to knock at the door, and not noticing Mrs Appleyard, Andrew ran straight into his mother's room, sinking to his knees by her bed and grasping her hand in his own. It was like something out of a film. Old Mrs Bird did one of her crooked smiles and patted him rather awkwardly on the head.

Andrew having returned, Mrs Appleyard slipped away. The district nurse came and settled the old lady down for the night. Though Theresa wanted to stay with her grandma, wanting to watch her like a hawk as though her eyes might be able to keep her from any thought of slipping away, the nurse was adamant that she should sleep.

'She'll be all right through the night, I'll be back

tomorrow morning. I know it sounds bad, a stroke, but it's common, these little ones, believe you me, and they just need a bit of help for the first few days, and then they carry on as though not much has happened . . . I see it all the time.'

'But how does she know?' Theresa wondered as she brushed her teeth. 'She doesn't know . . . she can't *know*.'

Once ready for bed, she slipped back into her grandma's room. She was still propped up on the pillows which the nurse had arranged for her. She was not as she normally looked. Her eyes were closed and her head slumped forward and she was snoring slightly.

There was no indication, no sign either way. She stood there, until suddenly she was tired and she wanted to be in bed where she fell instantly into a deep sleep.

23

It was simply the last possible thing she had
expected. She rose to the surface of the day with
the thought of her grandmother pulling her up and
she leapt straight out of bed still riding that upsurge.
She ran to Grandma's bedroom door, tapped perfunctorily and opened the door before she could
dread what she might find.

She was sitting up. Theresa could see instantly
that she was more alert in the way she sat. But the
surprise was Mary sitting by the bed, Mrs Appleyard's blue plastic beaker in her hand.

Theresa, too punch drunk to speak, stood there
waiting to be released.

'Theresa . . .' For once Mary seemed lost for
words too but her face was not hostile.

'I heard . . . I'm so sorry . . . I feel dreadful, honest
I do, and if you hate me for ever it wouldn't be
more than I deserve.'

'It's OK,' Theresa said and advanced towards the
bed.

'I just came to say hello. You all right, Grandma?'

The old lady had already turned her head towards
her. She smiled that lop-sided smile and said, a little
slurred and indistinctly:

'I'm perfectly fine.' And then she added. 'And how are *you*?'

'Me? Oh, I'm perfectly fine too! I just woke up,' she explained remembering her short T-shirt and bare legs. 'I'll just go and get dressed, Grandma . . . I can see you're in good hands.'

She was washing her armpits when she heard the phone ringing in the distance. It barely registered, it was answered so quickly. But when she heard Andrew's door open and his voice yelling up the stairs, she understood instantly.

'Theresa!' She met him halfway up the stairs.

'That was the hospital.' She nodded. 'I'm off! It seems it's not a false alarm now . . . I don't think anything else can happen. You've seen Mary?'

Theresa nodded.

'Thank God for Mary!'

Theresa frowned.

'I'll phone!' He ran down the last few steps, stopped, then returned to where Theresa was standing to kiss her, a big wet kiss on the cheek.

'I don't know what I'd have done without you, Trees.'

There was a catch of emotion in his voice.

'Go on! Get off! Got some money? Clean handkerchief?'

He checked his pockets immediately before breaking into a smile.

'And . . . hope it all goes well,' Theresa added.

She took a deep breath before returning to Grandma's room.

'Dad's gone to the hospital,' she announced. 'I think it's all started.'

Again her grandma's head swivelled round to gaze at her. Their eyes met. Hers seemed much more alert, clear.

She lifted an arm and held it out to Theresa who went towards the bed and took it.

'Poor Theresa,' she mouthed. 'Some holiday!'

They smiled at each other.

'It was never meant to be a holiday, Grandma, remember.'

Mary cleared her throat.

'Don't worry, my love, I'm here for as long as you need me. You go and get some breakfast inside you.'

The cornflake packet only had a few disappointing broken flakes in the bottom. This was not a good omen.

She was forced to have muesli which tasted dry and plain and smelt like Polyfilla.

As Theresa munched it, she thought of her father speeding along the country roads. Naomi, God only knew what was happening to her. It was something she hadn't really wanted to think about before, but it would happen, wouldn't it? They'd be back, she and some squalling brat. Theresa thought briefly about Rosie. Rosie, poor Rosie ... not her fault. Maybe she should send her a card or something; she'd like it here – the harbour, fishing for crabs from the steps with pieces of string; the fishing boats; and the sea gulls in the Church Meadows ... and she'd love the beach! All the rock pools and the cockles and seaweeds and they could make seaweed gardens on the rocks and then play houses, carving out rooms in their imaginations from the fallen slabs, like she used to do with Grandma. Grandma would come to visit her and she'd make pretend scones in her pretend oven and take the best china from the shelves in the rocks where the sea anemones stuck like lumps of brown jelly, and the limpets which she tried so hard to prize from the rocks . . . it would be better with Rosie here . . . not so lonely . . . someone to play with . . .

She was wondering what to do when the phone rang again. Andrew.

'Just got here. Nothing to report. Could you give Pat a buzz for me . . . I rang her last night and promised I'd give her a call after the doctor called. Her office number is on the pad in front of you and, if she's not there, call her mobile phone. That number's there too. OK?'

'OK, Dad.'

'Sorry – money's running out. I'll . . .'

'Call you later,' she finished for him.

Mary came clattering down the stairs with the tea tray and caught Theresa in the hall. Theresa averted her eyes and was on the point of going up the stairs, just to avoid her, when Mary said:

'You got a moment, my love? I just want to explain myself.'

Somewhat reluctantly, Theresa followed her into the kitchen. Fortunately, even through their conversation, Mary worked away making pastry, washing vegetables and peeling and slicing them, diving into her shopping bag and coming up with packets of mince which she turned out onto a dish to breathe.

'Now Theresa, I hardly know where to begin . . . I feel that bad . . . not your grandma . . . well, I don't mean I don't feel bad about that, of course I do . . . I'm talking about . . . you know . . . that other business . . . the boat and all that . . .'

'Oh.' Theresa flushed. 'That!'

'Yes, that. You see I was too hasty, I admit it, but that's what I was told see, and there were witnesses and the bracelet and all. And, like I said, I was too hasty . . . and now it turns out I was quite wrong.'

Theresa lifted her eyes and looked at her, and she seemed to be attacking the pastry, rolling it very thin with great swipes of her wooden rolling pin.

'Last night it was too late, or I'd have come straight round. Well, I didn't even know about your grandma then, not till this morning when Mrs Appleyard looked in . . . wanted to see my dad about something . . . Anyway I felt double bad then, I can tell you. No, it was last night late.' She lifted the pastry from the table and slapped it down in a dish and piled apples and raisins into it. She cut round the edge and then scooped up the cuttings and twisted them into curls for the lattice top.

'I was in bed . . . but Paul come in and he woke me up . . . down I went and there was Paul downstairs with this other girl . . . in floods of tears she was . . .'

'Susan,' Theresa said quickly.

'No . . . not Sue . . . it were Jill Pidgely . . . well, I know her . . . know her mum . . . there she was blabbing like a baby . . . and Paul was being all rough with her . . . so I told him to lay off or we'd never get any sense out of the situation . . . and he said that Jill had something to tell me . . . and what she said was that Sue had confessed that *she'd* been the one . . . she'd seen you two go off . . . and then she'd bided her time . . . and then I guess she'd gone right out to the boat and done what she done . . . and then she told everyone it was you she'd seen and then other people who saw it . . . well, you don't look so unlike her . . . and in the dark . . . well, that was it, really . . . except of course Jill said Sue would kill her . . . but Paul said he'd kill Sue if he got to her first . . . and I said I'd kill the lot of them if they didn't grow up!'

Theresa smiled.

'Still, that's about it. And my husband went round Sue's dad's house, he's in the Coast Guard, known him since he were a lad, and they come to some agreement. Turns out it's not so bad anyway . . . just the one seat damaged . . . split the plastic with a knife . . . and then all the innards come spilling out . . . it'll mend!'

Theresa smiled again at the thought of the one little tear which they could patch up so quickly.

'Don't know what it was all about mind!' Mary was saying. 'That's your business . . . yours and hers . . . And Paul's, I suppose . . . but there's just one thing I can say in my own defence . . . you never should have got him drunk with all that whisky, whatever the provocation!'

Theresa drew breath but she found herself

exhaling the air again without bothering to defend herself. It was enough. She didn't have to be lily white, so long as the worst of the tarnish was removed.

'So, now I'm going to try and make it up to you all. I know how close you and your grandmother were . . .'

'Were . . .?'

'Are . . . are . . . I just meant, I know it's difficult for you.'

'But she is looking better today isn't she?' Theresa asked urgently.

'Well, I didn't see her yesterday . . . but she's quite alert now I'd say.'

The doctor came. The nurse came and went. Dr McCloud agreed that she *was* looking better.

'We'll keep a good eye on her for a day or two . . . and then I think we'll try to get her up and about before her limbs get lazy . . . maybe tomorrow . . . I'll get Mary to persuade her into her chair . . . something like that . . .'

'I could do that,' Theresa said at once, wondering if she could.

'Oh yes, I just meant . . . You know, old ladies look as though they're about to blow away but they're a dead weight,' he said, seemingly unaware of the words he was using.

'Is your dad around?' he asked vaguely.

'Oh no . . . he had a call from the hospital. Naomi's started I think . . .'

'Crikey! That's all you need!' he said rubbing his

hands together gleefully. 'Ah well, fitting in a way, isn't it . . . new life and all that sort of thing.'

Theresa looked at her feet.

'Well, must be getting along . . . funny how all the visitors get sick as soon as the rain starts. Too busy enjoying themselves on sunny days or burning themselves or getting half-drowned, of course. Tell your father to ring me, to exchange news!' he called to Theresa.

As soon as the doctor had gone, Theresa returned to sit at her grandmother's bedside. She seemed to be slumped in sleep. For a time she sat just staring at her, trying to see behind the frail eggshell exterior the robust figure she held so strongly in the very centre of her mind and memories. It was difficult to see that now dissolving, petering away, without feeling something disappearing, melting away inside herself.

It was easier to read a book. Not stare, not think. How she wished she had something more involving than *The Camomile Lawn*!

Once the old lady's eyes flickered open. They seemed to register what they saw for she mouthed:

'What are you reading?'

'It's rubbish,' Theresa told her.

'Read to me,' she asked her. 'Read Alice.'

Theresa knew where the book was, of course. It sat on the book-shelf still in its cardboard slip box, marbled in maroon to match the leather of the book itself: '*Through the Looking-Glass.*' The pages were edged in gold. Every page she remembered, every illustration, the black and white woodcuts and the full colour plates, and the way the words looked on the page. She remembered the smell of it too, and the little maroon tape which marked their progress each night.

'Which bit?' she asked.

'Oh, let's be hopeful – start at the beginning.'

'One thing was certain,' she read, 'that the *white* kitten had nothing to do with it.'

It was always the black kitten Theresa sympathized with; she loved that little dark illustration of it tangled up in the ball of wool.

She wasn't sure how much her grandmother heard, how often she faded away, but it was that sort of a book anyway. Theresa herself remembered coming in and out of it, through childhood fevers, and nights when she couldn't sleep, when an owl was hooting too loudly in the tree outside her window, or when the thunder had woken her, or the wind and the rain. And now *she* was reading it to *her*, and that seemed right too.

Mary looked in at about noon with a lunch tray.

'Do you fancy a little something, Mrs Bird . . . I've done you a bit of soup.'

Theresa slipped Alice back into its cardboard cover and seizing her chance she said to Mary:

'I just want to go and get a card for my sister . . . is that OK? I'll only be half an hour.'

'You run along. I'm not going anywhere. Not till you get back anyway. Get along with you.'

It took Theresa some time to choose her card. She would have sent a herring gull, but she'd drawn that one for her mother; the views of the village, the harbour, the sunsets, the beaches weren't right. On the far side they had a rack of cards which had nothing to do with anything ... kittens, field mice in pretty clothes, fey women in cornfields, blurred reproductions of Old Masters.

'That'll do.' She picked one out with a naughty black kitten sitting in a flower pot.

Next she went to the Post Office. On the counter, among the litter of registered delivery forms and Giro Bank slips she wrote.

'Hi Rosie! Isn't it cute! Ahhh! You'd love it here. Ask Mummy if you can come one day. Hope you miss me. I miss you, love Theresa.'

She bought a stamp and put it into the letter box, first class delivery, and quickly set off up the hill.

When she saw the blue flashing light and the white ambulance parked at an angle on the hill, Theresa realised she had vaguely heard its siren from inside the Post Office. She quickened her step until she realised it was in fact drawn up outside the cottages. The black door of the Haven was open. She saw the ambulance man struggling out backwards, holding one end of a stretcher. On it, strapped round like a parcel of meat, was someone wrapped in a cherry red blanket.

Immediately a terrible guilt flooded Theresa's body. The poor old lady, kicked out like that, and that terrible wound on her forehead! She should have told someone!

But it wasn't her. As the stretcher was manoeuvred into the back of the ambulance, Theresa saw the white, almost skull-like head of an elderly man, his cheeks sunken, eyes closed, lips a dark purple.

Before the men closed the doors, the old woman came hurrying down the pavement, pulling her arms into the sleeves of a drab overcoat. There was a dark bruise on her forehead.

'I only turned my back for a minute. I *knew* he'd do this one day. I *knew* it would end like this!'

'Not ended, love. He'll be OK. Cry for help more like!' the ambulance man told her cheerfully, helping her up the step and into the interior.

The ambulance pulled away up the hill, its light flashing, siren wailing and had quite disappeared from sight before Theresa continued her way up to the house, following a trail of dark spots on the ground which led from where the ambulance had been, to the front step of The Haven.

24

During the afternoon, there were two further phone calls from the hospital. The second announced they were on their way to the delivery suite as Naomi was two centimetres dilated. Theresa deliberately formed no concept, didn't even register what the words were referring to, and just said: 'Right, Dad!'

There was a constant stream of visitors. The nurse called again, and the doctor. The Vicar stopped briefly and Mrs Appleyard arrived with a bunch of flowers from her garden.

Unannounced, a large Volvo drew up into the forecourt at about six-thirty. It was Pat.

She flew into the house, a long expensive Burberry coat, unbuttoned, flapping behind her. She wore a silk scarf round her neck, a smart white blouse and well-cut trousers.

'My God . . . I just couldn't get away . . . but in the end I just jumped up in the middle of a meeting . . . drove like a bat out of hell . . . and here I am . . . can't think why I didn't come earlier . . . if you ask, they always say no . . . how is she?'

'Not too bad. Mary's just giving her some tea.'

'Tea! Oh, thank the Lord!'

Pat streaked up the stairs and soon afterwards Mary came down carrying a tray.

Later, Theresa read her grandmother another chapter of Alice, 'The Garden of Live Flowers'.

' "Oh Tiger-lily! I wish you could talk!"

"We *can* talk when there's anyone worth talking to!" ' read Theresa.

'Show me, show me!' her grandmother said and when she turned to the picture of the tiger-lilies and the red roses with their white faces, and the yellow and white daisies, she smiled. But by the time Theresa turned to the picture of Alice meeting the Red Queen, she was deeply asleep.

Carefully, she marked the page with the maroon ribbon, closed the book and slipped it into its protective cover.

'Night, Grandma!' she said, kissing her lightly on the forehead.

Pat was downstairs and the kitchen was full of smoke. On the table in front of her was a dish of half-eaten pasty, the peel of an apple, a saucer of ash and half a cup of coffee.

'I think she's asleep,' Theresa told her.

'I'll go up in just a sec. Must get the hounds in, they'll be going potty.'

'Hounds?'

'Had to bring them . . . no time to arrange anything else . . . anyway . . . just don't know how long I'll be holed up here. Andrew can't stand them, still, other things on his mind, I hope.'

She stubbed her cigarette out and got to her feet.

'Hold on to your hat!' she cried.

Theresa heard the scrabbling and the excited yaps but she was not expecting the size of the invading party. Big as ponies they were, thin and scraggy and they leapt through the house with two bounds and disappeared into the hall where they met Cuthbert. A growling and a screaming and excited yapping resulted until Pat went streaking after them.

'Down! Leave the poor old bugger alone . . . Dennis, Desmond . . . come!'

She came into the kitchen leaning slightly to one side, holding both dogs by their collars.

'Theresa, this is Dennis and this is Desmond.'

'What are they?'

'Irish wolf hounds. Aren't they adorable?'

Desmond, without having to stretch, proceeded to help himself to the remains of the pasty crust on the table, Dennis had found Cuthbert's bowl and was slurping noisily from it.

'Poor loves, they must be famished . . . past their supper time.'

Pat disappeared to the car and returned with two washing up bowls and a box of Chappie and a giant size bag of dog biscuits.

'Costs me a bloody fortune to feed them,' she admitted cheerfully.

From under the dog biscuits she pulled out a large bottle of brandy. 'I think we deserve it don't you?'

Theresa smiled and to her own surprise found herself shaking her head. Pat shrugged.

'Don't mind if I do?'

Theresa clenched her fists so hard she could feel

the nails digging into her flesh. Water gushed into her mouth forcing her to swallow, though it was hard to do so.

'That's better!' Pat said as she downed the brandy in one long gulp. She pushed the dogs' bowls one to one end of the kitchen, and one to the other.

'Have to separate them, Denis wolfs, pardon the pun, his down and then gets Desmond's. He's such a sissy, aren't you, my love?'

She slumped into a chair and reached for her cigarette packet. Theresa sat feeling strangely clear-headed and calm and yet, strangely, as though she was watching herself with curiosity.

'I can do it!' she thought to herself, feeling suddenly elated. 'It's easy. No problem!'

Cuthbert came moodily into the kitchen. He sat by Theresa and put his head in her lap and gave her a look which said everything.

'I know Cuth . . . I know,' she sympathized gently.

Pat spent the evening popping in and out of her mother's room. Once she found her awake and asking for tea. Otherwise she was peaceful.

'Less stressed I think,' she told Theresa. 'Still, wouldn't you be, snuggled up in bed, waited on hand and foot . . .'

'Doubt it.'

'No, maybe not . . . Youth!'

Theresa settled down with the dogs to watch *One Foot In the Grave*. She wished it wasn't called that. Funny how you only noticed when something like this was happening.

They watched a film about an invasion of giant ants.

'This'll do fine,' Pat said. 'Doesn't matter a toot what rubbish we watch so long as it's not real.'

Real it certainly wasn't.

By the final credits, their eyelids were drooping.

'I'll never pour boiling water on an ants' nest again without thinking of the awful revenge they might wreck,' Pat confessed. 'Got to let the dogs out, then I'm turning in – *if* I can find anywhere *to* turn in . . . I'll pop in on Mum. You look ready for bed.'

'I am.' Theresa yawned and stretched and slowly dragged herself up the stairs as though her legs had turned to lead.

She woke from sleep to find the phone was ringing.

Flinging back the bedclothes, she raced down to the office.

'Theresa! You've got a brother! Weighed in at just over two kilos half an hour ago. Mother and baby doing well, thank the Lord!'

'Oh, that's great, Dad . . . what time is it?'

'Time? About one-fifty . . . I thought you'd like to know right away!'

'Oh yes . . . of course.'

'Grandma all right?'

'Yes . . . and Pat's here . . .'

'Pat! That's grand. Well, you get back to bed. I'll come back soon. Get some sleep, I'll tiptoe in.

'Oh Dad . . . Dad!'

But he'd rung off.

Pat appeared at the top of the stairs. She'd been sleeping in Naomi's bed and she had Andrew's dressing gown on.

'That was Dad.'

'And?'

'Oh, yes ... a boy ... mother and baby doing fine.'

'A boy! I've got a nephew. Well, I never ... and you've got a brother.'

'Yes ... half-brother ...'

'We'll tell Mum in the morning. Night, night, sweet,' Pat yawned and stumbled back to bed.

Theresa didn't fall instantly back to sleep. A brother. A half-brother. No, stupid that ... a brother ... a little baby. A baby brother.

It was hard to know quite how to think about him. It was strange to lie there and know that he existed suddenly, where he hadn't existed before.

Tiptoeing in might have been Andrew's intention, but the noise of the barking dogs, his swearing and his loud efforts to calm them woke her again. She smiled to herself and had just turned over to go back to sleep when she was roused again by his voice from the landing.

'My God, Pat ... you gave me a shock ... what are you doing?'

'Nowhere else to sleep ...'

'And what in God's name did you bring those dogs for?'

Theresa rolled over onto her side.

And if Andrew had had any thoughts of sleeping

in the next morning, he must have abandoned them. The dogs were up and barking noisily from six a.m.

Theresa heard the car door slam and the barking fade away as Pat's car drove off out of the drive. But before she had time to realise she had fallen back to sleep, they were back again and the cacophony resumed.

They barked for breakfast, they barked for water, they barked at Cuthbert, they barked for pleasure and when Theresa appeared, defeated at the bottom of the stairs, their barks of joyous greeting redoubled.

The rugs were all scuffed up. One lay curled in the corner of the hall and now, unimpeded, the dogs raced up and down, skidding at the corners and ricocheting off the walls.

'Morning!' said Pat brightly. 'Hope we didn't disturb you. We're a bit excited this morning, aren't we?' she said, scratching Dennis on the head as he whizzed past her. The back door being open, they raced in and out, tearing the length of the garden before returning to the house.

'Pity it's a wet morning,' Pat said eyeing the doggie footprints. 'No point in clearing them up . . . they'll just mess everything up again,' she said. 'Cup of tea?' Theresa nodded. 'Haven't you got a dressing gown . . . you'll freeze. Mum's awake. I took her a cup. She's got the radio on . . . but not quite with it if you know what I mean . . .'

'Don't think *I* am!' Theresa confessed.

Andrew surfaced a few minutes later. He was

wearing the same dressing gown Pat had appeared in in the night.

His eyes shone, though his face was grey with exhaustion.

'Well done, Dad!' Theresa said, feeling that wasn't quite what she wanted to say.

He came and put his arms on her shoulders and kissed her on the top of the head.

'A little brother, eh? How about that! Did you want a brother?' he asked anxiously.

'Hadn't thought about it,' Theresa said which was the truth.

'What's its name then?' Pat asked.

'Well, I want Richard and Naomi wants Seamus . . . so either it's Richard Seamus or Seamus Richard . . . we'll see who wins.'

'Better than Theresa.'

'What's wrong with Theresa . . . I approved, though I must admit it was your mother's choice. I wanted Clare as I recall.'

'Clare!' Theresa exploded. 'God, I hate the name Clare!'

'You're not a Clare,' Pat told her. 'Mind you, I always hated Pat, especially when I discovered they had hoped for a boy and had already decided on Patrick.'

The dogs returned from a garden excursion, seeing Andrew, who had not been greeted properly, they started barking again and bouncing round him wildly.

'For God's sake, Pat . . . do something with these beasts, like put them down preferably.'

'Dad!'

'Well, honestly, if you had to have dogs, why not chihuahuas, why choose Shetland ponies?'

Pat tried to clamp her hands over Desmond's ears. 'Don't listen, boys, he doesn't mean it.'

'I damn well do! I'm going up to see Mum, tell her the good news . . . have you taken her a cuppa?'

Pat nodded. 'I didn't tell her . . . left it to the proud father.'

The dogs gave the postwoman a greeting she would never forget and then they met Mary coming up the gravel drive. Theresa was looking out of her bedroom window. At the expression on her face, Theresa burst out laughing.

'It's all right, they won't hurt you!' she called out. Mary looked up, relieved. 'Hold on. I'll come and rescue you.'

She led Mary into the kitchen with her heavy bag of shopping.

'Nearly gave me a heart attack,' she said. 'What are they, wolves?'

Theresa laughed again.

'No they're Irish Wolf Hounds. They're Aunty Pat's.'

'I knew it, the way they came at me, I thought it was wolves . . . now, any news?'

'Yes . . . a boy . . . Richard or Seamus.'

'A boy! Oh how lovely!' Mary clasped her hands under her chin. 'Oh, your Dad *will* be pleased! A boy! Well, well! And does Mrs Bird know? She'll be thrilled!'

Andrew told her and it was not that she didn't

seem to understand. She repeated the word 'boy' but she just nodded.

When Theresa came into the room her grandmother seemed to look at her with a penetrating look and then she seemed far away again. She didn't say anything.

Later in the morning after the doctor had been, Mary and Pat struggled to get her into her chair. Standing outside the door, Theresa could hear her whimpering and moaning. When she glanced in she saw the frail old lady, hanging like a scarecrow between their arms. They sat her on the chair, wrapped in a rug but looking uncomfortable, slumped at an awkward angle.

As Mary and Pat left the room, Theresa slipped in.

'Back to bed!' her grandmother said distinctly.

'I can't, Grandma. The doctor said, just for a short while.'

The old lady pulled at her arm.

'Why?' she mouthed.

'I don't know . . . to get your legs working maybe.'

'Why?' the old lady said again.

Theresa couldn't answer these questions.

'Shall I do your hair?' she asked.

She picked up the tortoiseshell brush from the bedside table. Her hair was sticking up like a nest. Gently she smoothed it and untangled it. It was as fine as spiders' webs and covered her skull in a fine grey sheen.

'Shall I read to you?' she asked.

Her grandmother shook her head.

'Bed,' she moaned, pointing clearly to where her bed lay neatly remade, with the sheet turned down and the quilt in place.

'I can't, Grandma . . . I'm sorry, I just can't.'

It was raining outside, this she knew, but Theresa suddenly needed to be out in the drizzle and the damp.

In the hall she met Andrew looking through the post on the hall table, on the point of leaving for the hospital.

'Might even be able to bring her home . . .' he told her. 'They don't keep them in longer than they can help it nowadays.' But when he saw the way the dogs had rearranged the hall furniture and the muddy skid marks on the floor, the umbrella stand on its side, he added:

'But maybe, in the circumstances, I'll try and get her another twenty-four hours. Oh, by the by,' he fingered his car keys. 'Do you want to let your mother know? You can ring her if you like – or I will.'

'You,' said Theresa quickly.

Theresa slipped out of the back door while Pat distracted the dogs. They wanted to accompany her.

'I'll take them later on, down to the beach . . . but I want to see someone,' Theresa promised.

'You telling me or them?' Pat laughed. 'Go on, I'll give them a Good Boy choc drop . . . they're crazy about chocolate.'

She crossed the road before The Haven, not wanting to see again the dark spots on the doorstep. Beyond the church, Theresa turned down the lane presuming it would cut through to the Estate. It was damp and musty and still full of last year's leaves. The hedges of brambles and the nettle banks had encroached and she had to push her way through at one stage, although there were signs of bent branches, even a green cut in the stouter branches, which showed someone had been down here recently.

It did come out on the far side of the town, traversing the road which led up from the far quay to Paul's house. She could see it meandering on towards the old railway line, but she headed uphill.

The house was very quiet, but she rang the bell anyway and strained her ears to hear sounds of movement. The door opened just as she was about to give up, not by one of the children but by Old Joe. He had his waders on and that old flecked sweater with the holes in the elbows. He wasn't wearing his cap though, and she saw his white hair was thick and curly.

'Is Paul in?' she asked.

His eyes were as clear as sea water.

'He is not. Have to make do with me.'

She had been about to back away, but he was obviously inviting her into the front room by the way he stood back, opening the door wide.

She sat down at one end of the long dining room table. He sat at the other. There was a big brown teapot in front of him, and a loaf of bread and a slab of cheese on the bread board which he pushed towards her.

'Help yourself.'

He fetched two mugs and a pint of milk and settled himself down to pack his pipe.

'Sorry to hear about your grandma . . . how's she doing?' he asked between sucks. The match burned so near his skin, Theresa was about to shout out when he shook it with a quick flick of the wrist.

'I don't know really . . . she seemed better yesterday . . . but they got her walking today, you know, sitting in her chair . . . and she wasn't very happy about that.'

He nodded.

On the wall, above the sideboard, was an oil painting of the harbour slipway. In the silence, Theresa found herself staring at it, trying to identify in her mind the position of the boat she and Paul had rowed across the harbour. Joe followed her gaze.

'That's where we all used to "hang out" as you call it, years ago, your grandmother, Gillie and George, Nance and I. That old stone wall could tell a secret or two . . .' He winked at Theresa.

'Joe,' Theresa hesitated. 'Will you tell me about it? About George and the murder . . . I nearly know, but not quite . . .'

He smiled at her, paused, poured the tea slowly into the mugs and passed her one.

Down on the slipway where the smaller boats are moored they huddle. With the water out, the boats are pitched in the harbour mud at strange angles, their ropes hanging slack in the slime. It is a dark place, a private place for the youngsters to come, away from the snug of the public house, which casts a great slice of light over the quayside. In the lee of the wall they can sit and tangle, throw stones into the water, laugh, tease and flirt, with just sufficient light to catch the look in an eye. And where once, as children, they dared each other to race to the edge of the sea, to walk along the lines of ropes like trapeze artists, to pirate the boats, or lie low and stow-away, now, their games are of a different kind of excitement, a different kind of daring.

The wild girl, she with the tangle of hair and the glistening eyes, has something secreted beneath her skirt – a bottle, a dusty bottle, one she found and stole from her father's store behind the lobster pots. She pulls the cork with her teeth and puts the bottle to her lips and pours the fire down her throat. No choking, though tears spill over her cheeks. She passes the bottle to the pale girl, who shakes her head at first, but then takes a sip and explodes in strangled choking, and passes the bottle to the boy who puts a brotherly arm round her. He drinks, gulping twice before putting the bottle down. The second and third boy take furtive turns, but the wild girl is impatient with them, wresting the liquor from their hurried mouths. She takes the bottle, looks at the first boy who looks at her. She takes another mouthful and passes the bottle to him. As he stands there, by the old stone wall, she turns away and running through the slice of light thrown onto the quay, she plunges into the shadows beyond. The boy, with a moment of hesitation, one backward glance at his pale sister, follows her.

But up in the secret shadowland away from the light, the boy and girl are not unseen. Someone whose eyes are well accustomed to dark places watches them, sees the way they drink, lips meeting lips first over the top of the

258

bottle, and then . . . but he cannot see . . . he must look
away . . . for a red blood is fountaining from his heart.
He is cut. He is pierced. He is overcome by a wild rush
which takes him away, moving like a flame along a fuse
wire, first to the shop, where among the strong blood
smells and the sawdust he picks out cold steel and then,
following the line he waits in the darkest silence of the
lane, for the boy will come this way, that he knows. And
he is happy, unsteady a little, humming, his heart lifted
and bursting with an excitement that still makes him
smile . . . And the moment detonates as it has to: the
smile and the hum exploding into a scream and a wild
contortion of pain. Blood, cold steel, insanity, and cruelty,
the madness of love and passion and jealousy dying in
one act, taking, in that moment, so many lives.

'August 2nd,' said Theresa.

Joe paused and thought for a moment. 'Now, you
been doing your homework . . . it was indeed August
2nd 1931. How d'you know that?'

'Grandma sends flowers to the church.'

'Does she now, I never knew that. Well, course it
was a terrible thing to happen . . . a killing in a small
place like this. Things were never the same. There
was the trial of course, and the poor bugger got sent
away . . . not fit to plead . . . sent him to Broadmoor
or somewhere like that. Then that grandfather of
yours came along. Never knew him, the rest of us,
being up the hill and that, and off at boarding school
and whatnot, but he'd had his eyes on Tilda May
along with the rest of us. So that was that. Francis
Bird just swooped down and whisked her away. She

had her reasons, though. Always the strong-willed one . . . and poor Gillie never really recovered.'

Joe shook his head sadly and sighed.

The pale woman, hair unkempt as the briar in the hedge, eyes wide as a dead cod's, stands on the town's bandstand waving an empty bottle and howling like a wolf. She spits like an alleycat and flails her arms and throws obscenities more jagged than stones at anyone who approaches her.

'Poor thing . . . not the same girl . . . turned her mind . . . and the drink too . . . like half of her was cut away . . . mad with the grief . . .'

It is the young bride from the top of the hill who is fetched. She runs quickly down the hill, summoned by the young man from the boats in his blue oiled jersey. He pulls her urgently by the hand but stands back as they approach the crazed woman, and the crowd pull back, quietly, knowingly, to let her through. She walks right up to her, and there are no words. The pale woman's fury is spent, her rage is turned to docility. She gives the bottle from her grasp, she takes the proffered hand and together they walk quietly away, along the quay and turn up the hill.

'*It won't happen again,*' *she tells the overwrought parents.*

'*There won't be a next time,*' *she tells the Vicar and the policeman who sit at her table in the big house where she lives now.*

And when a sceptical eyebrow is raised she explains:

'*I have made arrangements.*'

Joe paused, sighed deeply, then concentrated on relighting his pipe. Theresa sat quietly knowing he hadn't finished his story.

'Tilda May wanted to do the best for Gillie. But the best don't always come cheap. Francis Bird married our Tilda May and Gillie spent her life in a pricey private hospital . . . that's the long and the short of it.'

His pipe had gone out so he struck another match and sucked away again, placing his thumb over the bowl until the tobacco seemed to draw.

'I'm going to tell you something now,' Theresa said. 'You know The Haven, Paul told me that's where William's sister moved?'

He nodded. 'That's what I heard,' he confirmed.

'I think Willie Spedding tried to kill himself today. I saw a man being taken away in the ambulance. And Esmie was there too. Do you think it could have been him?'

'Could well be. Poor old bugger,' he added.

'Maybe he's escaped?'

Joe smiled and shook his head.

'Oh, I expect they let him home now and again . . . or maybe he's out for good now. Life's a long time. We all do things we're not proud of, take a wrong turning here or there, and like I said, you don't always leave things behind as you'd like to . . . they come with you. He's not had a very good life, has he?'

'No, but George had a very short one.'

'So he did, and that's a tragedy. That's what it's like being old. All of us old-timers feels we're living on borrowed time ... we all knew so many who didn't make it, see, and some say we're the fortunate ones.'

He paused and sucked his pipe reflectively.

At that moment there was a key in the latch.

'Ah, that'll be young Paul now. Well,' he paused and sighed deeply, 'I'll be putting up a prayer for the old girl, she can count on that. But she's a lucky one remember that, she can look at you and see something that wouldn't be walking around if it hadn't been for her ... and you can't ask for more than that, can you?'

Paul opened the door and stood not knowing what to do.

'On second thoughts ...' the old man grinned. 'Only joking! Come on in, boy, or go out, make up your mind, don't just stand there like a great pudding.'

Paul shifted uneasily but it was Theresa who rescued him.

'Look, I've got to get back ... will you come with me?'

'OK.'

She grabbed her coat.

'Thanks,' she said to Joe, 'you know ... for what you said.'

He nodded and smiled.

'*Dew genough-why! Bennath Dew!*'[1] he said.

'Come on.' Paul took her arm. 'Don't mind him.'

_____
[1]Goodbye! God bless you.

262

'Let's cut up the back way,' she suggested as he was on the point of turning down the hill.

'Gives me the creeps, those alley-ways,' he confessed.

'They're OK. Anyway, no one will see us,' she added.

Theresa saw his discomfort as he turned back to follow her.

'I saw Esmie and her brother twice,' Theresa told him. But that was all she told him.

Paul looked up, interested.

'He escaped or something?'

'Probably not . . . released or home leave or something. Funny, to think of him, you know, just down the street, and Grandma keeling over like that just up the hill.'

'Yeah, sorry about that,' Paul mumbled.

'She's old.'

Paul nodded. 'My gran died couple of years back.'

'I didn't say she was dying,' said Theresa sharply.

They walked in silence, pushing back the overhanging brambles and nettles with their sleeves.

'Got a new brother.'

'Oh, that's good.'

'Maybe.'

'Look.' Paul stopped in the track in front of her, turned and took her arm. 'I'm really sorry . . . I was really dumb . . . I didn't think that Sue'd do anything like that . . . especially cos you and I weren't up to anything . . .'

'*We* know that,' Theresa laughed.

'I told her, but she didn't believe me. I don't understand it, really I don't.'

'Well, people do crazy things.'

'I told her, if she thinks that is going to make me like her . . . I don't want anything more to do with her. I mean she's so stupid. If she thought for one minute she could make me . . .' He was speechless and ended up blowing air through his cheeks like a horse.

'I never meant to make any trouble, but sometimes it just seems to happen to me. Suppose it runs in the family,' Theresa said slowly.

'You sound like my grandad now, talking in riddles.'

By the entrance to the house, Paul stopped.

'There's a party tomorrow night . . . at the Beach Bar will you come along?'

'Probably not.'

Paul scratched his neck. 'Well, if you can . . .'

'Things are a bit difficult.'

'I know . . . but my mum could always . . .'

Theresa laughed. 'You leave your mum out of it.'

'What d'you mean?'

'Never mind. Look, gotta go. OK?'

'Come if you can,' Paul called after her.

In the driveway, there was a mini car; on the back window there was a sticker which said: Jesus Saves; but there was no sign of the two Volvos.

There was no sign either of the hounds, only evidence of where they had been. Cuthbert, exhausted, lay by the Aga, opened one eye and thumped his tail as he saw her.

On the table there was a note.

'Exercising the beasts. Proud father with new son.'

From upstairs, she could hear the sound of voices. A door opened and there followed footsteps on the stairs. It was Mary.

'Mucky old day init? Look at you with cobwebs in your hair . . . I'd give that a good rubbing with a towel if I were you . . . your grandmother's got visitors.' She mouthed the words as though she were veiling a secret.

'Oh?'

'Mrs Appleyard. But she's got someone with her.' She pursed her lips and spoke in an overly careful way.

'Who?'

'I'm not saying nothing . . . my lips are sealed . . . but I did say I'd take them up some tea. And if you're very good I'll let you take the tray up. How's that.'

Mary ran up the stairs in front of her, to open the door, though Theresa said she could manage.

Her grandma was propped up against the white pillows. The lamp on the bedside table was on. Although it was still afternoon, the day outside was grey and cheerless. Mrs Appleyard was sitting in the little button-back chair but sitting on the bed, holding her grandmother's hand was another elderly woman whom Theresa had never seen before.

She was wearing a green felt hat with a bunch of drooping felt violets fastened onto the hat-band by a visible safety pin. Her cream macintosh remained firmly buttoned up and belted. Wisps of white hair had escaped imprisonment from under the hat, and against the light from the window, they framed her head in a silver light.

Theresa knew who it was immediately. She set the tray on the bedside table without saying anything. There was a deep stillness in the room. Even Mrs Appleyard was silenced.

Before Theresa turned to slip quietly away, she saw those two old hands firmly locked – old, beautiful hands, brown with liver spots, knuckles pronounced, nails opaque as pearls; and on the sheets beside them were the two halves of the poem, together now. She just paused long enough to read:

> *'Glad days – sad days*
> *are all the brighter made*
> *with the Happy Knowledge*
> *that our Friendship will not fade.'*

It was Gillian.

25

She died in the small hours.

Theresa woke suddenly, not to noise, but to silence and emptiness. She woke completely and immediately. Her eyes were wide open so she could see the dark.

There was a certain feeling that she had gone, that a light had been extinguished. But with the light blown out, the after-image burned clearly, even with closed eyes. Theresa lay very quietly and very awake.

She heard doors opening, running of feet, Pat's voice called out: 'Andrew!'

She heard a low mumbling of voices, more running up and down stairs, a dog barking once, but sleepily. Some time later, a car arrived and she heard more footsteps, more voices.

She heard muffled sounds of sobbing but she herself felt very calm.

Eventually, she must have slept and her dreaming was as hectic and confused as her waking moments had been composed. There was a lot of running to catch up with something, to get away from something else . . . and the thing she wanted got away from her and the thing she didn't want caught up with her. There were long tunnels of red and green, and her heart was about to burst from her chest and nobody seemed to care. And there was her mother running away and this black figure behind her threw a big net over her, like a fisherman, and she was being pulled back and she was struggling and crying and her heart was pounding.

'Oh!' She woke horribly to find her father's hand on her shoulder. He sat on the bed. His face was tired and his eyes were sad.

Theresa was already crying from the dream.

'You were having a nightmare,' he told her.

'I know.'

'Grandma died,' he said.

'I know.'

It was a grey wet day.

When she drew her curtains, she said to the sky: 'Good. I'm glad.'

She put on her clothes quickly and ran down the stairs, passing Grandma's bedroom door without glancing at it. In the kitchen Pat was sitting at the table with her head in her hands. A lit cigarette burned in the saucer in front of her.

The dogs greeted her with an ecstasy of energy, quite unsubdued by the atmosphere around them. Pat lifted her head. She went to grasp her hand, but Theresa said quickly:

'Thought I'd take the dogs down to the beach. OK?'

'Great idea. They'd love that . . . only have to get locked in the car otherwise . . . you know . . . with all the coming and going . . .' Her shoulders shuddered again.

Theresa turned quickly, whistled to the dogs, slapped her legs a couple of times and then set off crunching over the gravel driveway.

They went for miles, over the fields where she and Grandma had walked together so recently, past the turning to Trenance's Farm.

'Never did have that cream tea.'

One of the dogs lifted its head at the sound of her voice. She picked up a stick that was lying in the hedgerow and hurled it as far as she could. Both dogs bounded after it. They circled the fields time and again, eating up the distance with their huge bounds. Sometimes they almost disappeared from view into the mist, and then they loomed back again, grey and bedraggled, their mouths smiling, eyes bright.

Together they scrambled down the slippery rocks to the beach. The tide was out revealing great stretches of dull gold sand, deserted now as the rain redoubled its strength.

A wind was lifting the surface of the sea, whipping and teasing it to white plumes, and the waves were thunderous and strong.

Theresa kicked off her shoes and walked as close to the edge as she could. She loved the way the waves just went on and on and on as they always had and they always would. For ever.

It was here they used to come . . . when she was little . . . here she would paddle . . . leap over the creamy playful waves, scream and tremble as the sun

269

warmed her back to honey brown. And Grandma would be standing there: 'Not above the knees!' And she'd be holding the towel, and when eventually, and always too late, Theresa would run to her, blue, teeth chattering like castanets, she would rub her vigorously with that hard salty sandy towel until the tears came.

And now the tears came again, hot and agonizing, and Theresa was glad of the slashing rain and the wind which carried away her chokes and howls. There were only the gulls to hear her. Theresa was so used to listening to their wailing, it was their turn now. Not that they were in the least perturbed. Their eyes were as flinty as ever, their sleek bodies untouched.

Had there not been all the diversions and surprises of the beach, the dogs might have been more affected. When she cried out, if they were near enough they lifted their heads, sharpened their ears to questions, but quickly turned away, drawn by another smell, another excitement.

It was misery Theresa felt, the misery of being as small as she ever was, and as in need of her grandma as she ever had been.

'I want you!' she cried and stamped her foot. 'Don't go. It's not fair!'

Now there was only the wind to wrap round her body and the salt air to rub her hair.

'I need you!' she called out, face lifted to the sky, and all around her was a huge misty emptiness and a blurred horizon.

Eventually, Theresa quietened, the need to cry

out gradually sapped, leaving a deep quiet inside her. She continued to walk, and her feet tracing the very edges of the waves seemed far away.

Her monologue, when she continued it, was inside herself.

'I know you *have* gone,' she told Grandma. 'Please don't go any further away. Just stay with me, inside, like this.'

When she turned round, the sea had already covered her footprints.

'Tide's coming in!' she warned the dogs, but they were miles away exploring the far edges of the beach, savouring its width and its breadth, stretching out to fill it.

At the end of the beach, she whistled the dogs to her and together they squeezed through the pass of purple and green rocks which divided this beach from the next. They would be cut off soon and forced to return over the cliffs. But that way the sand would be cleaned from the dogs' coats and she would be able to look down on it all. See things from a height. Take a bird's-eye view.

One of the dogs found something on a rock and stood and barked furiously and would not leave his find. She returned and saw a dead crab stranded on its back.

'Leave it!' she said.

She took it in her hands and hefted it into the sea.

At first the dog thought she was playing and he started to tear in the direction of her throw, but he would not go into the sea where the waves were crashing down. He stood, ears flattened, and looked at her for guidance.

'Come on!' she called.

At once he turned and put all his energy and enthusiasm into chasing his companion up the narrowing stretch of sand to the steps cut into the rock face.

On the remotest part of the cliff, she scrambled down away from the track to the more precipitous rock face. There she sat on a tuffet of dense grasses watching the sea below her. Against the black rocks it curled hungrily, breaking itself in a white explosion of anger every now and again before, defeated, it drained back into itself. You might think it had given up, changed its mind, but no, suddenly it would swell and hurl its liquid rage against that immovable rock face.

It would never stop, always be the same, keep on day after day. Deep inside her mind she knew this and it was a comfort. Always the same and gradually different. She knew this by the broken headlands, fragmented rocks, arches and blow holes, stacks, the places where the cliffs had crumbled; by the fact that the route she and her mum and dad used to walk was now a ghostly path hanging out over space and a pile of bare rocks on the beach below.

A herring gull flew out from behind the lea of the headland, flying at exactly the height she was sitting at. For a moment their eyes met, only a few feet apart.

She did not know how many hours she was gone. A fair time, she hazarded, by the way the dogs' tongues lolled in their mouths, and the way they chose to trot only a few yards in front of her. She hadn't thought about it, but as the buildings of the town came into sight, she realised that *part* of the hollowness inside was her stomach, groaning for food, and *part* of the emptiness in her head was a faintness from lack of sustenance, and *part* of her coldness was the fact that she was wet through.

26

Mary was in the kitchen peeling potatoes.

She looked at Theresa as she came in, anxiously. Theresa smiled at her and Mary, encouraged, said:

'Well, life goes on . . . got to eat . . . it's all I can do now . . .'

There was a catch in her voice which Theresa did not want to trip on.

'Got the dog's towel, Mary? We're all soaked!'

She dried the dogs, only perfunctorily, and led each to the Aga where she tied them to the rail. They hated being tied and whined in protest, shivering, ears sagging miserably.

Cuthbert, warm and dry moved out to his spot in the hall.

'I think I'll have a bath,' Theresa said. 'But I'm starving hungry, is there anything to eat?'

Theresa accepted the hunks of bread and cheese and pickle that Mary put in front of her.

'Fancy some soup?'

Theresa nodded. 'I'll take it up with me. Where are the others?'

Mary spoke in a low voice as she heated the mulligatawny in a pan.

'They've taken her away . . . Mr Gilby came for

her . . . she's gone to the chapel of rest . . . your dad and Pat's gone too . . . there's things they have to do . . . papers, certificates and so on.'

'Is the water hot, do you think?'

'Oh, I should say so, they've not had their minds on baths, my love. Here you are.'

Theresa took the mug from her. Its warmth made her realise how cold she was.

She soaked long and deep, pouring some of Naomi's 'Bain Moussant' into the water. It was turquoise and coloured the water a faint sea green. It smelled of peppermint and lavender and tea-bags and frothed at the surface like egg whites. She lay among the bubbles, sipping her mulligatawny and just felt warm.

When she heard a car door slam, somewhat reluctantly she heaved herself out of the water and wrapped herself in a towel, warm from the linen cupboard.

'Wish I had some more clothes, I'm sick of you,' she told her grey shorts and black top. She wanted a thick sweater and big socks. Maybe Andrew wouldn't mind. She padded over to his room. The room at the top of the stairs, her old room, was open. She stopped and peered round the door. Someone had been here. It was warm and there were a couple of brand new whiter-than-white towels tucked over the radiator. The little whicker cot had its polythene cover removed and someone had prepared it. A quilted cover lay on the top. Someone had taken the covers from the plastic bath and leant it against the wall, and the contents of the

Boots bags, and arranged the bottles of lotions and the powders and the cotton wool and the tiny nappies, size one, on the chest of drawers. Theresa opened the top drawer. There were just a few items here, folded neatly. She took one out, a tiny vest, the size she used to put on her doll Belinda, the size Grandma used to knit for her.

Quickly she shut the drawer, tiptoed out of the room, leaving the door ajar as she had found it. From the chest in her father's bedroom, she took out a pair of grey mountaineering socks from his sock drawer, and a huge Fair Isle sweater from the bottom drawer. Dressed in these and taking a deep breath, she went downstairs.

Pat was telling her story to Mary.

'They couldn't have been nicer, couldn't have been kinder; but three quarters of an hour we had to wait . . . in that draughty lobby and they only had one chair . . . no loos . . . nowhere to have a cup of tea. It would make anyone feel miserable, even if you didn't have good cause.'

She turned to see Theresa.

'You're a gem,' she told her. 'You've shot to number one favourite with my boys. Had a whale of a time, they told me.'

Theresa smiled. 'Where's Dad?'

'Gone to see the baby. I told him it would do him good. He was going to ring Naomi and tell her he couldn't, but I told him, there's nothing more we can do now. Just go!'

It had been Naomi's intention to return that day but when Andrew returned, he was alone having postponed her reappearance until the next day. It would give him time to 'get things done' in the morning and then be able to concentrate on her home-coming.

Theresa's job, the next day, was to answer the telephone, a job which she had underestimated in terms of volume of work.

'Could you let your mother know?' Andrew said to her just before he and Pat left to visit Mr Gilby's and make all the arrangements.

Just after they had gone, and Theresa had settled herself in the office, Pat reappeared.

She hovered at the office door.

'Umm, Trees ... I just wondered. Do you want to see her?'

'Who?'

'Grandma.'

'No.'

'People do you know ... to say goodbye ...'

'It's OK. I've said goodbye.'

'Right ... just wanted to, you know ...'

'Thanks.'

Theresa smiled at her and swallowed down a lump rising in her throat.

It was with a strange hollow feeling in her stomach that she dialled her mother's number. But when the Ansaphone answered, she felt a sudden deep anguish that brought the tears pouring down her face.

'Mum ... it's Theresa ... Grandma's dead ... that's it.' She put the receiver down and abandoned herself to weeping.

But not for long. Several incomprehensible business calls for her father forced the drying of her tears. There were two calls for Aunty Pat from her boss: one furious with her for failing to meet some deadline; the next full of apologies because he'd only just heard – someone had failed to tell him – deepest condolences. It wasn't a word she had known before 'Condolences', but by the time she had written it ten times on the message pad, she felt familiar with it. It seemed to be a special word you used when someone died.

Mrs Appleyard arrived at lunchtime and gave Theresa a big hug which Theresa had not been expecting. It was like hugging a cushion, a springy foam-filled cushion.

'You're being a tower of strength,' she told her. 'A tower of strength. Isn't she, Mary?'

'One in a million,' Mary beamed at her.

'I'm only answering the phone,' Theresa said.

Just before Mary left, when Pat had returned and taken to her bed for a rest and Andrew had departed for the hospital, she opened her handbag to put in tomorrow's shopping list and gave a gasp of annoyance.

'Oh, mind like a sieve I got . . . nearly forgot. They'd have killed me for that.'

She held in her hand a fistful of cards, two of which she had sorted out for Theresa.

She left the others, written in similar handwriting, on the table.

The first card was from Paul. It was black-edged and said 'In Sympathy' on the front. Inside it said:

'Sorry about your Gran, Paul.'

'Bet Mary bought it for him,' Theresa thought.

The second was a plain postcard and in copper-plate lettering on one side was written: '*Gans treger-eth.*[1] *Bennath Dew.*'[2] and on the other side: 'To Tilda's Granddaughter from Joe.'

Naomi and Seamus Richard or Richard Seamus arrived back late in the afternoon. The rain had just stopped and there was a definite break in the clouds, a pink, soft breach in the grey to the west. Pat had locked the hounds in her car a good half-hour in advance of their return, Andrew having phoned and alerted her from the hospital. She had been doing some sorting in her mother's room and had emerged, eyes rather red-rimmed, to have a cup of tea before they returned. She carried the brandy bottle with her and a tiny glass. The bottle was nearly empty.

Theresa thought she would offer to take the dogs out and miss the actual event, but when it came to it, she found herself still sitting at the kitchen table.

Pat bounded out like one of her dogs and Theresa stayed where she was. Naomi came in first clutching a mohair cardigan round her shoulders. Theresa's first impression was how fat she still seemed, almost as though she was still waiting, but she said nothing, just beamed and allowed her cheek to be kissed. Naomi's eyes shone with unshed tears.

'It's so good to be back home,' she kept repeating.

[1] In sympathy.
[2] God bless you.

'Oh, it's so good. It's true . . . there just is no place like home!'

Andrew carried the baby in his Moses basket. He put him down on the kitchen table.

'Well,' he said to Theresa. 'Here he is!'

Theresa got slowly to her feet and peered into the deep folds of blanket. He was lying on his side. All she could see was a shock of black hair and a tiny, very pink forehead. His eyes were closed and just above the line of the blankets she could see his minute pink nose. He was snuffling slightly.

She felt she should say something.

'He's very small.'

'Didn't feel like it, let me assure you,' laughed Naomi.

It was a strange evening. They sat and ate the celebration meal Mary had prepared. Pat slipped out onto the garden to 'admire the sunset' a few times, but came back smelling of smoke. She and Theresa took the dogs up to the field before dark. The telephone hardly stopped ringing.

When they returned from the field, Naomi and Andrew were opening cards and letters. On the mantelpiece in the living room, Andrew arranged the cards with their black edges, with their pansies, or scrawly black lettering: 'In Sympathy', 'Condolences'. On the sideboard Naomi arranged a contrasting display: 'It's a Boy!! Congratulations!' Blue bunnies and baby chicks and cartoons, misty mothers leaning into draped cradles, chubby-faced cherubs looking not in the least like the tiny pink object Theresa had peered at in the basket.

They sat in the living room for a while, the baby in its cradle, a new and tiny presence; but the more tangible sense was the space, the gap, which was huge and everywhere.

Sometimes they talked. No one suggested turning on the television, though Theresa thought of it.

'What about this name, then?' asked Pat. 'What am I to call my nephew?'

'I want Seamus,' said Naomi. 'Or I did . . . I don't really mind any more.' She bent over the cradle, putting her finger out to touch his cheek. 'Do you think he's a Seamus or a Richard?' she asked Pat anxiously.

'I have to say I think he's a Richard.'

'Yes, call him Richard, then he'll be Dicky Bird,' said Theresa.

'Oh no!' cried Naomi. 'We can't have that. I hadn't thought. Seamus it is. Seamus Richard.'

'Well, he'll still be Dicky Bird,' Theresa pointed out. '*I* had to put up with it, Trees jokes all my life.'

'But at least you're not Theresa Green,' said Naomi.

'Well, Seamus it is then, but we can't make people call him that . . . and anyway he can decide for himself later on,' Andrew said.

That decided, Seamus Dicky Bird started to wriggle and snuffle and without much build-up launched suddenly into a series of impressive wails, high-pitched, long and shuddering.

Immediately Naomi picked him up and held him to her but his protest was not assuaged.

'I'll go and wash and feed him and settle him down. Say goodnight, Seamus!' she said as she went.

Pat reached for the brandy bottle and, holding it up to the light, announced with some relief: 'Just enough for a night cap, Trees. Go on, do me favour, help me finish it, . . . our medicinal.' She smiled a wry smile.

'Well, all right then,' said Theresa. 'But just one!'

27

Into the depths of her dreams, somewhere, Seamus's cries had penetrated. Theresa woke finally to that high shivering cry which cut through every device to keep it out. It was the kind of sound which shot high voltage down the central nervous system.

'Just like Rosie,' she moaned, remembering. And as her brain seemed to have switched into recall mode, the thought of her grandma came immediately and strongly to her.

'You wouldn't have liked it, Grandma... it wouldn't have been right for you to put up with this.'

She lay for a while trying to pick the sounds up behind the screaming: people noises; dog noises; the raucous rooks and little chirping hedge birds; the seagull on the roof, tapping his morning ritual. There were footsteps on the gravel drive and then the sound of the letter box opening and a faint whoosh, like rain, as letters poured onto the mat. The dogs barked at a higher pitch. The footsteps retreated. And suddenly the wailing stopped.

It was in this quiet that Theresa rose and washed. Moving quietly past Grandma's door, she reached the door at the top of the stairs. She put her ear to the door jamb.

'That's better isn't it . . . my little water baby . . . that's lovely, isn't it, beautiful warm water . . .' Faint sounds of lapping water punctuated the words.

'You can go in.' Andrew appeared behind her.

She straightened. 'It's OK.'

'No, Naomi would like you to. Come and see.'

He opened the door. Naomi was sitting on the floor holding Seamus in the crook of her arm in his white plastic bath. She had spread one of the fleecy towels on the floor in case he splashed. He was so tiny, so skinny, like a frog, or perhaps a tadpole with newly developed legs. Attached to his tummy was a small frizzled piece of something black, like a piece of seaweed.

'This is killing my back,' Naomi told them cheerfully. 'Out you come.'

She lifted him, dripping, and lay him onto the towel. His skin hung loosely on his body as though it were a size too big and his flesh had a purplish bloom to it until Naomi covered him in talc like one of Mary's scones.

And how huge and surprising was his scrotal sac, big and full. Had Andrew not been in the room, Theresa would have remarked on it.

It took him time to realise things felt different – that there was space round his limbs instead of warm water, and it didn't feel so good.

'From content to utter fury in less than a second,' Theresa told Pat in the kitchen, having retreated when the wailing began. She didn't particularly want to see Naomi's breasts either. It had been bad enough with her mother.

Both dogs came and sat by her as she ate her cereal. Their ears were flat and there was an unmistakable look of reproach in their eyes.

'What's up with you two?' she asked.

'Don't like the noise,' Pat told her.

'Don't blame me,' Theresa told them. 'I didn't do it. I hate it too.'

'Also, they feel their dignity has been undermined by spending a night in the car when they knew damn well that old Cuthbert was having it cushy on the nice hall rug. Only allowed in cos it's sunny and I've promised Andrew I'll clear up all doggie traces, and they'll be put away as soon as Naomi appears.'

'Could you do something for me, Trees?' Andrew stuck his head round the door.

'What?'

'Nip down to the newsagents and get the papers – *The Times* and *The Telegraph*, *Independent* and *Guardian*.'

'What for?'

'They should be in today . . . the announcements: Grandma and Seamus.'

Theresa scraped her bowl carefully, put it in the dishwasher and turned to go.

'Oh, no money,' she looked apologetically at Pat.

'Sorry love, here.' She fished in her purse and took out a five pound note.

It was welcome, the sun again after all these wet days. The roads still shone like black jet and there was moisture lingering on the fuchsias and geraniums in the hanging baskets down Mariner Street. Briefly she glanced up at The Haven. It was very still. Outside the cottage next door, a woman was standing on a chair watering her hanging basket. On impulse, Theresa stopped.

'Excuse me. Do you know if the man next door is all right. I saw the ambulance,' she explained.

'I thought I'd seen you somewhere . . . well – "all right" – that's a question. Not dead if that's what you mean. But I'm not saying that's a good thing myself. Don't know how many times he's tried it over the years. Poor old thing!'

Past the church she went and then past the remaining houses until the shops started.

Outside the butcher's a lady stepped out in her path.

'So sorry to hear about Mrs Bird!' she said.

Theresa had never seen the woman before. She smiled and thanked her.

In the newsagent's, she picked up the four papers and took them to the counter.

'Sorry about your gran, dear!' said the lady who took her money.

On the way back up the hill, the door to the printer's shop opened before she reached it and a woman in brown slacks and a floral blouse gave her a card: 'For the little boy! I'm so pleased.'

Just before she reached the house, Theresa took one of the papers and opened it. Obituaries . . . she glanced down . . . always an advantage of her name, never far to look . . . BIRD. Without reading further she turned to the column of births: BIRD.

She closed the paper and turned into the gravel drive.

Parked behind Aunty Pat's Volvo was a pale blue Peugeot.

For one moment she stood shocked by recognition and then the shock seemed to turn to an instant thrill.

Running into the house, she threw the papers on the table and her mother, standing in the hallway with her back to her, was just quick enough to turn and catch her in her arms.

Theresa didn't think anything, she just held on to her while gradually she became aware of how small her mother seemed, sensing how her head fitted over her mother's shoulder, her cheek was against the skin of her mother's neck.

She didn't know if it were *her* saying sorry, or her mother, or if it were both of them – or what they were sorry about. But they both seemed to be – for everything.

Eventually, they broke apart.

'God, Mum, what a shock!'

'Yes, everything's a shock isn't it? Poor Grandma! Poor Theresa! I never should . . .'

'It's OK, Mother.' Theresa threw her a warning look.

'Yes . . . I know . . . you're right . . . I'm not starting all that . . . it's just . . . I've missed you, Theresa, I really have.'

'Yea,' Theresa managed to say before looking away. 'Me too.'

Anxious to be active, she went back into the

kitchen and picked up the papers. Her mother followed her. She stood awkwardly, one hand on the table top steadying herself, the other twisting the button on her cream cardigan.

'Darling, let me explain. I've come to take you home, if you'd like to come . . . or not, if not.' She hesitated. 'We'll come back for the funeral . . . or not . . . just as you like. You can make up your own mind. We both want you, Andrew and I, he's told me how wonderful you've been. You may want to stay, I know how you love this place; but I want you home . . . if you want to come.'

'OK. Let's go,' said Theresa quickly, startling her mother who was unprepared.

'You mean that? Do you want some thinking time?'

'No.'

'I mean it *is* still holiday time, we could still all go away somewhere together . . . whatever . . . Sam can get some time off and I could do with a break. We could pick up some brochures.'

'I don't want to go anywhere,' Theresa said decisively.

'No?'

'Just home. And I want to get a job.'

'A job! That's not necessary, darling, really.'

'It is. I want a job. I want some money and I want some new clothes.'

Her mother looked at her jacket. 'Yes. Whatever happened to your coat?'

'Long story.'

'But you can have some money and some clothes, darling.'

'No, I want to, Mum – McDonald's.'

'McDonald's! How could you, it's slave labour . . . rush you off your feet . . . dress you up in those ridiculous uniforms. You don't even like hamburgers!'

Theresa laughed. 'You said I could do what I want. That's what I want.'

Her mother's mouth was open to protest, but she closed it and smiled a resigned smile instead. With a gesture of helplessness she said:

'I give in.'

'Hold on. Just get my stuff.'

Pushing her few items of clothing back into the rucksack did not take Theresa long. Her scan of the spare room was brief. She just needed to go.

At the top of the stairs she bumped into Andrew.

'You're going then?'

She nodded. 'I'll come to the funeral. At least I think I will.'

'She wouldn't mind.'

'Oh I know . . . not for her . . .'

He hesitated.

'We never did get out in the boat.'

'No.'

He put his arms round her and pulled her to him. She allowed him to.

'It's been hard,' he said. His dressing gown smelt slightly of sick.

'Yes.' She pulled away from him and busied

herself with adjusting the strap on her rucksack. 'It was meant to be, wasn't it? Short, sharp, shock.'

'No, not really. I couldn't have managed without you, Trees . . . and nor could Grandma. She loved you, you know that.'

'I know it.' Theresa was trying hard to be brusque and brief.

'Say goodbye to Naomi . . . and Seamus,' he told her opening the nursery door.

Naomi was standing at the window, a tiny fuzz of back hair on her shoulder.

'Bye you two,' Theresa said quickly from the doorway.

She lingered longer over Cuthbert who once again was happy lying in a shaft of warm morning sunlight. On her hands and knees, she nuzzled her nose into his whitening fur.

'Bye Cuth . . . don't let them bully you. They don't mean anything, they're only young.'

He thumped his tail, lifted his head and rolled onto his back, waving his paws imploringly at her.

'Oh, no, I'm not getting into that,' she said straightening up.

In the kitchen Mary had arrived; she and her mother were deep in conversation.

'Where's Pat?' Theresa cut across this praise to ask her mother.

'I think she went upstairs – maybe doing some sorting. I said I'd help her, but apparently they can manage.'

'Don't you worry about that Mrs . . . oh, I was going to say Bird . . .'

'Cussons!'

'Mrs Cussons. I'll be helping, and Mrs Appleyard. We're used to this kind of thing down here. We won't let her overdo it, don't you fret.'

Pat was sitting on the empty bed. The box was in front of her. She was sitting reading a letter when Theresa popped her head round the door.

'Look at this lot. All tied up in ribbon, bless her! Look at this old Valentine: *Roses are red, violets are blue – Tilda May, I love you. Joe.*'

Theresa squinted briefly at the old signature and smiled.

'Isn't it sweet!' said Pat. 'Perhaps I shouldn't be reading them. I suppose they're her secrets, but maybe it doesn't matter any more.'

Theresa was eager to be away.

'And look at this.' She handed Theresa a little card with a small rather tarnished satin bow pinned to the corner.

'What is it?'

'Read it!' Pat told her.

It was written in her grandmother's spidery script, though the letters spoke of a young woman's hand and the paper was flimsy and faded:

'Signed the pledge at the Band of Hope Meeting in the Methodist Hall today – October 2nd 1931.' Theresa smoothed the tiny satin bow between her finger and thumb.

'Explains a thing or two – like the whole of my life!' Pat said cheerfully. 'Vowed not to touch a drop of intoxicating liquor – and never did, as far as I know. I wonder what on earth made her do it!' she added.

Theresa said nothing.

'I'm going back with Mum, Aunty Pat. I'll be back, probably.'

'Oh, yes, I thought you would. And so would I in your place. There's only sorting things out left now, I've made a good start. I think I've found out who this George and Gillie were, by the way – look!'

She held up a curled photograph of three teen-agers. In the centre was a young girl with wild brown hair; she was laughing. She had her arms round a girl, about the same height but thin and pale with a blonde bob and an innocent smile, and a boy with a mop of dark hair and that same open smile. On the back was written Gillie, Tilda, George: June 1931.

Theresa handed it back to her.

Pat got up from the bed and put her arm round Theresa's shoulder as they walked downstairs.

'I'll be sorry to see you go. I'm glad I've caught up with you again after all these years. Always something good comes out of something . . .' she chose the word carefully '. . . difficult! I was saying to your mum, you must all come down and visit me soon. The dogs would love it and so would I.'

'Where are the dogs?'

'Confined to barracks I'm afraid.'

Still with her arm round her, she led her to the car. In the Volvo, the dogs were slumped sulkily on the floor in the back. As Theresa pressed her nose to the window, they raised their heads hopefully.

'Bye Dessie, bye Den. And don't give old Cuthbert too much stick . . . he's old remember! Bit of respect.'

Mary pressed a bag of cake into her hand.

'For the journey,' she said.

'Say goodbye to Paul and your father from me.'

'I will,' she promised.

Andrew, still in his dressing gown, appeared on the front porch. At first, he seemed to be focused on opening and shutting the old front door, trying to find where it was sticking on the tiled floor. But eventually, he left the door and stood studying his feet. His big toes were bursting out of his plaid slippers. Theresa's mother, having unlocked and opened the driver's door, saw him standing there and went up to him.

'Bye Andrew . . . and thanks.'

She stood awkwardly as he leant forward and pecked her on the cheek.

'Take care,' he said, squeezing her arm.

'*You* take care.' For one extended moment, she allowed her eyes to engage with his before turning briskly away.

She slid into the driver's seat, put on her dark glasses, hitched up her powder-blue skirt, kicked off her smart heeled shoes and pulled on a battered pair of flat slip-ons.

'Belt up!' she told Theresa.

'I haven't said anything!' replied Theresa in a flat routine response.

Her mother smiled.

'How I've missed your sense of humour, Theresa. Want to change your mind?' she asked with mock seriousness. 'Look! There's Naomi.'

At the upstairs window, the window which Theresa had looked out of every morning for the last five weeks, Naomi's head appeared. She was waving her hand from side to side like a small child.

On the tip of the rooftop, a lone herring gull stood watching the scene, his eyes emotionless.

'I bet that's the bird who's been beating a military tattoo on the roof at some ungodly hour every morning,' said Theresa as they swung, spitting gravel, out of drive.

She turned round once more to wave and saw the gull, rising effortlessly, and with one slow beat of its wings sweeping gently away across the fields in the direction of the sea.

The *S*huttered Room

by Christine Purkis

Open up THE SHUTTERED ROOM, a compelling story of love - and hate - by Christine Purkis.

Life is sweet for Alison. A long, hot summer nannying in France is bound to brush up her French, top up her tan and - who knows? - maybe even pep up her love life too! But things aren't so simple, as Alison quickly discovers...

'My God! This is terrible!'

The words sounded loud, strange in this silent room.

At first she felt she wanted to do something. She sprang up and went to the window. Rain drops were sprinkling down, though the real storm was still rumbling over the other side of the valley.

It was here, she found herself thinking. It was here. I know it. It has to be. On this bed. These curtains... a night like this... I can't sleep in here! she thought wildly.

But as she stood in the room, staring at the crumpled quilt, at the impression of her own body where she had just been lying, she knew she had no choice.

RED FOX paperback, £3.50 ISBN 0 09 947231 7
THE BODLEY HEAD hardback, £8.99 0 370 31916 8